D0520653

THE LAST CONFESSION

THE LAST CONFESSION

SOLOMON JONES

Minotaur Books ⚏ New York

This is a work of fiction. All of the characters, organizations, and events portrayed in this novel are either products of the author's imagination or are used fictitiously.

THE LAST CONFESSION. Copyright © 2010 by Solomon Jones. All rights reserved. Printed in the United States of America. For information, address St. Martin's Press, 175 Fifth Avenue, New York, N.Y. 10010.

www.minotaurbooks.com

ISBN 978-0-312-58020-9

First Edition: November 2010

10 9 8 7 6 5 4 3 2 1

To LaVeta, my angel

ACKNOWLEDGMENTS

First I'd like to thank my Lord and savior Jesus Christ, who snatched me off the streets and gave me a second chance at life. I'm grateful to my wife, LaVeta, for being drop-dead gorgeous and for sharing the brilliant ideas behind this and so many of my other stories. I appreciate my children, Adrianne, Eve, and Solomon, for helping me learn the true meaning of manhood. I'm indebted to my parents, Carolyn and Solomon Jones, for life and love, and to my aunt, Juanita Bryant, and my grandmother, Lula Richards, for their loving guidance. I thank my late grandfather, Gerald Richards, for passing his work ethic down to me, and I'd also like to thank another special man who passed on as I was finishing this book. Mr. Rudolph Davenport believed in my work and was drawn to the wisdom I was able to share in my spoken word. Mr. Rudy, as we called him, often told me I should be on *Oprah*. He understood the power of encouragement, and he shared that power not only with me but also with many others. He will be missed. I thank my agent, Manie Barron, and my editor, Monique Patterson, for lending their considerable talents to mine. I thank Congressman Chaka Fattah for his support and encouragement. I thank Councilwoman Jannie Blackwell for her kindness in the days when I was one of thousands of nameless, faceless men on the street. I thank Philadelphia for being the place where my stories are born, and I thank you, the reader, for allowing me to share these stories with you.

THE LAST CONFESSION

CHAPTER 1

It was a few minutes after mass on a hot summer morning, and silence filled the cathedral as if the Lord himself had said, "Peace. Be still."

The quiet didn't last for long. As a breeze slipped between the cracks in the centuries-old walls, and the sun shone through the angels that adorned the stained-glass windows, the priest's heavy footfalls marched toward the confessional booth.

Father O'Reilly always walked with purpose to hear confession. He thought it was his most important duty as a priest. In helping his parishioners deal with their sins, he was more than a cog in the church's wheel. He was an instrument in God's holy symphony. That was why he loved to take his place in the confessional booth. It was there that he felt closest to heaven.

As he opened the sturdy wooden door and sat behind the screen, Father O'Reilly brushed his gray, thinning locks away from his eyes, fully prepared to play his part in the dance between sin and mercy.

By the time he closed the door, he could see that the first

confessor was already sitting on the other side of the screen. His face partially obscured, the man spoke before Father O'Reilly could even greet him.

"Bless me, Father, for I have sinned," he said in a thin, gravelly voice. "It's been five years since my last confession, and . . ."

The words drifted off into an awkward silence. Father O'Reilly glanced through the screen at a young man whose face was a mere shadow beneath his wide fedora. There was something familiar about him—something so otherworldly that it turned the sanctuary's whispering breeze into a chilling wind.

Father O'Reilly shivered in spite of himself. "Please, go on," he said, trying to sound reassuring. "It's all right."

"Is it really?" the man said, his tight smile evident in his voice. "Well, since it's all right, these are my sins. I've lied to those who've tried to help me, and hidden myself from people who love me."

Father O'Reilly felt uneasy about whatever was beneath those words. He folded his hands to keep them from shaking and asked the question whose answer he already knew. "Is there more?"

The man chuckled. Then a loud burst of laughter escaped his lips before he suddenly went silent.

Father O'Reilly went from uneasy to fearful. "Listen, perhaps you should—"

"Let me guess," the man snapped, the sound of his voice growing darker by the moment. "Seek professional help? Is that what you're suggesting, Father? Well, that's not what I need. I need forgiveness. Can you give me that?"

"Well, I—"

"Can you grant forgiveness!" the man yelled, his voice echoing through the sanctuary as he slammed his fist against the confessional wall.

The commotion got the attention of the sexton, who started toward the confessional booth from the other side of the vast cathedral. The priest, hearing the faint sound of the approaching footsteps, was relieved, and at the same time, anxious.

"God can grant forgiveness, if you confess," the priest said, his voice shaking as the sexton came closer.

"Then these are my *other* sins," said the man in a tone that was eerily calm. "I cut off a man's finger while he slept on a park bench. I sliced a child's leg when he wandered away from his mother at a playground. I'm sick, Father, and I don't know what to do."

"You're doing the right thing now," the priest said nervously. "You're confessing."

"That's not the problem, Father," the man said as the sexton drew near.

"Then what is?"

The man stood up and pulled open his jacket, revealing a sawed-off shotgun. "The problem is . . . I'm the angel of death."

The sexton opened the door and was about to speak, but the man never gave him a chance. He whirled on him and fired, the blast spattering the walls with the sexton's blood-soaked innards.

Father O'Reilly tried to make his way around the wall that separated him from the killer. As he did so, the gunman confronted a man and a woman who had just arrived to give their confessions.

When they saw the gun, they both tried to turn and run. Both of them were too late.

The gunman shot the man in the back. The impact of the shell threw him into the woman, who fell, face first, to the ground. By the time she pushed the man's dead weight from her back and stood up to run toward the door, the gunman was upon her.

"Please!" she said as she turned and looked at the killer's eyes. "Have mercy!"

"Mercy is God's job," the gunman said coldly.

The final gunshot echoed through the sanctuary as Father O'Reilly watched in horror. When the woman fell to the ground, the killer dropped the gun and walked slowly toward the cathedral's massive doors.

Father O'Reilly ran to the spot where the gunman dropped the weapon. Then he knelt down and picked it up. As he held it and looked at the bodies sprawled on the floor of his beloved cathedral, he was filled with a rage he had never known before.

Raising the weapon until he had the killer in his sights, the priest slowly squeezed the trigger. The angels looked down on him from the stained-glass windows. A statue of the Blessed Virgin watched closely through hollow eyes. The hammer clicked. The gun was empty. So was Father O'Reilly.

He dropped to his knees as grief overwhelmed him. Though he pursed his lips and squeezed his eyes shut, neither gesture could hold the pain inside. Tears poured down his face and he screamed in anguish as the reality of the moment set in.

When the police arrived, he deliriously whispered that the gunman was the angel of death. They took the gun from his hands and lifted him to his feet. They shook his shoulders to stir him from the shock. However, the more they tried to rouse him, the deeper he seemed to fall. It was as if the floor of the sanctuary had opened and hell had risen up to swallow him.

He cried out to God as he fell into the enemy's hands. He yelled for his Father to save him from the torment he faced. He looked up to heaven as the tears poured down his cheeks. Then suddenly, someone reached down and snatched him up.

That's when Michael Coletti awakened. As always, the nightmare left the detective disoriented. He looked around expecting to see the cathedral, but there were no marble statues, no magnificent arches, and no stained-glass windows. There were only the threadbare furnishings of his one-bedroom apartment and the odors of stale smoke and sweat.

He ran his hands over his face and felt the wetness of the tears he'd cried in his sleep. He wondered what had snatched him from his nightmare and transported him back to his own reality. More importantly, Coletti wondered if being saved had done him more harm than good.

Pushing his sweat-soaked hair back from his face, Philadelphia's most senior homicide detective flipped the covers off his naked body, propped himself up on his elbow, and looked at his alarm clock. It was 5:30 AM, August 25, 2009. Summer would be over in twenty-eight days. His career would be over in three.

He grabbed his Marlboros from his nightstand and lit one with shaking hands. The hiss of the burning tobacco filled the room as Coletti pulled the smoke into his lungs. He exhaled slowly and reflected on the things he'd seen in his years on the force: crime scenes covered with the blood of children; women brutalized by men who claimed to love them; adulterous lovers shot dead in the throes of passion. None of it had affected him like the Confessional Murders.

For ten years, his dreams wouldn't let him forget the crime. He wasn't dreaming now, though, so Coletti did what he'd done every day for the last decade. He went on with his life.

Groaning as he got out of bed, he turned on the news, tramping through the pile of dirty clothes that led to the bathroom. Once there, he pulled the string that lit the lavatory's single lightbulb and absently listened while a weatherman predicted a breezy late summer day with temperatures reaching the mideighties.

He puffed his cigarette once more before flicking the butt into the toilet and flushing away the evidence of his one-cigarette-a-day habit. Splashing his face with cold water, he looked at his image in the mirror that hung haphazardly above the sink.

At a stocky five-foot eleven, with a craggy face and ample lips, he was almost, but not quite, handsome. His features were dark and distinctly Mediterranean, from his brown eyes and sculpted nose to his curly mop of salt-and-pepper hair. His body wasn't as hard as it had been when he was younger, but his jaw, lined with stubble, was just as rugged.

As he stared into the mirror at the wear and tear of fifty-eight years, the light struck the tiny gold crucifix dangling against his chest, and his tired eyes wandered to his slight paunch. Coletti looked a mess. He didn't care, though.

He wasn't looking for a woman. After thirty-one years on the force, his job was his mistress. He'd be leaving her in less than a week. After that, he planned to spend time with the only other companion that mattered: himself.

Coletti looked away from his image and began brushing

his teeth while relishing the thought of being alone. Then he heard something on the television that stopped him cold.

"The Pennsylvania supreme court has refused to hear defrocked priest Thomas O'Reilly's final appeal in the Confessional Murders," the newscaster said in a tone of mock concern. "That means O'Reilly, who has always maintained his innocence in the decade-old triple murder, is scheduled to face execution this Friday—three days from now. In the words of his lawyer, 'Only a miracle can save him.'"

Coletti wiped his mouth with the back of his hand as a sick feeling bubbled in his gut. He remembered being the first cop to arrive at the cathedral. He remembered taking the weapon from the priest's quivering hands. He remembered hearing O'Reilly's repeated claims of innocence. Most of all, he remembered trusting fingerprints over feelings.

Now the priest who'd haunted his dreams for a decade was scheduled to be put to death the day Coletti was to retire.

As the lightbulb in his bathroom began to flicker, Coletti fingered his crucifix and wondered if the priest's execution would make the nightmares stop. Or if perhaps, like O'Reilly, Coletti would need a miracle, too.

At 7:00 AM, a well-dressed man stepped onto the platform of the Chestnut Hill Regional Rail station in Philadelphia's diverse and affluent Northwest. He looked to be about twenty-five, and he carried an almond-colored briefcase that was monogrammed with the letters *CLM*.

Standing on the crowded platform in the cool of the morning with his neat black dreads and sleek, athletic build, Charles

Leonard Mann looked every bit the young businessman. He had finished graduate school five years before, so the persona fit him, but it was just a charade.

Charlie Mann was a cop, one who was able to blend into environments that other officers couldn't. He could adjust his style from Brooks Brothers to FUBU, or his dialect from Ebonics to geek-speak. He was a new kind of policeman, and he was homicide's fastest-rising star.

Mann had been selected to go to the train station when homicide received a tip about a meeting between a suspected hit man and the drug dealer who employed him. The state police would be assisting on this one, and homicide couldn't afford any screwups, especially with hundreds of commuters on the platform and on the trains. Mann knew that, and while he wasn't about to violate the trust that they'd placed in him, he didn't intend to let the suspect get away, either.

Pulling his iPhone from its case, Mann opened his pictures folder and clicked on the mug shot of the person he'd come to arrest.

The suspect didn't look like a killer. His freckled face was framed by stringy red hair. He sported a silver stud nose ring. His lips were thin and chapped. From the look of him, he would be more comfortable with a skateboard than with a gun. Yet there was something haunting about his lifeless and cruel gray eyes.

Beyond those eyes was an addict who'd traveled to Philadelphia for the purest heroin on the East Coast and who'd learned along the way that drug dealers paid well for murder. Once he was armed with that knowledge, it was easy to transition from killing himself with needles to killing other people with guns. Over the last six months, he'd killed five times, and each time that he'd received his payment of drugs and cash, he'd come closer to dying himself.

As Detective Mann stared at the suspect's picture on the screen, the iPhone began to vibrate. The mug shot disappeared and was replaced with the words *Incoming call*. He reached up to his ear and tapped the button on his Bluetooth headset.

"Hello?"

"I think our boy's walking up to the platform," a woman's voice said in a calm whisper. "Jeans and a blue T-shirt, about thirty yards to your left."

"Yeah, honey, I miss you, too," Mann said, speaking in code as he moved through the crowd to get a better look at the suspect.

The blond-haired woman who was feeding him the information was sitting on a bench at the far end of the platform. In her pantsuit and heels, with Styrofoam coffee cup in hand, she looked to be just another passenger. In truth, Mary Smithson was the state police profiler who'd spent months studying heroin addicts from Philadelphia's drug-infested Kensington neighborhood, eventually narrowing the list down to a single suspect. She was there to provide technical support for the operation.

"So what are the kids doing?" Mann asked.

"We're in position," said the homicide lieutenant who was on the line with them. He was one of two officers hiding on the opposite platform. There was also a sharpshooter on a rooftop nearly fifty yards away.

"Where's Joey?" Mann asked, using the code name for the drug dealer.

"He's not here yet," the lieutenant whispered into the phone. "But we can't wait anymore. We've gotta move now."

"Okay, honey," Mann said, reaching into his jacket and gripping the butt of his gun. "I'll see you when I get home."

A train's flickering light rounded the bend, prompting most of the commuters to move toward the edge of the platform. Mann darted between them, pushing ever faster toward the suspect.

"Hey, watch it!" a woman said when Mann stepped on her foot.

"Sorry," he said, moving faster as the train approached the station.

The woman was about to turn away when she noticed Mann's hand in his jacket. She watched in horror as he dropped his briefcase, drew his weapon, and started toward the suspect.

"He's got a gun!" she shouted, and the platform exploded in chaos.

Women began screaming as Mann broke through the crowd. Men started pushing toward the arriving train. The suspect looked around, his face contorted into the pitiful expression of an addict in need of a fix. When he saw Mann charging toward him, his drooping eyes grew wide, and he bolted in the other direction.

The detectives on the opposite platform were trapped in their positions when the train pulled into the station. The sharpshooter on the roof was unable to get a clear shot. The commuters on the platform were screaming and running toward the train.

Mann was their best hope to catch him.

He sprinted after the fleeing killer, who reached into his waistband and grabbed a .38.

Mann took aim and hoped for a clean shot, but Mary Smithson had already beaten him to the punch.

"Stop!" Smithson shouted as she stood and aimed her weapon at the suspect.

Trapped between Mann and Smithson, the hit man did as he was told. He stopped, and as terrified commuters looked on, he held the .38 at his side.

"Drop the gun!" Mann bellowed from behind him.

A smile spread across the hit man's face. He closed his eyes and slowly raised the gun toward Smithson. As he did so, Smithson's finger tightened on her trigger, but Mann fired first.

The bullet exploded through the back of the hit man's head. As he fell to the ground, Mann fired another round through his torso.

There was a moment of tortured silence as the commuters absorbed what had just happened. Out of the hundreds of people who had witnessed the shooting, Mann was the first to speak.

"Are you all right?" he asked Smithson as the killer lay dead between them.

"I'm fine," she said, but her quivering hands said otherwise as she lowered her weapon.

With blood pooling against the platform and dumbfounded commuters watching in shocked disbelief, Mann and Smithson walked slowly to the body.

"Why didn't you shoot?" he asked without looking at her.

She was quiet for a few moments, trying to come up with an answer that wouldn't betray her fear. Then she remembered the information she'd gathered on the suspect's psychological profile.

"The mindset of a man who'd kill for drugs is the same as one who's suicidal," she said, masking her raging nerves with her matter-of-fact tone. "When he raised that gun, he wasn't trying to kill me. He was trying to kill himself."

An hour after the shooting, a disheveled Mike Coletti walked into homicide and sat behind his scarred metal desk. His mind racing with the news of Father O'Reilly's impending execution, he loosened his tie while drinking coffee from an old cracked cup.

The steaming brew was part of a morning ritual that he'd observed for the past thirty-one years. On days like this one, it helped him to quiet his mind and remember what was truly important, just the way it used to do for his father.

Even now, more than three decades after his father's death, the detective still remembered him clearly. A no-nonsense butcher who migrated to South Philly from Naples, Italy, Michelangelo Coletti, Sr., would begin each morning with a cup of his wife Gloria's freshly brewed espresso. He'd leave the house at sunrise to open his Ninth Street shop and butcher meat until well after dark to provide a good living for his wife and his only son, whose name they shortened to Michael.

The Colettis were simple people with an abiding sense of pride in their heritage and a core set of values that came from their native land. Honor and tradition, family and respect were enforced with Michelangelo's iron fist, encouraged by Gloria's velvet glove, and reiterated every Sunday at mass.

But even with all he learned at home and at church, the streets of South Philly taught young Michael the most. Living near the Italian Market, where blocks of rickety shacks brimmed with meats and cheeses and where hucksters sold everything from fresh milk to ice, he learned the value of hard work early on. However, there was a flip side to the neighborhood.

There were men who lived just blocks from his home who twisted the values of honor, family, and loyalty, and applied them to lives of crime. These mobsters convinced boys he'd grown up with to abandon childhood games in order to join South Philly's Mafia.

Michael resisted that temptation, graduating from South Philadelphia High School in 1968—a year that embodied all the turbulence of the sixties. Vietnam escalated. King and Kennedy were assassinated. Riots burned neighborhoods in Philadelphia and other cities.

For a year, Coletti watched it all on a black-and-white TV with rabbit ears as he worked in his father's shop. He wasn't picked in the draft lottery when he turned eighteen, thus avoiding the trip to Vietnam. But he couldn't avoid the internal war that determined the man he'd become.

He saw his father, Michelangelo, toiling for their home and family. He saw Frank Rizzo, the police commissioner from nearby Rosewood Street, fighting to maintain the status quo. He saw the mobsters killing and conniving for their piece of the pie. Then one day, he looked at himself.

He was twenty-three by then, and he didn't have a thing.

He didn't want to live that way, so he began weighing his options. He hated the mundane life of his father. He didn't want the responsibility of a cop. He was intrigued by the notion of taking what he wanted, so he contemplated joining the mob. When Michelangelo Coletti found out, his response was anything but mundane.

"You wanna shoot?" Michael's father said in his heavy Italian accent as he marched his son to the recruiter. "You shoot for your country."

Coletti always smiled when he thought of that day. That day was what allowed him to see a bit of the world during his four-year tour of duty as a supply clerk on bases in Italy and Germany. That day was also one of the last times he saw his father as the man he'd been.

When he came back to South Philly from overseas, his father's once-strong voice had been ravaged by throat cancer. In seven months, Michael Coletti's hero was gone. Five months later, his mother died from what could only be described as a broken heart.

After he buried her, Coletti sold the butcher shop that his father had spent his life building up, and something inside him changed. He got angry. He withdrew. Then he set out to keep his parents' memories alive by finding a way to enforce their values. He chose to do so by pursuing the very job he'd initially avoided. He became a cop.

For most of his career in the police force, he tried to serve with the honor and integrity he'd learned from his mother and father. He'd slipped a few times and made some mistakes, but he always worked hard to earn everything he ever got, just like his father before him.

In Coletti's mind, not everyone embraced such values, and that, more than anything, set him off.

"You all right, Coletti?" said a detective with a thick brown mustache and heavy eyebrows to match.

"Yeah," he said, taking another sip of his coffee. "I was just thinking."

"Did you hear what happened up in Chestnut Hill this morning?"

"Yep, Charlie shot a suspect with a hundred commuters in the line of fire," Coletti said, pausing for effect. "I wonder if he would've been that trigger-happy if he was shooting at one of his own."

"What's that supposed to mean?" a voice called out from across the room.

Coletti looked up and saw Mann walking in with a thin, blond-haired woman beside him. Mann looked angry, but Coletti wasn't about to back down.

"You went to college and you don't know what 'one of his own' means?" Coletti asked coolly.

"Yeah, I know what it means," Mann said angrily. "It means you don't think I belong here."

"You belong if you earn it," Coletti shot back. "But you don't make homicide just because somebody decides there's a quota."

A million answers went through Mann's mind, ranging in tone from eloquent to ignorant. When he'd considered every possible verbal retort and found them all to be lacking, he chose the only response he could.

His face clouding over with rage and his fingers curling into fists, Mann bolted across the room.

Coletti stood up, prepared to fight. Three detectives came between them a second before the first punch could fly.

As Mann and Coletti grunted and struggled to get past the peacemakers, Mary Smithson walked to Mann's side while carefully studying Coletti.

"Who the hell are you?" Coletti asked.

"Lieutenant Smithson, State Police," she said, nodding toward Mann. "I'm one of his own."

As she spoke, Mann jerked his arm away from the men who were holding him. A few seconds later, Coletti did, too. When they were sure that both had calmed down, the detectives who had restrained them stepped aside.

"What do you mean, you're one of his own?" Coletti asked while rubbing his arms where his colleagues had gripped them.

"You implied that he looks out for his own," she said in a level tone. "Well, I'm the one he looked out for today. As far as I'm concerned, he's the reason I'm still alive."

"Look, lady, I—"

"My name's Mary," she said, extending her hand.

He looked at her eyes. They were blue and bottomless, filled with curiosity and intelligence. It took everything within him not to stare.

"I'm Mike Coletti," he said, shaking her hand while forcing himself to look away.

"We came to fill out the paperwork on what happened this

morning," Mann said, his eyes scanning the room. "But I guess there's no need for that, since I don't belong here."

There was an awkward silence as the other detectives tried to decide who would answer first.

"Coletti doesn't speak for me," said the one with the bushy mustache. "As long as you do your job, I don't have a problem with you or anybody else."

A few piped up in agreement. Several more mumbled placating words. Then Coletti spoke.

"Look, kid," he said, clearing his throat as he searched for the right words. "I didn't mean it to come out that way. I've got a lot on my mind, and—"

"Save it," Mann said, stalking angrily to his desk as Commissioner Kevin Lynch walked in.

There were halfhearted greetings as the man who'd rocketed from homicide to the top of the department crossed the room and stopped at Mann's desk.

Lynch smiled, his bald brown head shimmering nearly as brightly as the stars on his shoulders. Unlike Mann, he relished the resentment of his former squad. It drove him to succeed.

"Mann, Smithson, I need to talk to both of you," he said, beckoning for them to follow him out to the hallway. "You too, Coletti."

Wearing a bewildered expression, the old detective walked out behind the other three. When the door closed, the commissioner turned to Mann and Smithson.

"Internal affairs, homicide, and the state folks are gonna need to interview the two of you about the shooting. Mann, you'll be reassigned to desk duty for a few days, and Smithson, I'm sure you'll be glad to get back to your desk out in Dunmore after all this is over."

"Actually, Commissioner, I was hoping to hang around here for at least a day or so," she said, smiling nervously before casting a furtive glance in Coletti's direction.

Lynch caught the look. Mann did, too, but he had more pressing matters to attend to.

"Sir, if I'm going to be strapped to a desk," he said, his jaw tight with anger, "I'd just as soon have it be in another unit, especially since homicide will be investigating."

"Angels from heaven could be investigating, Detective Mann. It won't make a difference. A suspect pointed a gun at a fellow officer. You shot to kill. Case closed. But if it'll make you feel better, you'll be on loan to the delayed police response unit— DPR. You'll take stolen car and theft from vehicle reports over the phone for a couple days, but you'll still be attached to homicide."

"Commissioner, I—"

"You think you're the only one who's ever had a hard time in homicide?" Lynch snapped. "Well, I've got news for you, Detective. You're not. When I came to homicide, *I* was the college boy who was rising a little too fast, and everybody hated me too, right, Coletti?"

"Nobody hated you," Coletti said to the commissioner before nodding toward Mann. "And nobody hates him, either. The kid just rubs me the wrong way."

"Why? Because I'm black?" Mann asked as Smithson shifted uncomfortably.

"No, because you're just like I was when I got to homicide. A smart-ass who thinks he's got it all figured out."

"Racists always have an excuse," Mann mumbled.

"Look, I'm not a racist," Coletti said, shifting his gaze from Mann to Lynch and back. "But I shouldn't have said what I said, and I'm man enough to admit I was wrong."

Clearly, Mann wasn't prepared to accept Coletti's apology. It was Lynch who broke the silence.

"Everything isn't always what it seems, Detective Mann. If you're gonna be a good cop, you need to learn that."

"Not from him," Mann said, staring angrily at Coletti.

"Oh, I think he'll be a fine teacher," Lynch said. "That's why I've decided to make the two of you partners. Mann, you'll make your appearance in DPR. After that, you'll work with Coletti. He's gonna share all the lessons he learned back when *he* was the young hotshot, and before he retires, he's gonna show you what it takes to be the top detective in this unit."

"And if I don't?" Coletti said.

"Somebody might lose your paperwork. I've heard pensions get held up for years when that happens."

Coletti was speechless as the commissioner turned to Mann and Smithson.

"You two need to get up to internal affairs now, and I need to get to a press conference about the shooting."

Lynch started down the hall, then stopped and turned around. "I almost forgot, Coletti. I heard they rejected Father O'Reilly's appeal. I know you'll be glad when that's finally over."

Coletti watched as Lynch walked to his press conference. A

second later, Mann headed up to internal affairs. Coletti didn't notice that Smithson was still standing there. He couldn't. The commissioner's mention of the Confessional Murders had taken him back to the nightmare from that morning.

"Are you all right?" Smithson asked.

"I'm fine," he said, but the thin film of sweat on his suddenly pallid face said otherwise.

Her eyebrows crinkled as her eyes moved from his chest to his face. "You don't look so hot."

"Thanks for the compliment," he said sarcastically.

Smithson chuckled. "Just calling it like I see it."

"Well, I wish you wouldn't see it so clearly," he said. "It's bad for my ego."

She smiled, and as Coletti tried to think of a way to end the conversation without making a fool of himself, she said something he didn't expect.

"Listen, I've got to go up to give my statement about this morning. But since we've both had a bit of a rough day, I was thinking we could take a walk down to Second Street after work."

Coletti looked at her quizzically. "For what?"

"I heard there were good exhibits here, and I've always wanted to see them. We don't really have many art galleries in upstate Pennsylvania, and it'd be great if—"

"I'm not really the art gallery type," Coletti said, turning to walk away from her.

"Okay, I'll make a deal with you. I won't drag you in and out of every exhibit, but there is one I want to see that I read about in the paper. It's at the Old City Art Gallery."

"I don't think so."

She placed a hand on his shoulder, and he turned to face her. Before he knew it, he was once again lost in her eyes.

"If you're too embarrassed to be seen with me . . ."

"No, it's not that."

"Good. I'll meet you outside on the corner of Eighth and Race at five o'clock," she said.

Coletti opened his mouth to protest, but she silenced him by placing a finger against his lips.

"I promise you'll like the exhibit," she said, her tone low and convincing. "It's called *Confessions*."

CHAPTER 2

Sergeant Sandy Jackson was on her way to spend the morning as she'd often done in recent weeks—studying at the diner at Seventeenth and Chancellor, just blocks from where she used to walk a beat.

She liked to go to the diner before reporting for her three-thirty shift, because being there spurred memories that made her study harder.

For her first two years on the force, Jackson had spent nearly every warm-weather sunrise conducting a tragic street opera between the old money in nearby Rittenhouse Square and the homeless who languished in the shadows of wealth.

The first act always began with a predawn call from a doorman near the park, whose fountain and copper statues punctuated Center City's most exclusive neighborhood. The final act frequently began with crass male supervisors sending Jackson and her female partner to investigate.

The calls most often involved homeless men bathing in the

fountain or drug-addicted prostitutes turning tricks on the benches. Having been admonished about leaving pornographic pictures in plain view of their female coworkers, the frat-boy complement of the ninth police district decided that sending women to roust naked men was the next best thing.

Such harassment forced Jackson's partner to take a stress-related medical leave, but it pushed Jackson to succeed. In just her fifth year on the force, she'd already passed the corporal's and sergeant's exams with the highest grades in the department. As a result, she'd been promoted to shift supervisor. Her radio moniker was 9A. She no longer took orders from men. It was she who decided what happened on the street.

In two weeks, she'd be taking the lieutenant's exam, and just as she'd done prior to the other two exams, she engaged in a ritual that served to keep the memories fresh. She walked the concrete path that wound through the grassy park and stopped at the fountain that she'd long ago rid of the homeless. Then she walked to the diner where her favorite waitress knew what she wanted.

Doing so was more than a reminder of her past. It was motivation for her future.

Of course, there was something else driving her. Or rather, there was someone. He was tall with dangling dreads and a smile that he saved just for her. He was intense and driven. He was smart and sexy. Most important, he was hers.

She'd spent the bulk of the morning trying to reach him after receiving word of the train station shooting. Her calls had gone unanswered.

As she walked into the diner and slid into her favorite booth at the front of the greasy spoon that had somehow survived amid sidewalk cafés and gourmet shops, she took off her hat, revealing reddish brown hair slightly darker than her cinnamon-colored skin. Then she took out her cell phone and pressed send, once again calling the only number she cared to reach that day.

It rang as the waitress smiled silently while sliding a cup of green tea in front of her. It rang while Jackson looked up with wide brown eyes and smiled back appreciatively. It rang while the sun shone dimly through the diner's dirty window, and rang again while Jackson worriedly rubbed her right temple.

"Hey, Sandy," he said, picking up on the seventh ring.

She exhaled, unaware that she'd been holding her breath. In that moment, she was soft, vulnerable, worried about the man she loved. That lasted for a few seconds, and then the tough veneer she'd developed as a cop resurfaced.

"Don't 'Hey, Sandy' me," she hissed. "I've been calling you since I heard about what happened this morning. Are you all right?"

"Of course I am," he said. "I've just been dealing with some stuff down here at homicide."

"What do you mean, 'stuff'?"

There was a pause. She noticed it. Clearly he was going to try to hide something from her. That wasn't a wise move.

"Nothing I can't handle," he said, his voice filled with the self-assurance that had drawn her to him in the first place.

But she heard a slight tremor in his voice when he spoke. It wasn't fear. It was the kind of rage she'd held in far too many times herself. Rage she thought might boil over someday, in a time and in a place she least expected.

"Let me guess," she said knowingly. "Coletti and his minions are at it again."

"I don't want to talk about it," Mann said quickly. "Actually, I *can't* talk about it. I'm on my way to internal affairs right now to give my statement about the shooting."

"Well, here's *my* statement," Sandy said. "Don't take any crap from anybody in that homicide unit. You're the best detective this department has seen in a long time, and I'll be damned if they're gonna treat you as anything less."

"Listen Sandy, I—"

"No, Charlie, *you* listen," she said, her neck rolling as her finger pointed in the air almost reflexively. "I've seen people get run outta this department by the old boy network. I'm not gonna watch them run you out, too."

"There's only one place I'm running," Mann said with a mischievous smile.

She could hear the flirtation in his voice, and her cinnamon skin flushed red.

"I'm glad to hear that," she said with a grin, the seductive tone in his words relaxing her finger and steadying her rolling neck. He was the antidote to her attitude. The bass in his voice brought out the soprano in hers. When she spoke again, the acidic tone was gone. It was replaced by something velvety and smooth that the men she supervised never heard. It was a tone she saved just for him.

"I've got some studying to do before I go to work," she whispered. "I'm going in early today, but when I get off, I'm going home and run myself a hot bath. Then I'm going to wait for you to come over and investigate the scene. I want to see if you're as good at solving cases as you think you are."

"You're crazy," Mann said.

"You like it," Jackson said, biting her bottom lip and grinning. "Now remember, don't let them get to you, especially that damn Coletti."

"Be nice, Sandy. Mike Coletti's going to have a special place in my life now."

"What do you mean?"

"Oh, I guess you didn't hear," Mann said as he approached the door to internal affairs. "Commissioner Lynch made us partners."

Sandy Jackson usually knew just what to say and when to say it. This time, however, she couldn't do anything but sit there with her mouth agape, trying to imagine how her man could work with someone like Coletti.

As he disconnected the call and walked into internal affairs, Charlie Mann read the apprehension in Jackson's silence. He couldn't imagine working with Coletti, either.

By five o'clock, Coletti was standing outside police headquarters, gazing across the street at the abandoned hospital that had been converted into condos.

He wondered if the young professional residents with their hybrid cars and doctorates knew that the building and nearby playground had once been home to rats and homeless drug addicts. He doubted that they would care. After all, the city had given them thousands in property tax breaks to become urban pioneers. In the face of such a windfall, what did a few rat turds matter?

His own presence there was a little more difficult to figure. With his matted hair and worn-out sport coat, Coletti wasn't much to look at. Yet Mary Smithson—a woman who seemed to have more in common with the Birkenstock-clad crowd across the street than with him—had asked him to meet her there.

Perhaps it was some kind of joke, he thought. Maybe Ashton Kutcher was somewhere close by.

"Mike Coletti, you've just been punk'd," he muttered, his face creasing in a wry smile.

"What'd you say?"

Coletti turned to find Smithson standing behind him.

"I was just, uh, wondering what was taking you so long," he said, averting his eyes so she wouldn't see his embarrassment.

She smiled. "Thanks for waiting."

"My car's in the lot," he said, starting back toward police headquarters.

She placed a hand gently on his chest. "I thought we could walk. I've been cooped up in that building all day."

Coletti nodded, and the two of them started down Race Street, silently taking in the sounds of cars on the nearby Ben Franklin Bridge and the laughter of children in the playground across the street.

"So I guess they grilled you about the shooting today," Coletti said, stuffing his hands in his pockets and staring at the ground in front of him.

"It's like the commissioner said. There wasn't a lot to tell. The guy pulled a gun on me and Mann shot him."

Coletti's brow furrowed. "Yeah, I remember you said that. I was a little confused, though. If the guy pulled the gun on you, why didn't *you* fire?"

"I hate guns," she said, lowering her eyes and forcing a tight smile. "I can't bring myself to use them unless I absolutely have to. I guess that's kind of strange for a cop, huh?"

"That depends. Are you a cop who happens to be a profiler or a profiler who happens to be a cop?"

Smithson thought about it for a moment. "I guess if I had to choose one of the two, I'd be a profiler first. That's why I got my doctorate in criminal psychology—to study criminal minds."

She laughed absently. "Five years ago, when I realized the FBI would actually want me to work cases before recognizing my genius as a profiler, I applied to the state police. They cut me a deal. I could be a profiler, but I'd have to carry a gun. It was a trade-off that worked out pretty well until this morning."

Coletti stared at her as she spoke. Her face was soft and supple, with fine wrinkles at the corners of her eyes and mouth, and deeper lines extending across her forehead. Her shoulder-length blond hair framed a wide, rounded jaw, and her lips were barely full enough to kiss. She was more handsome than beautiful. That is, until she looked at him with those eyes.

"Do you study everybody that way?" she asked when she caught him staring. "Or were you saving all your weirdness for me?"

"I'm sorry. I was just wondering why you . . ." Coletti hesitated. He didn't want to make himself sound like the loser he knew he was.

"Why I asked you to go to the gallery with me?"

"Well, yeah."

"You're not wearing an undershirt," she said with a mischievous grin.

"You saw my flab, didn't you?" he deadpanned as he stopped and turned to her. "Please don't tell me you're attracted to flab."

She laughed. It was a high-pitched, pleasant sound: one that Coletti could get used to. "Actually," she said coyly, "I noticed your crucifix."

He looked down at his chest self-consciously. Then, as they started walking again, he glanced at her with a question in his eyes.

"Your shirt's kinda cheap," she explained, her face contorting into an amused apology of sorts. "It's easy to see through it without an undershirt, especially from the side."

"So you asked me to go to the gallery with you because you like old guys with cheap shirts and crucifixes. Is that some kind of fetish or something?"

She slapped his arm playfully. "No, silly. I just—I don't know. It's interesting running into other practicing Catholics, I guess. Makes me feel like I'm connected to something bigger than me."

He was quiet as he contemplated what she'd said. When he spoke, it was with seriousness that he'd thus far been able to avoid.

"I hate to disappoint you," he said soberly, "but I haven't really been a practicing Catholic for years. So, if you're looking for some kind of connection . . ."

"Whoa, there, Mr. Coletti," she said, raising her hands in

mock surrender, "I didn't ask you to marry me. I just wanted somebody to talk to."

"Let me guess. You picked me because of the great rhetorical skills I showed back there with my new partner."

She chuckled, but this time the sound was empty and humorless. "Actually, I thought you were a jerk back there," she said bluntly.

"So you like jerks?"

"No, I like men, and it takes a man to apologize when he's wrong. Plus, I'm a bit of a sucker for reclamation projects. Maybe it's the psychologist in me. I think I can fix people."

"Even if they don't want to be fixed?"

She smiled. "Everybody wants to be fixed. Most people just don't know it."

"Well, don't waste your time trying to fix me," Coletti said with a grin. "I'm not the one who's crazy."

"And I am?" she asked, raising an eyebrow.

"You're out with me, aren't you? That can't be a good sign."

She laughed as the two of them crossed Sixth Street, passing the stately slab of glass and concrete that was the National Constitution Center. As they crossed Fifth Street, then Fourth, they grew more enamored with their surroundings, and a bit more relaxed with one another.

They passed by Quaker meetinghouses that held the graves of colonial Philadelphians. They examined streets where the ghosts of Franklin and Washington mingled with those of British redcoats. They walked among the ancestral memories of slave and free, indentured and conscript. They walked through history, and as they did so, each of them wondered what their place in it would be.

By the time they turned on Second Street and strolled a block and a half south, they'd walked past the nation's oldest street and into the city's newest fad—an art exhibit fashioned out of secrets.

"Welcome to *Confessions*," said a smiling blonde with freshly coifed hair and glasses that made her appear almost professorial.

Coletti greeted her with a curt nod, while Smithson smiled warmly.

The hostess flipped her hair and pointed to a table propped up against the far wall. "There's Camembert and cabernet in the back," she said, exaggerating the French pronunciation of both the wine and the cheese.

Coletti wasn't impressed. The hostess noticed, and moved swiftly to say something that would correct that. "Personally, I would've served chenin blanc with the Camembert, but the gallery owners are new to the business, and—"

Coletti walked away before she could finish. Smithson's face turned red with embarrassment before she ran to catch up with him.

"Why were you so rude to her?" she hissed.

"Because I hate phonies," he said, grabbing a glass of wine from the table and taking a long sip.

"I think you hate everybody," she said, looking at him through squinting eyes.

"I don't hate you," he said, gulping down the remainder of the wine. "At least not yet."

Smithson shook her head disapprovingly and grabbed him by the arm. "Come on."

With six-foot potted palms intermittently placed along its carpeted floors and delicate flower arrangements on unvarnished pine tables, the gallery smelled of an earthy mix of wood, soil, and chemicals.

Silky, earth-toned fabric served as wallpaper. Paintings—mostly nudes and abstracts—were displayed beneath recessed lighting. White tags with sparse descriptions marked every painting, but none of them bore prices.

"I guess if you have to ask you can't afford it," Coletti mumbled as he admired a nude of a woman with flowing red hair and pale, freckled skin.

"Then don't ask," said an annoyed Smithson as she pulled him into the room where *Confessions* hung.

Foot-long stained-glass windows framed by ebony arches hung from the ceiling on wires. As people moved through the room, the glass spun, reflecting colored beams from tiny spotlights that illuminated handwritten notes arranged haphazardly on the walls.

The church-inspired imagery reminded Coletti of his dream. It disturbed him. Yet he was drawn to the exhibit by the same thing as those who'd never set foot inside a church—secrets.

"I hate my mother," the first ragged and soiled piece of paper read. "She hung me by my wrists in the basement."

"I slept with my wife's sister," said another. "My nephew is really my son."

"My daughter thinks her puppy ran away," the next one said. "I drowned it because we couldn't feed it anymore."

As they made their way around the wall, reading secrets on subjects ranging from gross cruelty to generational lies, Smithson seemed to become more engrossed. Coletti was bored, yet when he looked at the other patrons who'd come to see the exhibit, he saw faces filled with angst and contrition, disgust and remorse, and yet another expression that was universal among everyone there. They were riveted.

Coletti felt sorry for them. Then he felt annoyed by them. His eyes scanned the room until they fell upon the blond hostess and another gallery employee—a wiry man with spiked black hair and a collared shirt. The two of them were having an animated discussion in the corner, whispering urgently while engaging in a tug-of-war over a stack of confessions like the ones on the wall.

Coletti wandered over to them, leaving Smithson to read the last few confessions alone.

"All out of chenin blanc, huh?" Coletti said, interrupting their conversation.

"Please, sir, we really need a few moments, if you don't mind," the man said politely.

"Well, I sorta do mind, because if you're looking at something more exciting than the crap on the wall over there, you need to share it with the rest of us."

"Look, Grandpa, mind your own damn business. We've got a crisis here."

The blonde's genteel pronunciation and manner were gone now. She sounded like a broad who'd spent more than her fair share of time in bars.

"Crisis?" Coletti said, flashing his badge self-righteously. "I deal with crisis all the time."

The hostess exchanged a worried look with the spike-haired man. They were quiet for what seemed like an eternity. The man was the first to speak.

"I'm the curator. My name's Peter Bloom. Seems we have a confession here that's a little different from a lot of the others. I saw some guy leave it on the desk a couple minutes ago."

"Well, what does it say?" Coletti asked as Smithson came alongside him.

The man hesitated, and Coletti snatched the sheets of paper from him. He read the first one quickly and tossed it aside. He did the same with the second. When he got to the third, the blood drained from his face.

"What is it?" Smithson asked worriedly.

Coletti looked at her with fear and uncertainty in his eyes. "It says, 'I'm the angel of death. I escaped Coletti ten years ago, and in less than twenty-four hours, I'll kill again.'"

With that, the detective leaned hard against the wall. A million fractured thoughts went through his mind: the blood on the floor of the cathedral; the shotgun in the priest's hands; the sight of the killer's bared teeth. Those thoughts came forth in a whirlwind. Then they disappeared in a flash of light, leaving him with nothing but anger and fear.

"You look like you've seen a ghost," Smithson said.

Coletti pushed himself away from the wall. "I'm fine."

She looked in his eyes and immediately knew he was lying. Then she looked at the note and instantly knew it was real.

"This angel of death must've done something terrible for you to react this way."

"He did," Coletti said through clenched teeth. "He got away."

A moment later, he was on his cell phone, calling dispatch and telling them he needed an assist. In doing so, he brought every cop in the area flying to his aid. When he disconnected the call, Smithson touched his shoulder in an effort to comfort him. Coletti was too preoccupied to notice. He looked once more at the words scrawled on the paper. Then he did something he hadn't done for nearly ten years.

He prayed.

By five forty-five, dozens of police cars lined Second Street, their red and blue dome lights flashing against the gallery's walls as the curious looked on from nearby shops and coffee bars.

In Philadelphia's Old City, where Betsy Ross's house and Ben Franklin's printing press are flanked by nightclubs and sidewalk cafés, they'd seen disturbances before, but they'd never seen anything like Mike Coletti.

"You mean to tell me you didn't notice anything else about the guy who dropped off this confession?" an agitated Coletti snapped at the exhibit curator.

"I already told you," the man answered, nervously regarding the two detectives and four uniformed officers who'd joined Coletti and Smithson in a back room at the gallery. "People drop confessions off all the time—here and in the boxes we've placed around the city. We don't take down people's descriptions."

"So how can we be sure you saw this guy?"

"He walked in the front door," the curator said in an agitated tone. "He was kinda hard to miss."

Coletti flipped through his notepad. "So you said he was white, kinda stocky, and wearing a dirty blue down jacket and jeans?"

"Yes," the curator said, hoping the questioning would stop. "He looked like he could've been homeless."

The description didn't match anything Coletti remembered from ten years before. More important, it didn't jibe with what he'd seen in his dreams. "You're sure the guy was stocky?"

"Yeah, I looked right at him. He left the note on the desk and walked toward Market Street."

Coletti turned to one of the uniformed officers. "Get the description on the air. Have all units use caution. This guy might have a gun."

"*Might?*" boomed a familiar voice. "You called for an assist because you thought some guy *might* have a gun?"

Coletti's face flushed as he turned and saw Lynch walking in.

"It's not about a guy who might have a gun," Coletti said, holding up the note which had been placed in an evidence bag. "It's about a murderer who's about to kill again."

Lynch read it and beckoned for Coletti to follow him into another room. When Lynch closed the door behind them, he wheeled on Coletti with fire in his eyes.

"Why would you call the whole sixth district in on this?"

"I already told you. I think there's a killer on the loose."

"Because some crazy homeless guy wrote something on a note?" Lynch asked cynically.

"No, it's more than that," Coletti said, closing his eyes and rubbing his temples. "I, uh, I've been having these dreams."

Lynch was incredulous. "Come on, Coletti, you don't expect me to believe—"

"The dreams are about the Confessional Murders, and in those dreams the killer isn't the priest. He's a skinny white man dressed in black."

Lynch stopped at the mention of the ten-year-old case. In the context of those murders, Coletti's reaction to the note almost made sense. Almost.

"Look, Mike, we all have cases that bother us," Lynch said. "I mean, nobody wants to believe that a priest would kill three people in a cathedral, but . . ."

"I know it sounds crazy," Coletti said. "And you're right. I never wanted to believe Father O'Reilly was guilty, especially the way I came up, watching Father Carducci saying mass in South Philly. Back then, the priest was the most respected man in the neighborhood. Even the Mob would cease fire if he said so. But things changed over the years, and I changed, too. When I came back from the army, my parents died and Father Carducci died, and I didn't want to go to church anymore because I felt like God had abandoned me. Then in the nineties, even before it went public, I heard whispers about priests from the guys in the special victims unit. All that made it easier to believe it when I found Father O'Reilly with that gun. But something about that case always felt wrong. Now I know why."

Lynch looked at Coletti, and for the first time, he saw what the case had taken out of him. The commissioner tried to put it back.

"I remember coming to homicide as a young detective," Lynch said quietly. "I was always ranting about the way we went after black suspects because they were easy to convict. Do you remember that, Mike?"

Coletti nodded.

"One day, you got tired of hearing it and told me—told everybody, in fact—that our job was to gather evidence and make arrests. It was up to the DA to prove the case and up to juries to determine guilt. If someone went to jail for something they didn't do, that was on the courts, not us. Back then, you said knowing that helped you to sleep at night."

Coletti smiled weakly. "It did."

"So what's different now?"

Coletti's smile faded as he looked at Lynch. "Those guys were guilty," he said softly. "Father O'Reilly isn't."

"How can you be so sure?"

"Because that so-called crazy homeless guy called himself the angel of death."

"So?"

"When I arrived at the cathedral that day, Father O'Reilly said the murderer called himself the angel of death. That was the only time he used that phrase. He never said it under questioning, he never said it at trial, so the only other person who'd know that phrase would be the killer."

Lynch stared at Coletti in disbelief. "Are you saying you think the man you helped put on death row for those murders is innocent?"

"No," Coletti said. "I'm saying I *know* he is."

The two men stood there, wondering what the truth about

the murders would reveal, and wondering if they really wanted to know.

A moment later, there was a tap at the door. Lynch was still trying to digest what he'd heard. Coletti felt strangely free, as if a weight had been lifted from his shoulders.

He squeezed past the commissioner and cracked the door. Mary Smithson's blue eyes were on the other side.

"They think they found the guy who dropped the note," she said. "They're in pursuit."

Sergeant Sandy Jackson was already in her car, having driven from Rittenhouse Square to answer the art gallery assist.

Police radio had declared the situation under control before she could get there, and she was now on her way back to the ninth district. In many ways, she was glad she'd missed the assist. If she'd seen Coletti face to face, she might've said something ugly. Being phony wasn't her strong suit.

Though Sandy's sharp tongue was her weakness, her strength was her sixth sense. It was that sense that caused her to notice the man who was running down Market Street as befuddled tourists watched.

Even before the alert tone was broadcast on police radio and the dispatcher described him as the man involved in the art gallery assist, Sandy Jackson knew that something wasn't right. She skidded to a stop at Fifth and Market.

"Stop!" she yelled, jumping out of her car with her gun drawn.

The suspect looked back quickly. Then he ducked into the mass of people who were walking to the train entrance at Fifth

Street. Using rush hour commuters and wide-eyed tourists as human shields, he waded into the crowd, stuffed his jacket into a trash can, and popped out the other side as Sandy sprinted to catch up.

"Stop now!" she shouted, as two other officers fell in behind her.

Knowing that the police couldn't shoot into the crowd, the suspect bolted down Market Street, weaving through throngs of tourists who'd come to see the Liberty Bell and Independence Hall.

He ran while the sound of sirens filled the air, his fists pumping and his legs churning as adrenaline made him move faster than Sandy and every cop who joined the chase.

Sandy knew that he could hear the heavy footfalls of the pursuing officers. She knew that he could hear the radio chatter that betrayed his location. She knew that he was desperate.

As she watched him dodge in and out of the crowd of commuters and tourists, she knew something else, as well. If they didn't catch him soon, an innocent bystander would be hurt.

With sweat streaming down her face and cramps locking up her muscles, Sandy ran harder, even as her lungs were ablaze and her breath came in heavy gasps.

With rush hour traffic clogging streets too small for heavy volume, and commuters flocking to subway platforms and bus stops, she caught sight of the suspect once more. As she and other officers closed in, the suspect took advantage of the chaos around him.

Stepping into the midst of the crowd at Ninth and Market,

he threw his head back. "They're shootin'!" he shouted as loud as he could.

At that, the people around him ran in every direction. As they did so, he moved toward a flight of steps leading to the Gallery shopping mall. Sandy saw him at the last moment, just as he disappeared down the steps and through the mall's rotating glass doors.

To the suspect's right were kiosks and a sandwich shop, a bookstore, and a dimly lit passage to the Market-Frankford Elevated's Eighth Street stop. To his left was the passageway that would lead past the food court and toward the Twelfth Street exit.

"There he is!" Sandy shouted as she ran through the doors behind him.

The suspect ran to his left, knocking down an old woman with a two-wheeled shopping cart and jostling a young boy whose heavy book bag nearly tipped him over. He smashed into a kiosk filled with cell phones, sending the glass display tumbling to the red brick floor.

Shards of shattered glass popped up toward his face, and one of them opened a gash near his eye. Still, he kept running, even as police officers came toward him from the escalator at Tenth Street.

"West in the Gallery food court!" Sandy shouted into a radio as she ran to catch up with him.

Her legs felt like tree stumps. Her chest burned with exhaustion. But as Sandy struggled to catch up to him, the suspect labored, as well.

The blood that dripped from the wound over his eye left a

trail in his wake. His legs flailed wildly. His arms swung desperately. He stumbled toward the Twelfth Street exit like a man about to fall from his own momentum.

When five officers came through the Twelfth Street doors and ran in his direction, cutting off his route of escape, he did the only thing he could. He veered left at Eleventh Street and ducked into a passageway filled with commuters going to and from the Market-Frankford Elevated.

As he lumbered toward the glass doors that would lead him to the trains and an underground tunnel to City Hall, the bleeding that had begun with a slow drip came down in a steady stream.

Commuters saw the sweat and dirt mingling with blood on his face and clothing, and they stepped aside in horror. Conversations ceased. Eyes went wide with shock. Mouths flew open in disbelief. Brows furrowed with confusion.

When Sandy came up behind him and the people realized that the blood-soaked man was being chased by the police, they backed away and made room for the inevitable.

Sixth district officers caught up with the sergeant. Transit cops moved in as well. Before they could wrestle him to the ground, the suspect fell in a bloody heap, losing consciousness as his head bounced against the floor with a sickening thud.

A few seconds later, Sandy Jackson cuffed him.

CHAPTER 3

As news of the suspect's capture made its way back to the impromptu staging area at the art gallery, Coletti and Lynch remained in the back room away from the others. Lynch was making calls. Coletti was preparing to question the suspect, but first he questioned himself.

He wondered if his nightmares had jogged his memory or replaced it. He wondered if what he'd seen in the cathedral that day was real. He wondered if saving Father O'Reilly could absolve him of his sins, or if he'd need to make a few confessions of his own.

As Coletti lost himself in the past, Lynch hung up the phone. "They took the suspect to Jefferson Hospital," he said, breaking into Coletti's thoughts. "You can meet them over there."

"What about Father O'Reilly?" Coletti asked. "Can we get them to put the execution on hold?"

"I just got off a conference call with the mayor and the governor's office. The governor's ready to give us whatever help we need. But they can't grant a stay of execution until we come up with something more than a note that could be from a copycat."

Coletti sighed impatiently. "Kevin," he said, addressing his old colleague by his first name. "There isn't a copycat in the world that would know what Father O'Reilly said to me ten years ago."

"Where's the evidence that he said anything about the angel of death? In fact, where's the evidence that he said anything at all? Is it in the court records? Do you have it on tape? Is it in your report?"

"My word's not good enough for you?"

"Doesn't matter if it's good enough for me. The governor already signed the warrant setting the execution for Friday and he needs more than a note and your word to grant a stay, especially with the media all over it."

"So we're just gonna let Father O'Reilly die for something he didn't do?"

"Don't get all sanctimonious on me now, Mike," Lynch said, his eyes smoldering. "Up until this note surfaced, you were perfectly fine with letting the execution happen."

"That's not true."

"It *is* true! If you were so sure he was innocent, you had ten years to say something."

"I could never find any solid leads," Coletti said earnestly. "That doesn't mean I never looked."

"You could've come to me. You could've reopened the investigation. You could've asked for help."

"Based on what? A priest who said the killer was the angel of death? A handful of dreams? You would've looked at me like I was crazy, Kevin, and you know it."

"Yeah, but you never tried, Mike, did you? So stop wasting time talking about what might've happened, and go get the evidence we need!"

Lynch snatched the door open, and Smithson was standing there wearing a shocked expression.

She was about to say something, but Coletti pushed past her before she could get it out.

"Wait a minute, Mike." She caught up to him before he got to the door. "I can help you get that stay of execution."

He stopped and turned to her. "You can help me by minding your own business."

"I wasn't trying to eavesdrop."

"I know," he said sarcastically. "You just happened to be standing at the door."

"I'm trying to help you!" she said angrily. "And apparently you need it. Now, you can stand there and act like you've got it all under control, or you can let me tell you what I found."

Coletti rolled his eyes impatiently as she held up the plastic evidence bag containing the note.

"I took another look at this note while you and the commissioner were talking," she said as she handed it to him. "The handwriting leans slightly to the left, so I think our writer's left-handed. They also pressed really hard. The pen almost went through the paper."

"What's your point?" Coletti said, pocketing the note and heading toward the door.

Smithson grabbed his arm. "Whoever wrote it was angry, and angry people usually act irrationally. But there was nothing irrational about this. If the note was really written by the same person who did the Confessional Murders, he's had ten years to channel that anger and put together a plan."

"Yeah, well, I have a plan, too," Coletti said. "I plan to save an innocent man, and whatever I've gotta do to make that happen, I'm gonna do it. Now, if you'll excuse me, I've got a suspect to question."

"He's not the murderer," Smithson said flatly.

Coletti stopped in his tracks. "How do you know that?"

"A man who's gotten away with a ten-year-old murder would never be careless enough to drop a note and get caught. And if he's arrogant enough to tell the cops he's planning to kill again, he isn't about to be outsmarted."

"So what are you saying?"

"I'm saying your suspect might've talked to the murderer. He might've even seen him, but he's not the man you want. He's just a pawn."

"You seem awfully sure of yourself," Coletti said skeptically.

"I'm only sure of two things," she said softly. "I'm sure I'm good at my job."

"What's the second thing?" Coletti asked.

"I'm sure I'm curious about you," she said, gazing into his eyes. "I've never seen a man so intent on correcting his mistakes. It's almost like you're the one who's the angel."

It was six o'clock when Commissioner Lynch drove Mary Smithson back to police headquarters. As she stared out the car window in the wake of the chase, everything looked different from the way it had with Coletti.

The National Constitution Center was foreboding rather than majestic. The vibrant sounds of the streets were only noise. To Mary, Philadelphia no longer felt historic. It simply felt old.

"Do you ever get used to it?" Smithson asked, as she watched a businesswoman stepping over a prostrate homeless man.

Lynch knew what she meant without looking: the mingled scents of greasy food and day old waste; the grime that had taken centuries to accumulate; the city.

"You don't get used to it if it's home," he said grimly. "You just work like hell to make it better."

"Is that why you stay?" she asked. "To make it better?"

"I stay because I like it," he said as he turned onto Ninth Street. "Liking it makes it easy to see past the blemishes. Kinda like you're doing with Coletti."

It took her a moment to recover from the commissioner's snide remark, but when she did, she came back swinging.

"Is that part of the commissioner's job?" she asked with an edge to her voice. "Sticking your nose into your officers' personal lives?"

"No, Lieutenant," he said with a tight smile. "Forget I said that."

They both were quiet as Lynch pulled into the parking lot. As they were about to get out, Smithson spoke up.

"You're right about Coletti having blemishes, you know. We all have them, but at least his are right out front."

"Yeah, with him, it's take it or leave it," Lynch said wistfully. "Most men I know tend to respect him and take it, but over the years every woman he's known eventually decided to leave it."

"Sounds like you're trying to talk me out of spending time with him."

"No, that's not it at all. I figure you're, what, thirty-nine years old?"

"I'm forty-two, but thanks for the compliment."

"I just figure you're a lot younger than him and you've got options. If you're going to do the older-man thing, you should know what you're getting into. Not for your sake, but for Mike's."

"Why do you care?" she asked. "From what I can see, there's no love lost between the two of you."

"You're right," Lynch admitted. "We're not friends in the traditional sense of the word, but as much as he irks me, Mike's taught me a lot. Over the years I've kinda returned the favor by protecting him from himself. I won't be able to do that as much when he retires." He paused to look sternly in her eyes. "But I'll still be around if anybody tries to hurt him."

Mary reared back as if she'd been slapped. "I hardly know him. How could I hurt him?"

"Oh, I don't know," Lynch said, his tone nonchalant. "But I know what I heard about you. I heard you're one of the top minds in the state police. They say you showed up five years ago with a Stanford doctorate and changed the way they investigate murders. I figure a woman as smart as you could have some fun with a guy like Coletti, but you just don't seem like his type."

"And what type would that be?"

"The type with an hourly rate."

There was a moment of silence as Smithson tried to control her outrage long enough to digest what Lynch meant.

"So you think I'm too good for him," she said, staring into space. "Is that what you're saying?"

"No," Lynch said while opening the car door. "I think he's too good for you."

Mary's jaw dropped as Lynch slammed the door and walked away. She got out and caught up with him as he entered headquarters.

"Commissioner, I don't know what you think I am," she said, speaking quickly while she marched beside him through the corridor. "I thought I was doing a nice thing for a man who needed somebody to talk to as much as I did. You're trying to make it sound like something dirty."

He stopped and turned to her at the elevator. "If you like him and he likes you, the two of you can pass notes in class all day. I just thought you should know that Coletti has friends in the department who actually care about him."

"Commissioner, I like Mike, that's all. It's nothing serious."

"Then I guess you'll be leaving soon," Lynch said as he stepped onto the elevator. "Since the shooting investigation from this morning is pretty much over, you can get a jump on traffic for the trip upstate. I'm sure they need you back at the office."

Police officers flooded into the emergency room at Thomas Jefferson University Hospital, surrounding the curtained cubicle where the suspect lay on a gurney. His wounds were superficial, but when a scowling Mike Coletti strolled in and threw the curtain aside, the suspect's future looked undeniably bleak.

"So you're the grim reaper," Coletti said with a wicked grin.

"I don't know what you're talkin' about," the suspect said, wincing as his bandaged head throbbed.

Coletti's grin widened until it was almost a smile. "You know, it's funny. About a half hour ago, I was out with a lady for the first time in years. Had a little wine, a little cheese, a little conversation. She actually seemed to like me. And these guys can tell you," he said, gesturing toward the two officers in the cubicle, "*nobody* likes me."

Coletti grabbed the suspect's medical chart and read the name that had been scrawled there by one of the overworked emergency room physicians.

"So, Mr. Bobby Robinson," Coletti said as he flipped through the chart, "you can imagine how pissed I am. First date in years, a woman who actually likes me, and I had to leave her to come here and deal with you."

"I didn't make you come here," the suspect murmured, his face contorted in pain.

"Actually, you did," Coletti said, pulling out the plastic bag containing the note from the *Confessions* exhibit. "You made me come here when you left this on the desk down at Second and Arch."

The suspect scowled at Coletti. "I look like I hang in art galleries to you?"

There was a moment of protracted silence as Coletti smiled again. "I didn't say anything about art galleries," he said, moving closer to the gurney. "But since you mentioned it, why not tell me the whole story? You can start with how you committed the Confessional Murders."

"You mean the case they keep talkin' about on the news?

The one with the priest who's about to get executed? I didn't have nothin' to do with that."

Coletti lifted the bag so the suspect could see the note. "So, you're saying you didn't write this?"

The man ignored him.

"You don't know anything about the contents of the note you dropped off at the Old City Art Gallery this afternoon? Is that what you're telling me?"

Again, the man refused to respond.

In a flash, Coletti was at the side of the gurney, grabbing the suspect's face with one hand and forcing the man to look at him. "There's a reason nobody likes me," he whispered, as an odd sort of madness played in his eyes.

The two cops in the cubicle moved to subdue him, but Coletti raised his other hand, signaling for them to stop.

"Why did you write the note?" he said, peeling his lips back from his teeth as his hand slid from the suspect's face to his throat.

The man looked up at him defiantly, but as his windpipe began to close, defiance was replaced by fear.

"I've got two cops outside who'll keep the doctors out, and two cops in here who'll help me finish the job," Coletti said, his tone low and threatening. "It's not about wanting to answer me. It's about wanting to live."

Coletti held on for a few minutes longer, gripping the suspect's throat with all the rage that had been building up since the morning. He looked into the man's face and saw echoes of his own nightmare. He looked into that face and saw reflections of the past. He looked, and before the anger could consume his sensibilities, he released his hold.

When Coletti let go, the suspect took a ragged, desperate breath. With his chest heaving and his face shaking, he reached up unsteadily to grab at his throat and convince himself that he was still alive.

Coletti moved in until his face was just inches from the suspect's. "Why did you write this confession!" he shouted angrily.

"I . . . didn't . . . write it," the suspect said, gasping for air between each word.

"Then who did?"

The suspect took another deep breath and closed his eyes against the throbbing pain that moved between his head and his windpipe. Coletti took out his notepad and waited.

"I met him under the overpass down by Sixth Street last night," the suspect said slowly. "Buncha guys sleep down there near the expressway ramp."

"What did he look like?" Coletti said, his pen poised above his notepad.

"He came at night, when everybody was asleep. It was kinda hard to see, but he was skinny and white with a real rough voice."

"So he said something to you?"

"Yeah. He said he would pay me to drop that note on that desk. Handed me fifty dollars and said I would get another hundred today if I made it to Twelfth and Race at six o' clock."

"How would he know whether you dropped the note like you were supposed to?"

The suspect looked up at Coletti, and the fear in his eyes turned to outright terror. "He said he knew everything. He said he was the angel o' death."

Coletti looked at the other two cops in the cubicle. They were hanging on the suspect's every word.

"Did you believe him?" Coletti asked.

The suspect was quiet for a few moments. "I don't know. With the moon behind him like it was, it almost looked like he was glowin'. I couldn't see his body 'cause he had on this long suit jacket. I didn't know if he had somethin' under there or what, but I wasn't gonna try him and find out. I couldn't see his face either, 'cause he had this hat on. This hat with a real wide—"

"Brim," Coletti said, feeling like he'd just seen the ghost that had haunted his dreams for the past ten years. "The brim threw a shadow across his face, and it felt kinda cold when he was near you, like a breeze was blowing through your insides."

The suspect stared at Coletti. "Yeah," he said, his brow knit tight by confusion. "How'd you know?"

At that, sights and sounds fired through Coletti's mind: a piece of the killer's face beneath the shadow of the hat; the sound of the victims screaming as their bodies hit the floor; a shotgun blast; a gravelly voice; the priest on his knees looking down at the carnage.

Coletti felt himself sinking into the abyss he'd come to know in his nightmares. The room began to spin as the past rose up to drown him. But just like in his dreams, something reached down and grabbed him before he succumbed. This time, it was a voice from the other side of the curtain.

"Get out of my way right now so I can see my patient!" a doctor shouted as the cops guarding the cubicle blocked his path.

"I'm sorry, he's being questioned, and—"

"This is a hospital, not a police station. Now get out of my way!"

As the voices grew louder, Coletti stared at the suspect and thought back to what Smithson had told him. Indeed, this man wasn't the killer, but he was yet another piece of the puzzle. Both he and Coletti had seen the killer in different realms, and neither of them understood how. In truth, they were both afraid of the answer.

"Back away from the cubicle before I cuff you!" an officer in the hall shouted, snatching Coletti back to the moment.

Tearing his eyes away from the suspect, Coletti looked over his shoulder.

"It's all right," he said, his voice raised slightly. "Let the doctor in. Mr. Robinson's given his statement."

It was six twenty when Charlie Mann stepped out of internal affairs after several hours of filling out forms and answering questions. He was exhausted from everything about his ordeal. He was tired of reliving the sequence of events, tired of the gunshots reverberating in his head, tired of hearing that he'd done the right thing.

As much as he wanted to go home and lose himself in something far removed from his life as a cop, he needed the comfort of being at police headquarters.

"You're crazy," he said to himself as he walked toward the elevator.

A nearby clerk from the crime scene unit glanced at him as if he were just that. Then she scurried down the hall in an effort to avoid him.

He smiled uneasily and tried to think happy thoughts. The first one that came to mind was Sandy. He conjured an image of her waiting for him, her body slick with bath oils and her lips wet with anticipation. He knew that she could help him wind down, but in a strange sense, he didn't want to. Even as he tried to put her out of his mind, however, the halls of police headquarters were abuzz with her name.

"I heard Sandy ran him down," a corporal from the fingerprint unit told a patrolman near the elevator. "Chased him from Fifth Street to Twelfth like she was on skates."

"Yeah, that Sergeant Jackson is something," the patrolman said. "Who would've thought a woman that fine could run that fast?"

When they saw Mann approaching the two men grew quiet. They knew, just like everyone else, that Sandy Jackson and Charlie Mann were an item. And Mann knew, just like any man with a beautiful woman, that there were countless others waiting to take his place.

The elevator came and he waved them on. Then he took out his cell phone and dialed her number. She answered on the third ring.

"What's this I hear about you chasing people?" he asked playfully. "What are you doing, riding around looking for trouble?"

"No," she said with a smile in her voice. "I was going back to the Ninth from that art gallery assist, and this guy ran past. You know I don't like people trying to outrun me."

"You think you're still running the hundred meters for Spelman College, don't you?"

"Not the way my legs feel right now," she said. "For me to get out of this car before my shift ends at eleven thirty, all hell would have to break loose. Enough about me, though. How did it go at internal affairs?"

"They asked a lot of questions. I gave a lot of answers. They told me not to talk about it and said they'd get back to me."

There was a long silence on the other end.

"You still meeting me when I get off? I can rub your temples and you can rub my legs. Everybody wins."

He smiled and pushed the button for the elevator. "I'll be there," he said. "I just feel like I need to clear my head first. I haven't really had time to think about what happened this morning."

She knew what it felt like to shoot a suspect, and she was pragmatic enough to know that nothing could erase the image from Charlie's mind—not even she.

"Take all the time you need," she said, her tone empathetic but firm. "Just know you have to take what happened for what it was. If you do that, everything will be all right."

"Okay," Charlie said as the elevator arrived. "I'll call you later."

He disconnected the call and got on the elevator, riding to the basement to report to his new temporary unit—delayed police response.

The sergeant in charge knew who Charlie Mann was, and he knew what the young officer had been through that day. He cleared a space for Mann and ran him through a quick tutorial. The sergeant didn't need another officer to answer phones at the moment, but he knew that Mann needed to be there to clear his head.

As he donned his headset and answered the low-priority calls that came down to DPR from the radio room, Mann pondered the details of the shooting.

Could he have waited a second longer? Should he have stopped after the first shot? What if he had allowed the suspect to live? He asked himself those questions while wavering between guilt and self-doubt.

The other cops in DPR had their own inner conflicts and spent their time alternately cursing their misfortune and counting their blessings. The ones who'd been injured on duty swapped jokes and war stories about their days on the beat. The others were less apt to share, to laugh, or even to speak. These were the ones who'd taken shortcuts or, worse, taken lives.

Mann surveyed the room and saw cops he'd read about in the papers. One had been accused of colluding with a confidential informant to plant drugs and skim reward money. Another had been accused of shooting a hated neighbor under the guise of self-defense. There were a few he didn't recognize, including the one who came to sit next to him.

"I heard they're gonna stick you with Coletti," said the fat, red-faced cop as he slid into the cubicle.

Mann grunted in reply.

"Name's Frank Dougherty," the cop said, extending his hand.

Hesitantly, Mann shook it. "Charlie Mann's my name."

"I know who you are. You're the one who shot that guy in Chestnut Hill this morning."

"You know a lot about me for a guy I've never met," Mann said.

The cop laughed heartily. "I guess you haven't learned there aren't any secrets in the department."

"Apparently, there's a lot I haven't learned," Mann said, relaxing a little. "That's why the commissioner's making me work with Coletti. He says he's the perfect teacher."

"You could do a lot worse," the cop said. "Coletti's a good man."

Mann looked at him in disbelief. "They must've put you in DPR because you're crazy."

"Actually, they put me down here because I broke my foot chasing some kid."

"Sorry to hear that," Mann said, sitting back in his chair. He wanted to ignore the cop and lose himself in his thoughts, but his curiosity got the best of him. "So, um, how do you know Coletti?"

"We came into the Academy together back in '78."

"Thirty-one years is a long time," Mann said. "I'm sure he's a lot different than he was back then."

The cop shook his head. "People don't change, times do," he said in a faraway voice. "And it was a different time when Coletti and I went through the Academy. Most of the cops in Philly were just like us—white, blue-collar guys from row-house neighborhoods. There weren't many women or blacks, and there was nobody to tell us what we couldn't do, so things got kinda crazy sometimes.

"There was this one black cadet named Harry Williams who came through the Academy with us. He was short, kinda stocky, but you could tell he was a pretty sharp guy—serious about being a cop. Some of the guys didn't like that. They thought he was a little too uppity, so while everybody else was making friends, Harry was getting harassed. I still remember this one guy from South Philly kept calling him spade. He'd say it while we were doing a run or something, just loud enough for Harry and a couple other guys to hear. People would laugh and Harry would ignore it, but you could tell he was starting to get mad. Well, it took about a month for the whole thing to blow up. Harry caught the guy by himself and beat him up pretty good. Some of the guys from South Philly heard about it and they wanted to put Harry in his place.

"Naturally, they came to Coletti for help, since he was from South Philly, too. And the day it was all supposed to go down, Coletti was there, only he was standing with Harry. It was just the two of them against ten guys. I'll never forget what Coletti said when they asked him why he was with Harry instead of them.

"He said, 'My father came over from Naples and people laughed at him because he was different. He just wanted his little piece of America, and there was always somebody trying to keep him in his place. Well, Harry's different, too. But you're not gonna do to him what they did to my father. Harry's not gonna let you, and neither am I.'

"A few of them tried to get loud and the instructors came and broke it up," the cop said. "Coletti and Harry went their separate ways after that, but nobody bothered Harry again. And even though most of us never said it, we all respected Coletti for standing up the way he did. In fact, we all respect him to this day."

Mann sat for a few moments, trying to reconcile what he'd just heard with what he'd seen that morning. He couldn't, so he tried to get the cop to do it for him. "What made Coletti change?"

"He hasn't changed," the cop said insistently. "He's still a loner—he only had one partner that stuck in thirty-one years, and the two of them had some kind of falling out and Coletti started working alone again. But through it all, he always tried to stand up for people. That got him enemies. I think that's why Coletti never rose through the ranks. He stood up one time too many."

"Is that why he's so angry now?"

The cop thought about it for a moment. "There's more to it than that," he said. "Coletti's angry because he wanted to be the guy he was back at the Academy. He wanted to get justice for people who couldn't get it for themselves, but no matter how hard he tried, he could never get it right. To this day, he's still trying to make up for it."

CHAPTER 4

At six thirty, Coletti pulled out of the hospital parking lot as the suspect's words reverberated in his head: "He said he knew everything. He said he was the angel o' death."

It was only a few blocks to the overpass where the suspect claimed he'd encountered the killer. When Coletti arrived and got out of the car, it was almost like walking into his nightmares.

The air beneath the highway swirled like the breeze from the cathedral, and soft clouds hovered like angels in a stained-glass sky. The pillars beneath the overpass were statues in an unholy sanctuary, and the men who slept there were parishioners in a church of hopelessness.

He watched a scruffy man begging near the traffic signal at the end of the off-ramp, and his mind conjured the image of the priest. He turned and saw three men sleeping beneath the overpass and thought they were the bodies from the cathedral.

Coletti shut his eyes against the macabre daydream. When he opened them, everything seemed normal again. The scruffy man begged, and the sleeping ones were only dead in spirit. In some ways, the reality was more frightening than the vision, because a land of lost souls was the perfect place for the angel of death to appear.

As trash swirled behind passing cars, Coletti rubbed his temples in an attempt to clear his mind. Then he took the short walk to the spot where the three men lay.

"Yo," he said, reaching down and snatching the blankets off one of them. "Get up!"

"Leave me alone," the man said, trying to turn over.

Coletti bent down and put his badge in his face. "I'll leave you alone when I'm finished."

The man sighed in frustration. "They're roustin' us again," he said, awakening the two men sleeping next to him.

"No, I'm not," Coletti said. "I've just got a couple of questions."

All three men were wide awake now. Coletti stared at them and wondered how they'd wound up living in the shadows. Was it simply the bottles of alcohol that surrounded them, or was there more? Had they seen things they wanted to forget, done things they refused to remember? Or were they like him— men who'd tried and failed to right some monumental wrongs?

Coletti put his badge away. "There's a guy named Bobby Robinson who sleeps down here. Kinda stocky with brown hair. You guys know him?"

They all looked at each other, afraid to answer. Finally, the one closest to Coletti spoke up. "Look, we don't want no trouble," he said.

Coletti reached down and snatched a half-empty bottle of

whiskey from beneath one of the blankets. "You won't get any trouble if you answer my questions. But if you don't . . ."

They watched anxiously as he raised the bottle above his head. He was just about to drop it when the man farthest from him looked up with swollen eyes.

"We know him," he blurted out, his face pockmarked and red from years of drinking. "He hangs out here a couple weeks outta the month."

"When was the last time you saw him?" Coletti asked.

"Last night. Why? What'd he do?"

"It's not what he did," Coletti said, putting the bottle down. "It's what he saw."

The three men looked at each other. Clearly, they were uncomfortable. In fact, they looked downright afraid.

"I'm assuming he wasn't the only one who saw something out here last night," Coletti said.

The men remained silent.

"Look, we can do this the easy way, or we can do it the hard way. It's up to you."

The men still refused to talk.

Quickly, Coletti reached under his jacket and took his radio from his belt. "This is Dan 26. I've got three prisoners. I'm gonna need a wagon."

"Wait a minute," said the man in the middle, speaking up for the first time. "I'll tell you what you wanna know."

Coletti waited half a second before telling the dispatcher to disregard his call. When he did, the man in the middle threw off his blanket and the detective got a good look at him.

His salt-and-pepper hair was in a crew cut, and he hadn't

shaved in days. He looked fit and strong, but there was something uneasy about his manner as he reached into his shirt pocket and lit a half-smoked cigarette.

"You'll have to excuse my friends," he said while exhaling the acrid smoke. "They get kinda nervous when cops come around."

"You look a little nervous yourself," Coletti said.

"Post-traumatic stress disorder. I had a Humvee blown from under me by a roadside bomb near Tikrit. Watched three guys die right next to me." He took a long drag of the cigarette. "Stuff like that can make a man a little anxious. I guess that's why I sleep out here. It's safer than a shelter, cleaner than the VA, and you can always see what's comin'."

"Did you see what came last night?"

"Yeah, I did. I acted like I was asleep, though."

Coletti furrowed his brow. "Why?"

"Because Bobby does drugs and I don't wanna deal with the guys he hangs around. Most of the time I just stay under my blanket. That's what I did last night. At least, until the guy said who he was."

"That's enough, Frank," said the one with the pockmarked face.

The third man said the same thing with his eyes.

Coletti looked at the three of them and laughed nervously. "What are you guys so scared of?"

The man with the pockmarked face spoke in a conspiratorial whisper. "The guy said he was the angel o' death. You'd be scared o' that, too."

Coletti had been scared of it for a decade. He couldn't tell the men that, though. In truth, he couldn't tell anyone.

"It was about two in the morning when he showed up," said the one they called Frank. "He stood about four feet away. Bobby was the first one to notice him, and he didn't have enough sense to be afraid."

"What was there to be afraid of?" Coletti asked. "The way he looked? Did he have something in his hands?"

"No," Frank said. "It was his voice. It was rough and soft at the same time. When he talked, it was like he was whispering loud enough for the world to hear. It was scary."

"Do you remember what he said?"

"He offered Bobby money to deliver a note to some art gallery, and he told him there was more where that came from. Seemed too good to be true, if you ask me, but I guess when you're on drugs, you don't think about that."

Coletti nodded. "Did you get a look at the guy?"

"Yeah. I peeked out from under my blanket and saw him from the side. He was dressed in a black jacket, with a hat. His face was pale and his hair was blond. I couldn't see more than that, and to tell you the truth, I wasn't sure I wanted to. I've seen death one time too many."

It was nearly seven o'clock and Mary Smithson was sitting in a cubicle in homicide, fuming about the commissioner's veiled accusations and gathering her belongings as the detectives in the room watched her warily.

When she placed the last of her things in her purse and

slammed the metal drawer, a few of them muttered quiet good-byes. She ignored most of them and stormed out.

As she left the office and walked the curved hall leading to the building's entrance, she wondered if Mike Coletti was as special as Lynch had made him out to be.

She was lost in those thoughts when a man who was equally preoccupied walked into the building and nearly ran into her.

"Hey watch it!" she said before she looked up and realized who it was.

"Mary?" said a confused Coletti. "Where are you going?"

She sighed heavily. "We solved the case I was working on, so I'm heading back upstate."

"I know I was a lousy date," he said, his tone apologetic. "But you weren't even gonna say good-bye?"

"I was gonna call you later."

"What about the shooting investigation? Is that over, too?"

"Commissioner Lynch said it was pretty much open and shut," she said, her jaw tightening. "He, um, *advised* me that I should go back to the office. He thought you'd be better off if I wasn't around."

"Don't listen to him," Coletti said, playfully leering at her while rubbing his gut. "He probably thought you were after my luscious body."

Smithson tried to keep a straight face, but she couldn't and burst out laughing. "You're crazy, you know that?"

"I know, and I'm trying to get help," he said, his silly grin fading. "But I'm sane enough to admit that you were right about the suspect at the hospital. He's not the man I'm looking for, but he's seen the killer."

"How do you know?"

"Because I just left three other men who corroborated his story. They saw the guy under an overpass right off the expressway. They said he was thin, wearing a black jacket, and had pale skin and light-colored hair. It was just like I remembered."

"You mean you've seen the killer, too?" Smithson asked. "You never told me that."

Coletti hesitated. "That's because I didn't. . . . Well, not face-to-face. . . . Look, it's complicated, but if you stick around I could explain it over dinner."

"You don't have time for dinner," she said. "You've got a ten-year-old triple murder to solve, and I really do have to get back."

"Yeah, I know things are hoppin' up there in Scranton," Coletti said. "They desperately need a profile on the guy who keeps going out cow tippin' on Tuesdays."

"I'll have you know I work out of the Dunmore state police barracks," she said with a smile in her voice. "We don't take kindly to being called Scranton. And besides, they already caught the cow tipper."

"Okay, fine," Coletti said. "Do you think the folks up in Dunmore can spare you for a few hours so we can grab a quick meal?"

"Are you asking me out, or do you just want to use me for my profiling skills?"

"Both."

"I see," she said in a cynical tone. "But when I offered to help you before, you told me you had a plan, and I don't recall that plan including me."

"That was before I realized you knew what you were talking about," Coletti said. "I miscalculated, and I'm willing to make up for it by paying for dinner."

She looked at him with mock suspicion. "Are you trying to buy me, Detective Coletti?"

"You make it sound so dirty."

"Maybe it could be," she said in a sultry voice. "Depends on what you're offering in exchange for my company."

Coletti smiled. It'd been years since a woman had flirted with him. Yet there was Mary Smithson, teasing him with everything from her flashing blue eyes to her suggestive tone. He liked it.

"Not only am I offering you dinner," he said. "I'm offering you the chance to fix someone who doesn't want to be fixed. You're into that, aren't you?"

"I'm always up for a challenge," she said.

"Good. You help a stubborn old cop solve a case, and as a bonus you get to track down a murderer and save an innocent priest. It's a win-win."

She teasingly pretended to ponder his offer as passersby looked at them curiously.

"Come on, Mary," he said when he noticed other cops watching them. "Let's go outside before the rumors start."

She smiled as they walked out the front entrance. When they got to his car, he opened her door before walking around and opening his own.

"So what did you do with the note from the art gallery?" she asked when he got in.

"I dropped it at the lab right before I saw you. The paper's kinda rough to lift prints from, but I wanted to see if we could get an in-house handwriting analysis before we sent it down to Quantico."

"Smart move," she said. "The FBI would take weeks."

"That's why I need your help. We have to find something to make the governor's office stay the execution. If I can't get time on my side for something that important, the least I can do is get you."

She looked at him with eyes that spoke volumes, and for the first time, he didn't look away.

"I'll help you," she said. "But you've gotta promise to let me work."

Coletti hesitated. "Well, it's not like you'd be out chasing this guy, right? You'd be in the office doing psychological research or something."

"No, I'd be doing whatever I had to do to help you find him, even if it meant being in the line of fire."

"Look, Mary, I—"

"No, *you* look. If you want me to do my job, I need to be out in the street, so you have to ask yourself: Is it more important to protect me, or is it more important to find this killer?"

Coletti knew the answer, but he didn't want to accept it. Not that his acceptance mattered. The truth was the truth, whether he wanted to admit it or not.

"Okay," Coletti said. "So where do we go from here?"

The question had a double meaning, but Smithson wasn't about to take the bait.

"It's not about where we're going," she said with a knowing grin. "It's about where the killer's going."

"That's what I meant," Coletti said impishly. "You didn't think I was flirting, did you?"

"You're a man, so by definition, everything you do is flirting."

"I'm hurt," Coletti said with mock indignation.

"I'm a heartbreaker," she deadpanned. "Get over it, and let's go catch a killer."

"Okay, Lieutenant, you're the profiler. What's our killer thinking?"

Smithson sat back and pondered the question for a few minutes. "He's thinking he's invincible."

"What makes you say that?"

"He gave himself a nickname. Most killers get their nicknames from the media or the police. They rarely choose them for themselves. That tells me he thinks a lot of himself. I'd even say he has a God complex, and that makes me wonder if he purposely chose to kill in a church. Think about it—an angel with the church as a backdrop. The whole thing seems almost perfect."

Coletti nodded slowly. "I've thought about that a lot over the years. I always wondered if the church was a symbol for him: if he killed there to convey some kind of message."

"Maybe even a personal message," she said. "A message to somebody in the church."

"But if that was the case, he delivered his message ten years ago. Why would he come back now?"

"Maybe he didn't finish the job."

At that, Coletti thought of himself. He hadn't finished the job, either, and now the job had made its way from dreams to reality. If he was ever going to be at peace with himself, he had to do the one thing that he'd failed to accomplish. He had to finish.

Starting the car, he turned to Smithson. "I've got to talk to Father O'Reilly."

"Now? Suppose the killer strikes again while you're gone."

"We've got a whole police department to handle that," Coletti said. "But this is something I've been putting off for ten years. I have to do it now, and if you really want to help, I need you to do something for me."

"What's that?" she asked.

"Come with me."

It was seven thirty, and the man in black walked along Rockland Street near Tenth, slowly making his way through Logan, a once-prosperous neighborhood now plagued by poverty and crime.

The seemingly disconnected collection of black people, Latinos, and Cambodians who lived there knew the rhythms of the streets. They could tell when someone didn't fit. That's why they watched the young white man as he walked along Rockland Street. He didn't belong there.

They often saw white men like him—young and thin and dressed in black. The Mormon church on Broad Street sent them into the neighborhood to proselytize. But those young men traveled in pairs. They wore name tags and smiles. This one walked alone. He never smiled and didn't speak. They knew this because they'd seen him several times over the past few days.

He'd show up in the early evening, circling the neighborhood on foot, always ending up near Tenth Street. Unlike the

Mormons, who wore shirt sleeves during the summer months, he wore a jacket that extended past his waist. He also wore a wide-brimmed hat that obscured part of his face.

At first, the neighbors dismissed him as yet another of the mentally ill who sometimes wandered from programs and group homes. Such people would beg in front of stores when their Social Security checks and medications were gone. This one was different. He seemed to move with a sense of purpose far beyond that of a mentally ill beggar.

There was something frightening about him, and almost everyone who saw him felt it. Still, no one thought to call the police, because cops didn't respond to suspicions in neighborhoods like Logan. They were too busy responding to deaths.

As children on bikes rode by regarding him warily, the man in black walked calmly along the tree-lined street, watching as three people left their porch and started toward Broad Street.

For a moment they watched him, too. But he was walking in the opposite direction, and when he passed them, things went back to normal. The rumbling bass of a passing car filled the summer air. A loud conversation spilled out of an open window. Profanity punctuated an off-color joke. Children played tag, and their laughter was high-pitched music.

When he passed by, the neighborhood relaxed, and that was a mistake.

The man in black turned around at Eighth Street and followed the trail of the three people he'd been watching. There was no need for him to hurry. He knew where they were going, and he planned to meet them there.

As he passed Ninth Street, his gaunt, pale face took on a resolute expression. He was determined to fulfill the purpose for which he'd been called, and nothing on earth was going to stop him. Not even the black Crown Victoria that eased down the block and slowed near a group of young men on the corner.

The car's windows opened and the corner boys' eyes grew wide. Within seconds, all hell broke loose.

There was a loud, popping sound, followed by several more pops in rapid succession. The streets of Logan knew this sound all too well, and everyone reacted in unison. Children screamed and ran toward their mothers. Men dove to the ground and lay prostrate. Women held their babies to their bosoms, and through it all, the man in black kept walking.

The bullets lodged in trees and shattered windows. They frightened children and cleared the streets. The man in black ignored it all and walked through the line of fire. When the gunshots finally stopped, he was unscathed, and he kept walking.

He walked like a man who'd been called to fulfill a prophecy: a man who believed he was chosen for a specific task. In fact, he didn't walk like a man at all. He walked like something that was virtually invincible. He walked like the angel of death.

CHAPTER 5

Coletti called the commissioner and briefed him. Then he stopped at a downtown McDonald's, and for the first half hour of the ride to Graterford, he and Smithson drank huge Cokes and ate Quarter Pounders with large fries on the side.

"So this is the fancy dinner you promised?" Smithson asked while devouring the first of her two burgers.

"Nothing but the best for you," Coletti said while steering with greasy hands.

Neither of them had eaten a real meal all day, and they ate like it, spilling ketchup on the seats, getting mustard on their clothes, and tearing through apple pies like school kids. They laughed and poked fun, flirted just a little, and started to grow more comfortable with each other.

When they finished eating, they rode in contented silence, speeding north on I-476. As Coletti prepared to ask the priest the questions he'd been holding on to for years, Smithson posed the question she'd been contemplating for an hour.

"So, when did you see the killer?" she asked, sipping her soda.

In an instant, the atmosphere changed. It was bad enough revealing his nightmares to Commissioner Lynch, whom he'd known for nearly two decades. Coletti dreaded sharing them with a woman he'd just met.

Taking a deep breath, he tightened his grip on the steering wheel, and glanced at her before he spoke.

"Have you ever dreamed about something you think might happen?" he asked.

"Of course I have."

"Well, imagine dreaming about murders and seeing them through someone else's eyes. Only what you're seeing isn't something that's going to happen in the future. It's something that happened in the past."

He looked at her again to gauge her reaction. He didn't see any, so he went on.

"I saw the killer through Father O'Reilly's eyes," he said. "I know it sounds crazy and I can't explain how, but I saw him. He was dressed in black with a gravelly voice, and I watched him kill those people. Then I watched myself rushing past the bodies and pulling Father O'Reilly to his feet. He was holding the gun and looking confused, and he kept saying that the killer was the angel of death."

Smithson was silent as Coletti turned onto Route 63. She tried her best to take it all in, but she couldn't quite wrap her mind around it. "When did you start having the dreams?" she asked.

"A few months after the murders."

"And when did you start thinking the dreams might b[

"When they didn't stop," he said quietly. "That's wh[
started my own little investigation. I searched databases for th[
white males and looked through files for murders in churches. [
cross-referenced sawed-off shotguns with killers dressed in
black, but everything I tried was a dead end, so after a year of
trying to find the truth, I gave up."

"And you never told anyone?"

Coletti laughed bitterly. "I couldn't even tell my partner,
and he was my closest friend in the department. He would've
thought I was crazy to let dreams make me question a solid arrest and conviction."

"So if you couldn't tell anyone back then, why are you telling me now?"

Coletti looked at her. "You're the closest thing I've got to a
shrink," he said with a wan smile. "I guess that means I can trust
you."

Smithson nodded slowly. Then she turned and looked at
Coletti. "Can I ask you something else?"

"Sure."

"Is trust the only thing you feel when you look at me?"

Coletti glanced at her curiously. "Why does it matter?"

"Because a lady likes to know."

"Okay," he said. "You tell me what you feel, and I'll tell you
what I feel."

"What are we, ten years old?" she asked with a chuckle.

"No, but I'm not used to all this 'feelings' stuff. In my day
you dragged a woman off by her hair. You didn't have to bare
your soul."

u to. I'm just wondering what you want

back Pike and tried to think of an
question. When he couldn't, he took the

to be friends," he said. "If it grows into something
that's fine. If it doesn't, I can deal with that, too."

"A man doesn't look at a woman the way you look at me if he just wants to be friends."

"Maybe you're right," Coletti said as they turned onto Graterford Prison Road and parked in the prison's shadow. "But you made me promise to let you work. As far as I'm concerned, the work starts now."

By eight o'clock, the streets of downtown Philadelphia were eerily quiet. The city's Quaker roots, though in many ways forgotten, still demanded a certain piety when it came to drinking. Bars closed on Sundays, clubs shut down at two, and weeknight happy hours were never especially spirited, even in the heart of Center City.

This evening was no different. A few middle-aged men drank at the sidewalk cafés along Walnut Street, and young women from nearby office buildings kept them company. The girls were flirty, because the men's designer loafers and Cuban cigars made them look more prosperous than they were. Not that it mattered. For women in their twenties, a man who looked rich was sometimes enough.

Sandy Jackson knew better. Even from her squad car, she

could spot the frauds, and she often made a point of doing so, because people-watching made her workday go by faster.

As she cruised down Walnut Street in car 9A, she spied a brunette at Brasserie Perrier, crossing her legs seductively while fifty-year-olds panted at her feet. The girl knew how to play her first card, Sandy thought. But the sprayed-on LA tan and brassy New York attitude led Sandy to doubt the girl could play out her entire hand. Phony didn't fly in Philadelphia.

Smiling, the sergeant looked down Seventeenth Street at the little diner where she'd eaten earlier. Seeing the place reassured her that Philadelphia was still cheesesteaks with onions rather than foie gras and Brie.

She liked her city gritty, and in spite of the changes that had spawned million-dollar condos and gourmet restaurants, Philadelphia was still a tough town. It wasn't the boxing tradition or the bare-knuckled politics that made Philadelphia what it was. The most tangible manifestation of Philly's toughness was the street people.

By day, they begged for change to feed their vices. When evening came, they pocketed the contents of their cups and walked from trendy shopping and restaurant strips to neighborhoods where self-destruction was for sale.

Sandy knew most of those people by name, because they were the same ones she used to chase from the park as a rookie. There was Spider from Sixteenth Street, who loved to drink, and Easy from City Hall, who was in and out of shelters. Molly was a dope fiend who begged on the restaurant strip. Louie was a crack addict who sang Armstrong near the Kimmel Center.

Sandy would stop one of them every once in a while and try to convince them to do something different. Most of the time, they'd smile and nod politely while she spoke. Then they'd return to smoking or drinking themselves into oblivion.

Tonight, Sandy was too tired to preach. She simply watched from her squad car as they gathered quarters and wrinkled dollar bills and went to search for peace in bottles and plastic bags.

"Knock yourselves out," Sandy muttered to herself as she continued down Walnut Street and turned at Twenty-first, where a majestic church took up nearly half a block.

As she passed by the church and the two tiny streets that ran between Walnut and Locust, she noticed someone she'd never seen before. He was dressed in black and standing near an exclusive apartment building at the end of the block. He didn't have a cup and he wasn't engaging passersby. He was just standing, as if he were in a trance.

Sandy slowed down as she passed him. He didn't look up. He didn't look down. He didn't move. He simply stared straight ahead, his pale face obscured by a wide-brimmed hat that covered his eyes.

For a moment, Sandy wondered if the man was one of the lifelike statues that peppered Center City, like the man holding an umbrella in front of the Prince Music Theater. Then the wind blew, and the hat flipped up, revealing the man's right eye. It was bright blue, almost sparkling. Yet something about his eye was dead. It was as if the light was just an ember from his soul's dying fire.

Sandy stopped the car and backed up, nearly colliding with an SUV that had pulled up behind her. She contemplated letting it go. She was tired, and the man had done nothing wrong. Still, something about him wasn't right. That one glance at his eye had spooked her. She flipped on her siren and tried to back up again, but several cars had already lined up behind the SUV.

Suddenly, the man reached up to pull down his hat. Then he pivoted and walked quickly to his left, rounding the corner at Locust Street as Sandy got out of the car. She dashed to the corner and looked down the street. The man was gone.

She was about to go back to her car when she saw a tall, husky officer walking toward her from the other end of the block.

"Harris!" she said, jogging toward him. "Where did that guy go?"

"What guy?"

"The guy in black," she said, her eyes darting to and fro. "He just came around the corner. He was a skinny white guy with blue eyes."

The cop looked at her with a puzzled expression.

"He was coming right at you!" she said in an exasperated tone.

"I didn't see anybody, Sarge. You sure he came down Locust?"

She was about to press the issue, but she thought better of it. "Never mind," she said, grabbing her radio off her shoulder.

"This is 9A," she said, speaking into her handset. "Any units spotting a thin white male with blue eyes, wearing a black outfit and a large black hat, he's wanted for investigation. He was last seen going east on Locust from Twenty-first about one minute ago."

The dispatcher put the description out over police radio's central band, but no one heard it in Logan. That was too bad. They could've used it there.

It was eight fifteen and evening mass at Our Lady of Sorrows was coming to an end. Kannitha, Chavy, and Boran Seng were in attendance, praying with their neighbors for an end to the bloodshed in their neighborhood.

The Broad Street church, with its soaring spires and grand stone arches, had always served as the perfect house of prayer.

But on an evening when a drive-by shooting had occurred just after they'd left Rockland Street, the Sengs saw the church as a shelter. Not just from the bullets that had sprayed their street, but from the poignant memories of their homeland.

The two women, Kannitha and Chavy, had lived through Pol Pot's killing fields in 1970s Cambodia. They'd seen cities emptied out by the Khmer Rouge and people forced to leave their homes with nothing but the clothes on their backs. They'd seen daughters raped, fathers shot dead, and sons marched off to be dumped in mass graves. In short, they'd seen hell on earth.

When finally they were able to leave Cambodia for America in the late eighties, they chose Philadelphia because the name meant "City of Brotherly Love." They soon learned that the name didn't jibe with reality, but even with the violence that sometimes plagued the city, Philadelphia was better than what they'd left. That was why the two women had saved a portion of the money they earned at menial jobs and used it to send for their last surviving family member—their younger cousin, Boran.

For the last five years, the young man had lived in America with his cousins, and he'd joined them in their conversion to Catholicism. Since then, the church and the welcoming atmosphere created by the priest had helped them to endure life in the city.

That's why they stayed to talk with the priest at the end of every mass. He always gave them a measure of comfort.

But tonight, when they finished talking and the priest left to go to his office, the Sengs noticed a man in a pew near the door. His head was bowed as if he was praying. Something about him didn't fit, though. With the sanctuary empty and the homily a distant memory, the faith they'd felt just minutes before was quickly trumped by fear.

Though the brim of his hat obscured his entire face, they were certain of the stranger's identity. This was the man they'd seen on each of the last three days. This was the man who'd been following them.

Boran turned to his cousins and silently nodded at the door. Then he led them toward the exit. When the stranger didn't move, the three of them walked faster. The aisle of the church was long, however, and there was no way for them to run past him. He was too close to the door.

Boran considered turning around and running toward the front of the church, but by the time he moved from thought to action, the man was on his feet with a sawed-off shotgun in hand.

Chavy and Kannitha tried to run, but they stumbled over each other and fell. They managed to get up and run again, while Boran made a stand in the middle of the aisle, blocking off the gunman from the women.

The killer pushed the man aside and walked up to the

women, who were cowering between the altar and the first row of pews. He aimed the gun and was about to fire, but Boran jumped on his back.

Enraged, the gunman flung him off. Then he swung the butt of the gun with both hands, knocking Boran to the floor. The two women screamed and ran to shield their cousin with their bodies. Then, as the killer walked slowly toward them, the women began to pray.

Boran nudged his cousins aside as the killer stood over them, and he saw beneath the man's hat for the first time. His nose was straight as an arrow, and his lips were a thin, angry line. His jaw jutted out in a determined square, and his eyes were like blue, burning flames.

"What do you want?" Boran asked in an earnest, frightened voice.

"I want your souls," the killer said, his voice gravelly and strong.

"We haven't done anything to you," Boran said. "Why can't you just leave us alone?"

The man in black threw his head back and laughed. Then he aimed the shotgun at Boran's face as his cousins cowered in fear.

Boran tried to grab the gun, and the man in black shot him in the chest. When Boran fell, the killer fired two more shots that stilled the screaming women. Then he reached into his pocket and dropped a note on the dead man's chest. He was about to leave when something caught his eye. He turned around and saw the priest looking at him from a door beside the pulpit.

The killer held the gun at his side and took a few steps toward the priest. The priest, in turn, took a deep, trembling breath and stood his ground in the doorway.

"I'm the angel of death and this is a war," the killer said, his gravelly voice filling the church. "The note is for Prince Michael. Tell him I'll be waiting."

The killer turned and walked quickly down the aisle as the Sengs' blood soaked into the sanctuary floor. The priest watched him go and knew that the church was no longer pure. It was stained with the same blood that ran in the streets.

The killing fields had come to Philadelphia.

CHAPTER 6

Coletti and Smithson stood at the front desk at Graterford, making small talk with the guards while reading through the daunting list of rules: Vehicles must be registered, personal items must be placed in lockers, embracing is permitted only at the beginning and end of each visit, refusal to be searched may result in detention.

Though they weren't subject to those regulations, Coletti and Smithson were bound by the vagaries of prison procedure. The guards at the desk couldn't approve an after-hours visit to death row, and apparently, no one else could either.

After a few minutes, a captain from C Block came down to handle the problem, and the tall, rugged man was none too pleased that a cop from Philadelphia had arrived unannounced for such a visit. Like many Pennsylvanians from other parts of the state, he didn't like Philadelphia, and it showed in his demeanor.

"Can I help you?" he asked with a pasted-on grin.

"We're here to see Thomas O'Reilly," Coletti answered.

"So I heard, Detective, uh . . ."

"Coletti. Mike Coletti."

The captain's grin widened to a phony smile. "And who's this little lady?"

"Lieutenant Mary Smithson, state police," she said, glaring in response to his condescending tone.

"Well, Detective Coletti and Lieutenant Smithson, it's gonna be hard to facilitate your request. The governor's already signed O'Reilly's death warrant, and he's scheduled to be transferred to Rockville tomorrow."

"I don't care about the warrant," Coletti said, watching the captain turn red as Smithson and the other guards looked on. "Our department's been in touch with the governor's office. They're waiting for the results of our investigation before granting a stay of execution. So either you let us talk to O'Reilly, or I'll have the governor's office call the corrections commissioner at home."

The captain looked like he wanted to say something. Coletti looked like he wanted him to. Smithson and the guards looked entertained by the exchange.

As the game of verbal chicken stretched out for a few seconds more, Coletti stared the captain down and waited. After ten years of living with the Confessional Murders, he wasn't about to let a prison guard stand between him and the truth. He was determined to get the answers he'd come for, and he didn't care whom he offended in the process.

"Gimme a second," the captain said, knowing he couldn't risk a call from the governor's office.

The two other guards stood by silently, watching as the captain went into the back room to make a call of his own.

Coletti looked at Smithson, who nodded ever so slightly to show that she approved of his negotiation techniques.

When the captain returned from the back room, it was clear that the fight was over.

"You'll both need to leave everything down here, including your guns, badges, and cell phones," the captain said through clenched teeth. "Apparently the corrections commissioner already received a call, so I've been asked to escort you to the unit."

"Good," Coletti said with a tight smile.

He and Smithson handed over their belongings to one of the guards. A few minutes later, Coletti and Smithson were being whisked through locked doors and checkpoints leading to Graterford's infamous death row. When they walked through the final door leading to the two-booth visiting room, the captain directed them to two chairs in front of a glass barrier encased in a wood and metal booth.

"I'm gonna need you both to take a seat over there," the captain said. "Father O'Reilly will be out shortly."

Coletti and Smithson squeezed into the small space. That forced them to be closer than they'd been all day, and each was keenly aware of the other. Coletti could detect the faint hint of Smithson's fruity perfume. She could see an artery pulsating in his neck, and she knew that he was nervous.

After a few minutes, a steel door on the opposite side of the glass swung open. Father O'Reilly walked in and sat down.

In an instant, Coletti was transported back ten years. He

saw the cathedral, remembered the horror, and regretted the outcome.

The priest wasn't affected that way. He simply picked up the phone and stared through the glass with a blank expression. Smithson watched them both, trying and failing to get a bead on what they were thinking.

O'Reilly pointed to the phone on Coletti's side of the glass. Coletti picked it up and held it between himself and Smithson so both of them could hear.

"I'm not sure if you remember me," Coletti said quietly. "I'm Detective Coletti."

"I know who you are," the priest said. "But I don't remember her."

"My name's Lieutenant Smithson. I'm helping Detective Coletti look into your case."

O'Reilly studied Smithson's face for a few moments. Then he turned to Coletti. "What's there to look into?" he asked.

Coletti paused before he answered. He didn't want O'Reilly to think he was crazy, and he didn't want to relive it all in front of Smithson. Sensing his apprehension, she reached up and gently rubbed his back. He glanced at her with a hint of gratitude. Then he looked at the priest through the glass.

"I've had dreams about that day at the cathedral," he told Father O'Reilly. "In every one of them, I'm you, and there's a guy in the confessional booth who tells me he's hurt people. It kinda makes me nervous when he says that, but it's my job to take confession, so I listen to him. But then he starts to get kinda loud and the sexton hears him. Does that dream sound familiar to you?"

The blood drained from the priest's face, and as he sat there, his soul looked into a past he'd relived too many times. "How could you know that?" he asked in an anxious whisper.

"I don't know," Coletti said. "I just do. It's almost like I've lived the whole thing through your eyes."

"Well," O'Reilly said, "if you've lived the whole thing, then you know what happens next."

"I was hoping you could tell me."

The priest looked from Coletti to Smithson. Then he closed his eyes tightly. Neither of them could tell if he was trying to recall the images from that day or erase them. It wasn't clear which option he'd chosen until he spoke.

"The sexton started walking toward the confessional booth when he heard the commotion," O'Reilly said. "I could hear his footsteps coming across the sanctuary, and I was trying to keep the guy calm until he got there. But the more we talked, the more agitated he seemed to get. He finally admitted that he was sick and he didn't know what to do. I told him that confessing was the right thing to do, and that's when he stood up and said he was the angel of death. The sexton opened the door and . . ."

He didn't have to say what happened next. They knew it. The shotgun blasts, the killer's flight, O'Reilly's attempt to exact retribution. It all played out in their minds, in fits and starts, in flashes of red, in pieces of dreams.

"I thought you were in shock when you kept whispering about the angel of death," Coletti told the priest. "I thought it was your mind's way of dealing with what you'd done."

"So that's why you came here?" the priest asked. "To tell me what you thought?"

"No. I came to ask why you never mentioned the angel of death again."

"Because it was so traumatic, I wasn't sure that what I'd heard was real," O'Reilly said. "I knew I saw a man kill those people, but I couldn't be certain he'd called himself the angel of death, so I just stopped saying it."

"And because you weren't sure, you let it come to this?" Coletti asked in disbelief.

For the first time, the priest became agitated. "I got up on the stand and said I saw another man do it. What more could I have done? You think I wanted this? You think I haven't prayed every day for the last ten years that God would deliver me from this? Do you honestly think for one minute that I haven't hated you and everyone else for allowing this to happen to me?"

Coletti looked away, ashamed. "I can't blame you if you hate me," he said.

"But that's just the point," the priest said earnestly. "I don't hate you, and I don't blame you, either. Not anymore. Don't get me wrong, I still wish you would've looked past the circumstances and tried harder to see the truth. But about five years ago, in the midst of hating you for what you'd done, I realized that it wasn't about you. It was about me. As much as I used to love taking confession and seeing people set free from the things they'd done, I'd never truly grasped the one thing that confession is all about. I'd never truly learned to forgive."

As the priest's words hung in the air, Coletti turned to Smithson, who looked into his eyes and told him the very thing he needed to hear.

"Forgiveness is hard," she said gently. "Trust me, I know. But maybe you should follow Father O'Reilly's example, and start by forgiving yourself."

Coletti knew she was right about forgiveness being difficult. But she was wrong about where forgiveness began.

"Before I do anything else, I need you to know I'm sorry," he said, looking at the priest through the glass.

Father O'Reilly smiled. He finally had the chance to say the words he'd only spoken in a small still voice in his cell. "I forgive you."

With that, both men were loosed from the prison that had held them captive for the past ten years. They were freed to deal with the reality of the moment.

"The angel of death resurfaced today," Coletti said. "He dropped a note at an art gallery and said he was going to kill again in twenty-four hours. If we can link him to the Confessional Murders, we can get you a stay of execution and eventually get you out of here. But I'm gonna need your help."

At first, O'Reilly was shocked. Then he was elated, then hopeful, then frightened, and finally, he was resolved. Slowly, he looked from Coletti to Smithson and back again. "So he was real after all," he said. "What do you need me to do?"

"I need you to think back on what happened in the cathedral," Coletti said. "Do you remember anything distinctive about the killer? Anything that would separate him from a crowd?"

"Yes," O'Reilly said. "His voice was gravelly, almost guttural, but it wasn't very deep. He wasn't that tall, but he was strong for his size. He had to be. The recoil from that sawed-off never knocked him back."

"How about his face?" Smithson asked. "Did he have a tattoo, scars, anything like that?

"It was hard to see his face under the hat," O'Reilly said. "But, there was one thing about him. I was bigger than him. If I could've gotten to him, maybe I could've knocked him down. Maybe I could've even saved those people."

"You can't blame yourself," Smithson said. "I doubt there was anything you could've done."

"She's right," Coletti said. "And anyway, the past is the past. All we can do now is try to figure out the things we missed the first time."

"Things like what?" the priest said.

"In my dreams, the killer said he had hurt people before that day," Coletti said. "But I can never recall the exact words he used. Can you?"

"I've been hearing his words for years," the priest said, closing his eyes as he resurrected the memories.

"The killer said that he'd cut off a man's finger while he slept on a park bench, and sliced a child's leg at a playground."

Coletti and Smithson looked at each other, knowing that they now had something to go on. A second later, the door flew open.

"I hate to interrupt," said the captain from C Block. "Homicide's been trying to reach you, Detective Coletti. Three people were gunned down in a church. The killer left a note addressed to you."

It was nine o'clock when Commissioner Lynch got the call. As he listened to the homicide captain recount what he'd heard from the priest who'd witnessed the killings, his blood ran cold.

The killer not only matched the description Coletti had shared with him. He called himself the angel of death.

When Lynch disconnected the call, he turned to his wife, who sat next to him on the couch. She knew before he spoke that he wouldn't be staying through the end of the Bette Davis movie they were watching. Over the years, she'd come to understand that this was part of the territory.

"I'll be back," he said as he kissed her on the forehead.

"That's what you always say when you're about to cheat on me," she said with a smile.

Lynch kissed his wife again before heading off to yet another in the line of calamities that had taken him away from home over the course of his career.

He still remembered going back to the East Bridge housing projects, where he'd grown up, to solve the case of his friend's missing child. He remembered watching another police commissioner die in a battle between a man of faith and a man of the streets. He remembered chasing a beautiful killer after the mayor was murdered—and risking his marriage and career to chase her again.

Through it all, Jocelyn had been there, urging him on, lifting him up, and if need be, cursing him out. She was the constant in his life, and now that he was settled into the role of commissioner, neither of them was sure where his career would take him. They were certain of one thing, however. They knew that they loved each other. With a killer tearing apart the city he'd been charged with protecting, Kevin Lynch wasn't sure that love was enough.

He grabbed his cell phone as he left the house and called the governor's chief of staff on his BlackBerry. The chief of staff said that the governor had decided to err on the side of caution.

Based on the questions raised by Coletti and the similarities between the Confessional Murders and the latest round of killings, a stay of execution would be in place by morning.

That was the first good news Lynch had heard all day, but he still had to face the sobering reality that a killer was on the loose, and it was up to his police officers to catch him.

He drove down Germantown Avenue—from his affluent Chestnut Hill neighborhood to the gritty streets leading to Logan—with thoughts of the murderer swirling in his head.

Lynch knew that this killer called himself the angel of death, and seeing as the man had committed three—or was it six?—murders and disappeared without a trace, Lynch supposed the name fit. In truth, though, the killer didn't need to be an angel to vanish in Philadelphia.

The city's convoluted network of alleys, vacant lots, abandoned houses, and one-way streets offered refuge to killers and cost cops their lives. In keeping secrets and hiding treasures, providing shelter and hatching plots, the streets of Philadelphia were like heaven and hell, and their inhabitants were the forces that fought on either side.

As Lynch sped toward the crime scene with his black Mercury's dome light swirling against the darkening sky, he thought of the main lesson those streets had taught him: Things aren't always what they seem.

He whipped out his cell phone and called the delayed police response unit. When a sergeant answered, he spoke quickly. "This is Commissioner Lynch. Get Detective Mann on the phone."

A few seconds later, a nervous-sounding Charlie Mann came on the line. "Yes, Commissioner?"

"You're back on duty," Lynch said. "Go upstairs and get your gun and badge from internal affairs."

"Just like that?" Mann asked. "What about—"

"You let me worry about the particulars," Lynch said. "Right now I need my best detectives on the street. There's been a triple murder in Logan."

"I know. That's all they've been talking about down here for the last half hour. They say it's a copycat trying to make a name on the Confessional Murders."

"Coletti doesn't think it's a copycat, and I'm starting to agree with him, so we're going to get a stay of execution until we can sort things out."

"But I thought—"

"Don't think," Lynch said. "If you think, you won't believe. And you're gonna need some faith on this one."

"What do you mean?"

There was a long pause. "Coletti believes he's seen the killer," Lynch said matter-of-factly. "He's had dreams—visions, I guess you'd call them—and those dreams match what we've heard from witnesses who saw the killer in the flesh."

"With all due respect, sir, we can't stop an execution based on dreams."

"No, we can't," the commissioner said. "But we can stop it if we think we've got a serial killer on our hands. Get your gun and badge, Detective Mann. I'll see you at the scene."

Lynch disconnected the call as he approached the glut of traffic surrounding the church. He parked near three TV news vans that were positioned along the perimeter, their satellite dishes hoisted high. When he got out of the car, reporters shouted questions, but Lynch ignored them. He was too caught up in the ugliness all around him.

The church's magnificent edifice was marred by crime scene tape that fluttered in the evening breeze. Officers milled about. Neighbors strained to see. Squad cars lined the street with fire rescue trucks beside them.

The police cars' dome lights spun slowly. The lights on the rescue trucks were still, primarily because there was no one left to save.

While bystanders looked on worriedly, hoping that their loved ones weren't inside, Lynch walked to the foot of the church steps. The officers guarding the scene stepped aside to let him through.

A priest with dark brown eyes, a slight frame, and thinning black hair walked down the steps to meet him. "I'm Father Douglas."

"I'm Commissioner Lynch," he said, shaking the priest's hand.

"I'm sorry we had to meet under these circumstances," the priest said in an anguished voice as he led Lynch into the sanctuary.

Once inside, the commissioner was struck by the contrast between the holy and the hellish.

A dozen nuns from the convent next door prayed beneath stained-glass windows filled with heavenly images. A crucifix stood at the front of the church, and candles stood behind the altar.

Less than thirty feet from the crucifix, the ethereal images were replaced by terrifying reality. Pools of blood smeared the sanctuary floor. Three bodies—each mutilated by a shotgun blast—slumped against the pews. What was left of their faces was twisted in the horror of their final moments. They looked like they died holding on to each other.

As officers from the crime scene unit dusted for prints and photographed the bodies, Lynch stood back and allowed them to do their work.

"We've got the description you gave us and we'll find the person who did this," Lynch said to the priest. "Two of my best detectives are on the case."

Father Douglas looked troubled by Lynch's assurance. "Is one of them named Michael?" he asked, almost timidly.

"Yes. His name's Mike Coletti. Why?"

The color drained from the priest's face. "The killer asked for him."

"What do you mean?"

"When I saw the killer he spoke to me in this rough, strange voice. He said he was an angel and this is a war. Then he said he had a message for Prince Michael."

The black Mercury sped down I-476 with sirens blaring, as Coletti tried to cut the fifty-minute trip from Graterford to Philadelphia down to twenty-five. Knowing that the killer had struck again gave him a sense of urgency, but seeing the priest face-to-face after all these years had sharpened his sense of purpose.

"What was it like to see him again?" Smithson asked, as if she were reading his mind.

"It was like walking into one of my dreams."

"Was it like you expected it to be?"

"No," Coletti said. "He was much more forgiving than I thought he would be."

"He's had a lot of time to think about it," Smithson said. "The killer has, too. That's why this pattern of killing people in churches scares me. He's established a ritual, and that's textbook behavior for a serial killer."

"So what else does the textbook say about serial killers?" Coletti asked skeptically.

"Most of them are white males who kill for the first time in their late twenties or early thirties," she said, ignoring his cynicism. "They work alone, they target strangers, and they don't venture too far from their hunting grounds. If this killer fits that mold, he would've been about twenty-eight at the time of the Confessional Murders. Of course, there's another possibility. We might not be dealing with a serial killer at all. We might be chasing a copycat."

"He's no copycat," Coletti said firmly. "This is the same guy from ten years ago. I can feel it."

"If you're right, that would mean he's in his late thirties or early forties by now," said Smithson. "And if he's anything like most serial killers, this whole thing goes back to his childhood."

"Meaning what?"

"He probably spent a lot of time alone as a child and developed a vivid imagination. Maybe he started out just thinking about the things he was going to do. Then as he got older, he might've gone out on a few test runs, like when he told Father O'Reilly that he cut a man on a bench and a child at a playground."

Coletti nodded.

"He probably spent years imagining the Confessional Murders before he ever made a move. I'm guessing that's why he's so hard to catch. He's a planner who imagines every contingency before he acts, and like I said before, he's got a God complex."

"You mean he actually thinks he's God?"

"Not necessarily. But if he really thinks he's an angel, he thinks he's got the power of God behind him, and maybe killing in churches is part of his ritual because he thinks he's doing God's work. Frankly, with the time he's had to map this whole thing out, I wouldn't be surprised if he thought he was working from God's plan."

Coletti was silent as the sound of the siren filled the car. He turned it off, flipped on the lights, and switched to the emergency lane.

"Funny how time affects people differently," he said as they sped down the shoulder of the highway.

Smithson looked at him. "What do you mean?"

"The killer spent the last ten years planning how to kill. Father O'Reilly spent the last ten years planning how to forgive."

"They say time heals all wounds," Smithson said.

"Yeah, but wounds leave scars."

She glanced at him curiously. "What scars do you have, Mike?"

"What makes you think I have any?"

"You're alone," she said. "A man your age should either be on his third affair or his second marriage. You're not on either, and the psychologist in me wants to know why."

Coletti shook his head. "I saw my parents' marriage. It's not for me."

"That bad, huh?"

"Actually, it was that good," Coletti said. "Mom was soft-spoken, but she kept my dad in line, even though he was the most stubborn SOB I've ever met. He worked long hours and had strict rules and I never once heard him say I love you, but he didn't have to. We saw it in his eyes.

"The two of them together were a perfect match. Right up until the time I left for the army, my dad was her protector and she was his right hand. But when I got back four years later, everything was different.

"My dad had been hoarse since that June. He said it was nothing, but by September his voice still hadn't come back. By the time my mom convinced him to go to the doctor, the tumor had almost closed his windpipe. Two months later he died from throat cancer. After that I watched my mom's heart break a little bit more every day. She was dead inside a year."

"Sounds like she loved him very much," Smithson said. "Some people spend their lives trying to find that."

"Yeah, they do," Coletti said soberly. "But I never want to need somebody so much that I can't live without them. I guess that's why the relationships I've had over the years have crashed and burned. I've spent my life trying to avoid becoming my parents."

Smithson didn't respond. She was absorbed in her own thoughts.

"So what about you?" Coletti asked. "Why aren't you married?"

"I guess I'm trying to find myself."

"I can help you with that," Coletti said. "You're sitting right there."

She punched him on the arm with enough force to make him swerve.

"Ouch!" he said, grabbing the wheel with both hands. "You're stronger than you look."

"That's what you get for teasing me," said a laughing Smithson. But then the laughter faded.

"My parents' marriage turned me off, too," she said. "They got along fine when we were little. In fact, our lives were like a fairy tale. We lived in a small town. We had this big, Irish Catholic family. Our house had a picket fence. Our parents seemed so in love.

"They'd take us to amusement parks and we'd come to Philly every once in a while to see the sights. Eventually, the city got too dangerous for that."

She stopped and looked out the window, her eyes becoming moist as she thought back to her time as a child.

"You don't have to talk about it if you don't want to," Coletti said.

"No, it's all right." She wiped her eyes and turned to him with a forced smile.

"My parents' marriage got shaky around the time I was twelve. Little arguments became big ones, but they always tried to make up. I guess that got too hard to do after a while, so they stopped trying. By the time the divorce came, nobody was surprised, not even me—the one who believed in fairy tales the most.

"When I got older I left town and moved to California. I guess I was trying to get as far away from the memories as I could. I married a guy in the psychology program at Stanford with the expectation that the marriage would fail, and in less than a year, it did. I stayed out there long enough to finish my doctorate, then I came back home to Dunmore and started my life over, hoping it would be better the second time around."

"Is it?" Coletti asked.

Smithson glanced at him, her red, tired eyes still moist with tears. "The jury's still out."

By nine thirty, when Charlie Mann walked into the church, his head was swimming. The day had been a whirlwind. He'd killed for the first time, been questioned at internal affairs, and learned things about Coletti that he'd never imagined were true.

Now he was standing at the edge of a sanctuary that had become an execution chamber, and the sight of it was surreal. The mere thought of bodies lined up against a pew seemed almost impossible, just like Coletti's dreams. But as he slowly walked the outside aisle, the bodies came into view. They were contorted and bloody, sacrificed near an altar where prayers had just been uttered.

Mann stood for almost a minute, pondering their final moments. Then his mind drifted to the man he'd shot that morning. Deep down, Mann knew that he was now a killer, too, and he wondered if he was any different from the one they were chasing.

"Charlie!" the commissioner called out.

Mann looked up at Lynch, who was standing about twenty

feet away, next to a priest. Then he walked over to the commissioner, who made the introductions.

"Detective Mann, this is Father Douglas," Lynch said. "He's the one who saw the killer."

"I heard the description on the radio on the way here," Mann said, turning to the priest. "But I'm also interested in what you can tell me about the victims."

"They were faithful members who loved to stay after mass and chat," Father Douglas said, sounding grief-stricken. "Tonight, they were the last ones here."

Tears welled up and perched themselves at the corners of the priest's eyes. One spilled over and rolled down his cheek, hanging on his chin before splashing against the floor.

"The woman in the black skirt was named Kannitha," he said. "The shorter one next to her, that's Chavy. The young man was named Boran. They were cousins. The two women worked for years cleaning houses to bring Boran over from Cambodia. He got here two months ago."

"Sounds like you knew them well," Mann said.

"I did. They lived on the northeast corner of Tenth and Rockland, in a three-story house with four other families."

Lynch thought for a moment. "Wasn't there a drive-by on that block a little earlier?"

The priest nodded. "That's one of the things they talked to me about after service. They were tired of all the shooting and they were saving up to move."

"Look into the drive-by," Lynch told Mann. "There's a chance this might be connected."

"Yes sir," said Mann, jotting down notes before turning to the priest. "So what else did they talk to you about, Father Douglas?"

"Nothing substantial," he said with a sad smile. "The weather, the Phillies, the neighborhood. We talked a lot, but most times we didn't say much. Talking to me was their way of practicing English without getting laughed at. And you know what? They were some of the wisest people I've ever met."

"What do you mean?" Lynch asked.

"They were Cambodian. They'd survived a regime that killed tens of thousands of people, including most of their family."

Father Douglas paused and wiped the sweat from his brow, the grief crumpling his face as his eyes grew vacant.

"When you come from a place like that, it makes you hard. Maybe that's why they were never afraid of anything that happened in Philadelphia. This was nothing compared to what they'd seen."

"Did they ever talk to you about what they'd seen in detail?" Lynch asked.

"Sometimes the women did. But Boran wasn't old enough to remember, and they never spoke of it in front of him. They just needed to get it out, I guess, and they trusted me with those horrible memories."

"How about the other Cambodians who live around here?" Mann asked. "Did they trust you, too?"

"They're Buddhists, mostly, so very few of them come here. From what I can see, they spend most of their time working and trying to fit in."

"What about him?" Mann said, pointing to Boran. "Did he spend a lot of time trying to fit in, too?"

The priest sighed heavily. "He was like most young people, struggling to find his place in the world. The streets move fast around here, and if you can't keep up, they swallow you."

"Maybe that's what happened," Mann said. "Maybe he fell in with the wrong crowd. Maybe the guys who did the drive-by were gunning for him and they came here to finish the job."

"Anything's possible, but I don't think so," the priest said. "First of all, he wasn't the type to hang with a crowd, and I couldn't see him doing anything to turn anyone against him."

"Maybe you're right, but grudges aren't always obvious," Mann said, as the door opened and Coletti and Smithson rushed down the aisle.

"This wasn't about a grudge," Coletti said, walking in on the tail end of Mann's comments. "And if it *was* a grudge, I doubt it had much to do with the victims."

"I see you made it back safely, Detective," Lynch said before turning to Smithson. "And I see you brought a guest."

"I was asked to come along," she said curtly.

"Good, we can use your expertise," Lynch said. "Father Douglas, meet Lieutenant Smithson and Detective Coletti."

Upon hearing his name, the priest stared at Coletti with a troubled look in his eyes. "So you're the prince," he said in a small, frightened voice.

"What do you mean?" said Coletti.

"The killer talked about you," Father Douglas said in a distant voice. "He called you a prince."

Blood rushed to Coletti's face and his skin grew hot. A

bead of sweat that had gathered at his temple trickled down over his cheekbone. "What else did he say?" Coletti asked calmly.

The priest began to shake as his eyes filled with the memory of the killer. "It wasn't just what he said, it was how he looked. It was almost like something out of scripture. His face was like lightning. His eyes were like fire, and when he spoke, his voice was strange, raspy, dead. It was a voice of multitudes."

Father Douglas paused and looked at Commissioner Lynch. Then he looked from Smithson to Mann before focusing his gaze on Coletti.

"He said he was the angel of death, and that this is a war. He left a note for you, and he told me to tell you he'd be waiting."

"What did the note say?" Coletti asked.

Again, the priest shifted his gaze to the commissioner, who nodded ever so slightly.

"It said, 'Prince Michael Coletti can stop this, but only if he believes in angels.'"

CHAPTER 7

It was nine forty-five, and Sandy Jackson was parked in her cruiser at Seventeenth and Walnut. The car's interior lights were on, and Sandy was sitting there, staring into space.

With the description of the Logan suspect being broadcast citywide at five-minute intervals, she was dazed and confused, because everything about the killer matched the man she'd seen on Twenty-first Street.

There was just one problem: It was eight ten when she saw him vanish in Center City, and eight fifteen when he murdered three people in a church seven miles away. In Philadelphia traffic, it could take five minutes to go one block. Traveling seven miles that quickly was impossible.

Since Sandy had broadcast the killer's description on police radio's central band five minutes before the murders, she knew homicide would come to her to ask what she'd seen. She also knew, from chatter in the district, that Mann had been reinstated and was working on the case.

Taking out her cell phone, she dialed his number repeatedly. He picked up after the eighth call.

"I'm in Logan at the crime scene," he whispered into the phone. "I can't talk now."

"That's too bad," she said frantically. "This can't wait."

Mann had never, in the three years he'd known Sandy Jackson, heard panic in her voice. This was the woman who was a better shot than any man he knew. She was the woman who had stood up to the old boy network and demanded that he do the same. She had chased a suspect down in a foot pursuit that was already legend. Yet here she was, on the other end of the line, sounding almost afraid.

Mann drifted away from Lynch, Coletti, and Smithson and found a quiet corner in the sanctuary. "What's so urgent that it can't wait?" he asked.

"I saw a guy who fit the killer's description. He was standing at Twenty-first and Locust."

"When?"

"About five minutes before the shooting at the church. I got out of my car to stop him, but he vanished."

Mann was quiet for a few moments, trying to understand what Sandy was saying. Clearly, it didn't make sense that the killer would simply disappear. Mann decided to steer her toward a more plausible explanation.

"Maybe the guy you saw was only dressed like him."

"He wasn't just some guy," Sandy insisted. "I think he was the killer."

"But that's impossible," Mann said, the confusion evident in his voice.

"I know. That's why I'm telling you first. I don't want to tell this story while I'm sitting across the table from some detective who thinks I'm crazy."

"Why would anyone think you're crazy?" Mann asked.

"You said it yourself. What I saw was impossible: a man standing on the corner of Twenty-first and Locust just minutes before shooting three people a half-hour away. I know it sounds crazy and I don't expect you to believe me, but I know it was him."

"How can you be so sure?"

"His eyes," Sandy said with conviction. "They were blue, but it wasn't a normal blue. It was almost like his eyes were on fire."

At that, Mann nearly dropped the phone. He remembered hearing that same conviction in Father Douglas's voice. More importantly, he remembered those same words. The killer's eyes were like fire.

"Charlie, are you still there?"

"Yeah, I'm here," he said absently, his mind racing through every possibility and finding none that made sense.

"Listen to me, Charlie," she said in a voice that was quiet but firm. "No man's eyes could have looked like that, no man could disappear like that, and no man could cross the city in five minutes, kill three people, and disappear."

"So if he isn't a man, what is he?" Mann asked.

"I hear he says he's an angel. And if I were you, I'd think about believing it."

When Mann disconnected the call, a look of apprehension settled on his face. He was nervous about what Sandy had told him, but he knew that she believed it to be true.

He fiddled with his iPhone, Googling "angel" and "eyes like fire" until he narrowed his search to several Old Testament passages. As he focused on the chapter that contained all he'd heard that evening, he looked around at his cohorts and considered whom he should confide in first.

Lynch was huddled with the homicide captain, preparing to make a statement to the assembled media. Officers from the crime scene unit were bagging and tagging evidence. Fire rescue workers were preparing to remove the bodies.

Standing off to the side were Coletti, Smithson, and Father Douglas. The three of them were looking up at the crucifix that stood tall in the front of the church. Mann walked over and stood beside them.

"You know, I never really thought about angels until tonight," Father Douglas said to no one in particular. "In my mind, they were just these beings who were there to praise God and protect man. But they never seemed real to me until tonight."

Coletti looked at him askance. "Do you really think the man who killed these people was an angel?" he asked.

"I don't know," Father Douglas said. "But he thinks he is."

"Maybe that's all that matters," Smithson said. "He thinks he's an angel, and that gives him the power to act like one."

"He might be doing a little bit more than acting," Mann said. "Sandy called me a few minutes ago. She saw a man fitting the killer's description downtown around the time he was here."

"That must've been somebody else," Coletti said dismissively. "No one can be two places at once."

"That's what I thought, too," Mann said. "But then Sandy

said the same thing Father Douglas did. She said he had eyes like fire."

Mann pulled out his iPhone and clicked on the link he'd found. "Eyes of fire appear a few times in scripture when people are talking about angels. The thing that separates this from everything else is the stuff about war and Prince Michael. It's from Daniel, chapter 10. That's where Daniel stands by a river and sees an angel who tells him about a great war."

Father Douglas looked up as if he was seeing things clearly for the first time. "Of *course*," he said, his eyes dancing about.

"So what does it mean?" Coletti asked.

"In a practical sense, Daniel's vision was about an angel fighting to free the Jews from slavery with the help of the archangel, Michael. But there's a deeper meaning. Some scholars believe the vision was a prophecy about a war between the forces of good and evil." Father Douglas paused to glance at the bodies of his dead parishioners. "I just wonder whose side this killer thinks he's on."

Lynch walked over to the four of them with the homicide captain beside him. "We're going to make a statement in ten minutes," Lynch said. "Smithson, I've been in contact with your barracks and you're officially on loan to the department for now, so you're going to stand with us to represent the state police. Mann and Coletti, I need the two of you on the street. We have to catch this killer before more people die."

At ten o' clock the bodies were removed amidst the incessant clicking of digital cameras. Shortly afterward, Commissioner Lynch came out for his impromptu press conference.

"Three people lost their lives here tonight," he said as Smithson and two captains stood solemnly behind him. "We're withholding their names until we can notify their next of kin, and we're taking steps to find someone whom we've identified as a person of interest: a blue-eyed white male wearing a black suit and a large black hat and carrying a sawed-off shotgun. We've also been in contact with the governor's office, and because of the similarity of this crime to the Confessional Murders of a decade ago, the governor has agreed to issue a stay of execution for Father Thomas O'Reilly while we investigate any possible connections."

With that, the assembled press exploded, pressing forward with shouted questions in an attempt to get details on the person of interest and the stay of execution. As they did so, Mann and Coletti slipped past them and jumped into Coletti's car for the trip to Tenth and Rockland.

They were silent during most of the seven-block ride to the victims' house, listening as the neighborhood paid its respects to the dead. Bass-heavy hip-hop grew quieter, loud conversations on porches became muted, and all eyes trained on the detectives who had come to speak of death in a place that had already seen too much of it.

"So, what do you make of the note the killer left for you?" Mann said, as they coasted to a stop in front of the house.

"The surface is too rough to get good prints, but maybe when they analyze it at the lab they'll find some of his blood or—"

"That's not what I meant," Mann said, cutting him off.

Coletti knew exactly what Mann meant, but he didn't want

to think about it, much less talk about it. However, since his young partner had asked the question, he decided to tell the truth.

"The note tells me two things," Coletti said with a look of determination. "He's underestimating me if he thinks the only way I can stop this is by believing in angels. And he's got me all wrong if he thinks I'm gonna play his game."

"Yeah, but you can't just ignore the fact that he's trying to communicate with you," Mann said earnestly. "That passage out of Daniel is a clue, and if he thinks you're part of some kind of prophecy, we ought to use that to our advantage."

Coletti sighed impatiently. Then he turned to his young partner and told him like it was.

"You know, Charlie, I used to be a lot like you," he said, his tone even and steady. "I came to the department from the army the same way you came from college. I thought I knew everything because I'd been overseas and seen a little bit more than other people. But in reality, everything I knew about life, I'd learned by watching people who came from South Philly just like I did. People like Frank Rizzo, who fought his way to City Hall before he lost an election, and died trying to make it back to the top. People like Angelo Bruno, who ran the South Philly mob from a little row house, 'til they shot him right in front of it.

"Now I'm watching you, Charlie, and it ain't a pretty sight. You know why? You're just like me. You think you can be top dog because you're smarter than everybody else, and who knows, maybe you are. But here's a little tidbit I learned from watching people rise and fall: You only get one chance to be on top. Don't waste it trying to school me on things you know nothing about."

Coletti got out before Mann could respond. Reluctantly, Mann followed, walking slowly up the steps of the corner row house and contemplating kicking his new partner in the behind. He looked around quickly and saw that the crime scene tape from the earlier drive-by shooting was gone, though the spots where the casings had fallen still bore chalk marks and the faces of the neighbors still bore pain.

Two Cambodian boys who looked to be about five years old watched the detectives from beneath a bright porch light. An old woman sat in a chair behind the boys. Two teenage girls stood on either side of her, their waist-length hair hanging limp against their backs. Their jeans were tight. Their faces were angry. Their eyes were lined with makeup.

Coletti pulled his badge and announced himself. When no one responded, he looked at Mann, who'd come alongside him.

Mann considered playing dumb, but this was his case, too, and he didn't have time to revel in Coletti's inadequacy.

"*Sues' day,*" Mann said haltingly, directing his words at the old woman. "*Soksabay che te?*"

"How do you think she is?" one of the teenage girls snapped in response to Mann's weak attempt to greet them in Khmer. "We lived with them. Now we hear they're dead. Shot like dogs in one of your churches."

Coletti ignored the blame in her voice. "Were you related to them?" he asked.

"They were our friends," the girl said.

"So they don't have any next of kin here?"

The angry girl shook her head no as Mann sized her up. She was seventeen, perhaps, but her eyes were much older. She was wearing a tight Bebe T-shirt that rode up at her hips, revealing smooth yellow-brown skin. A cell phone was clipped to her belt, and she was wearing designer sandals that showed off her French pedicure.

Her clothes said that she knew her way around these streets. Her understated makeup said she knew her way around men. Her tear-stained face said she knew at least one of the victims well.

"Were they shooting at Boran when they did that drive-by?"

She looked him up and down. "They were shooting at those nuts who hang on the corner. Boran wasn't about that. He worked hard, minded his business, and looked out for his cousins."

"Yeah, I know," Mann said cynically. "That's the stuff you tell the reporters when they come around. But you know a little bit more than that, don't you?"

"I don't know what you're talking about."

Mann looked at Coletti and nodded toward the girl with a knowing grin. His body language said he didn't believe her.

Coletti jumped right in. "How 'bout we call up Immigration and start running names through the system, starting with yours?"

"Wait a minute, Mike," Mann said, his voice filled with sympathy. "We don't wanna be too hard on her. She just lost the man who bought her that nice jewelry."

Her hand instinctively covered the tennis bracelet on her right wrist. Her face cycled through several emotions, from anger to self-consciousness to fear.

"You got five seconds, honey," Coletti said, looking around

impatiently. "After that, we bring INS in here and clear out this whole damn house."

She looked from Mann to Coletti and knew that they wouldn't leave until she told them something. She considered lying, but the look on the old one's face said he wouldn't accept anything but the truth.

"Look, I don't want any trouble," she said nervously. "Boran was sweet. He never bothered anybody. Sure, he liked me, and he told me that, but it never went anywhere. I already had a boyfriend."

"So was your boyfriend in the car with the guys who were shooting?" Mann asked.

"Tyrone never found out Boran tried to talk to me," she said defensively. "And even if he did, he's not the kind of guy to go around shooting people over something like that."

Mann and Coletti traded skeptical looks. The girl got even more defensive.

"Look, my boyfriend didn't have anything to do with what happened on this block or at that church. He's been at work since early this morning. He's doing a double shift at the Navy Yard."

"What's Tyrone's last name?" Mann said, taking out his notepad. "And what's your name?"

The girl was about to answer when the old woman held up her hand. Everyone on the porch fell silent, including Mann and Coletti. There was something in her manner that said she knew more than all of them. It was in the way she'd listened carefully, in the way she'd waited to speak. It was even in the way she looked.

Deep wrinkles crisscrossed her face like spiderwebs. Her wiry gray hair was long and straight, wrapped neatly in a bun and secured by a mother-of-pearl comb.

When she looked up at the detectives, it was with dark eyes ringed in white. There was wisdom in those eyes, and they knew it when she started to speak.

"You know the boy had nothing to do with any of this, don't you?" she said with a firm voice as she looked at Coletti.

"I only know what I see," he said, sounding more certain than he felt.

"You might know what you see," the old woman reasoned. "But you believe what you don't see."

"What's that supposed to mean?" Mann said.

"Your partner knows what it means," said the old woman. "Every material thing disappears, but love, faith, and hope, they never go away. Neither does evil."

The girl who'd been quiet spoke up for the first time. "Grandmom, do you know who killed them?"

"No," she said. "But I know they saw things in that church that we all seek. They were looking for light, and whenever you do that, darkness follows."

"How do you know that, Grandmom?"

The old woman sat back in her chair and took a deep breath. "Have you ever heard the story of the demon and the Buddha?" she asked.

The girl shook her head no.

"The Buddha's given name was Guatama," the old woman said. "When Guatama was seeking supreme enlightenment, he sat under the Bo tree, and a demon named Mara came there to tempt him. First, he told Guatama that his family had lost its throne. When that didn't work, Mara sent rain, rocks, ashes, and darkness, scaring away all the gods who had gathered to honor Guatama. Finally, Mara sent his three daughters, Thirst, Desire, and Delight, to seduce him. And even after Guatama achieved supreme enlightenment and became the Buddha, Mara tried to convince him not to preach the truth to the people."

The old woman sat back for a few moments, contemplating the question that no one wanted to ask.

"Wherever there are angels," she said gravely, "there are demons. No matter who you are, if you're looking for light, those demons will find you. They'll use lies, fear, pain, even desire. If none of those things work, they'll use death. I don't know what happened at that church, but I know that Kannitha and Chavy were named for angels. That's why it never surprised me when I saw the man in black following them. Darkness always follows light."

Coletti's ears perked up. "Did the man you saw following them wear a dark suit and a wide-brimmed hat?"

The woman nodded.

"Did you see that man today?" he asked anxiously.

She nodded again. "I saw him a few minutes before they died. He was heading toward Broad Street. In my heart, I knew he was following them to the church, and I knew I'd never see them again."

CHAPTER 8

When the press conference was over, Lynch asked Smithson to drive Mann's car back to police headquarters. She did it, although she was tired, and not just from the strain of that morning's shooting or the mental energy she'd expended on the case. She was tired from carrying the heavy weight of being a female cop.

When a woman froze in the line of fire, as she'd done on the commuter train platform that morning, her male counterparts clucked their tongues as if some feminine problem had contributed to the mistake. When a woman took an interest in a colleague, as Smithson did with Coletti, they were regarded as whores, destined to be passed around. In the male-dominated world of police work, being a woman sometimes meant being alone, even in the midst of one's peers.

In truth, it was that feeling of isolation that caused her to stand up for Mann that morning. He was the only black detective in homicide, which meant that they were both lonely figures in a world where they didn't quite fit.

As she maneuvered through the heavy traffic surrounding the cordoned-off crime scene, her thoughts were heavy, too. Surprisingly, they weren't about the suspect on the platform, or the shots Mann fired to save her life. They weren't even about the profile that she was still trying to shape in her head.

Her thoughts centered on Mike Coletti, and as she made her way down Broad Street, she wondered if he was thinking of her, as well.

His gruff manner was off-putting. His clothes were Goodwill-ready. He looked like an extra from a scene in *Grumpy Old Men*. Yet she remained drawn to him, partly because of his reputation as the best detective in Philadelphia, and partly because he seemed to be so much more—and so much less—than that.

In the twenty minutes it took her to get to Race Street, her mind wandered to the conversation she'd had with Coletti about marriage. And just as she tried to put those memories back into the space where they'd long been buried, her cell phone rang.

She rolled her eyes. The phone always seemed to be in her purse when she was driving. She reached over to the passenger seat to get it and fished it out in time to avoid rear-ending a Mercedes that had stopped at a red light.

When she looked at the number on the phone's display screen and saw that the call was from Dunmore—the tiny Scranton suburb that housed her state police barracks and her family— she took a deep breath before connecting the call.

"Yes, Dad?" she said, sounding slightly annoyed.

"I heard about what happened this morning. Are you okay?"

"I'm fine."

"I woulda died if something woulda happened to you. Those animals down there in Philly have already done enough to our family," he said bitterly.

She cringed when he said *animals* and wondered what he would think if he knew that one of the "animals" had saved her life.

"We asked Father Ryan to pray for you," he said. "I know you don't wanna believe it, but I won't be able to sleep 'til I know you're back home safe."

"It's not about what I want to believe, Dad," she said impatiently. "It's about the truth."

"The truth?"

"Yes," she said plainly. "The truth is we haven't seen eye-to-eye since I decided not to spend my life married to a good Catholic boy and having babies named Seamus and Molly."

It was her father's turn to cringe. They'd had the same argument too many times over the last twenty years. He didn't care why she'd left home anymore. He was just glad she'd come back.

"I don't want to argue, Mary. What you do with your life is up to you."

She knew what he meant. Her life, after all, was not what her family expected it to be. They'd always known that she was smart. They knew she'd go to college—maybe nearby Marywood University. They thought she'd marry a local boy, too, and move from working-class Sixth Street to the grand old homes in the Dunmore enclave the locals called Hollywood.

But Mary had defied their expectations twenty years ago,

leaving everything behind, from her family to her faith. Even after her brief marriage failed and she returned to the Scranton area, nothing was the same. She'd seen too much of the world, gotten to know people who were not Irish, Italian, Catholic, or any combination of the three. She came back with a worldview that frightened them, and though they lived in the same town again, Mary and her family were worlds apart.

"How's Mom?" Mary asked, trying her best to needle her father.

"I imagine she's worried about you."

Mary smiled, relishing the uncertainty in his voice before getting to the root of her anger. "That's right, the two of you don't talk much anymore, do you?" she spat. "Not since the bastard child and the divorce."

"Why won't you let it go, Mary?"

"Because you humiliated my mother in front of everyone," she said, her lip trembling with anger. "After all that mumbo jumbo about God hating divorce, you went out and had an affair with her friend. In a town as small as Dunmore, you shamed her. You shamed all of us."

The quiet came again. It was the sound of a strapping man being brought to his knees by guilt.

"I'm glad you're all right, Mary," her father said in a near whisper. "Be careful in Philadelphia."

She waited for the line to go dead. Then she held on to the phone for a moment, and as the traffic eased forward, she allowed the phone to drop to the floor.

Her father was a proud man with rough hands and a tender heart. He was strong when it came to his convictions, and he'd instilled in Mary and her five brothers a love for Catholic doctrine. No sex outside of marriage. No divorce. No birth control.

In the end, when he broke the first of those tenets, it was the third that did him in. Her half-sister's birth forced him to break the second, and in the end, he was left with nothing.

Mary's half sister was twenty-nine now. She'd followed in Mary's footsteps by leaving Dunmore as soon as she was old enough to drive. But her younger sister was a much wiser woman than Mary. She was smart enough to never return.

Mary had returned in more ways than one. After years of eschewing the beliefs that her father had instilled in her, she'd recently begun reconsidering her faith. When she saw the cross around Mike Coletti's neck, she wondered why he wore it. Was it just for decoration, or was he like her, searching for answers in a faith he'd all but abandoned?

Now, as she drove along Broad Street, she contemplated the tenets of that faith. There was a heaven and hell, a God and a devil, angels and demons. Good would triumph over evil in the end.

She stopped at a red light and smiled at the quaint simplicity of those beliefs. A man in the next lane saw her and smiled, too. His flirtatious glance reminded her of Coletti, whose eyes spoke volumes from the moment they met.

Mary loved eyes. They said things that mouths never would, and Coletti's were no exception. Every time they were alone, his eyes filled with lust, then uncertainty, then curiosity, as though he was wondering if there was a future for the two of them.

As the light turned green, Mary Smithson attempted to

forget the look in Mike Coletti's eyes, but no matter how hard she tried, she couldn't.

At ten forty-five, when he and Coletti left the house at Tenth and Rockland, Mann made two phone calls.

The first was to northwest detectives, the unit that investigates crimes in the fourteenth and thirty-fifth police districts. They told him that the Rockland Street drive-by was the result of a drug dealers' turf war, thus ruling out Mann's theory of a neighborhood grudge involving Boran. They said that the men from the nearby Mormon church were away on a weeklong religious retreat, which eliminated them as suspects. The girl's story of her boyfriend working at the Navy Yard checked out, too, according to a detective who knew him. That negated Mann's theory of a revenge shooting by a romantic rival.

With the conventional theories in tatters, Mann had little choice but to follow Coletti's lead and go with what they had: the notes from the killer, the priest's interpretation of scripture, and the old woman's stories of angels and gods. The spiritual underpinnings of it all forced a skeptical Mann to consider what Coletti had known all along—that the truth lay somewhere between dreams and reality.

That realization made the investigation personal for Mann, because the old woman and the priest weren't the only eyewitnesses to see the killer in the moments before and after the shooting. Sandy thought she'd seen him, too, and that's why Mann made his second call.

He reached Sandy on her cell and asked her to meet them

at the spot where she'd seen the man she believed to be the killer. Hesitantly, she agreed.

"She'll be there in fifteen minutes," Mann said to Coletti in the stilted tone he used with people he disliked.

"That's good," Coletti said in the same terse manner.

They sat in awkward silence for the next few minutes, listening to the engine's hum and the siren's wail as they drove toward Center City. They were both wondering if they could work together without speaking. Coletti didn't think so. He decided to make small talk.

"How'd you learn to speak Cambodian?" he asked.

Mann was mildly surprised. Not by the question, but by the fact that Coletti had decided to speak at all.

"I dated a girl from Phnom Penh in college," Mann said. "We didn't talk much. She was just using me for my body, but I learned how to say, 'Hi, how are you?' in Khmer."

Coletti looked at him. "So, how'd you go from that to a woman like Sandy?"

"What do mean 'a woman like Sandy'?" Mann asked defensively.

Coletti shrugged. "I mean a woman who's mature and confident," he said with a smile. "A woman who's too good for you."

Mann looked out the window, unsure of what to say. In truth, he'd often asked himself the same question, and no matter how many times he tried, he could never quite come up with the answer.

"She was working when I met her," Mann said, grinning at the memory. "It was three years ago, and I'd just joined the department two years before that. I guess I'd gotten into the habit of driving like I was in a squad car, no matter what time of day it was or where I was going. I figured I could always flash my badge if I got stopped, and for the most part, that's what I did. But then one night I was on my way to the old post office at Thirtieth and Market, trying to get a package in the mail before they closed at ten. I made an illegal left on Twentieth Street, and a second later, I saw flashing lights behind me.

"I pulled over, frustrated as hell, and whipped out my badge while I waited for this cop to get out and ask for my license and registration. So I'm sitting there for, like, five minutes, and the cop never gets out. And the longer I sit there, the more pissed I get, so I decide I'm gonna get out and show this cop my badge so I can be on my way. The minute I open the door, she gets on the speaker and says, 'Get back in the car.'

"By this time it's five after ten, and backup shows up, like they always do on car stops, and people are looking, and I'm livid. Another few minutes go by, and I'm sitting there rehearsing everything I'm gonna say, and all the supervisors I'm gonna call, and all the trouble I'm gonna make. Then all of a sudden this woman gets out of the squad car and she's standing next to my window and she's beautiful. Right then, my mind goes blank. I fumble around and show her my badge and she tells me to be careful next time. That should've been the end of it, but I couldn't stop thinking about her, so the next day I sent her two dozen roses at roll call and embarrassed her in front of everybody in her unit. Then I kept showing up at the district until she agreed to go out with me. Ever since then, she's never ceased to amaze me. She's smart and sexy and sure about everything she does."

Mann paused as Coletti whipped around City Hall and turned down Fifteenth. "I guess that's why it was so strange when she called me about seeing this killer," he said. "For the first time since I've known her, she seemed almost afraid."

"Didn't that make it hard to believe?" Coletti asked as he made a right on Walnut. "I mean, fear can do strange things to people's minds."

"I thought about that," Mann admitted. "I even tried to get her to change her story. But Sandy saw something on that corner tonight. Hopefully we can figure out what."

Coletti made a left on Twenty-first and parked behind Sandy's squad car. As he and Mann walked to the corner, Sandy got out and met them. A smile was the closest she came to a public display of affection for Mann. She showed her disdain for Coletti by rolling her eyes.

"Are you all right?" Mann asked.

"I'm fine," she said, glaring at Coletti before turning her gaze back to Charlie. "I'm worried about you. It's hard when you've got a partner you can't trust."

The hostility in her words wasn't lost on Coletti. He tried to smooth things over. "Look, Sandy, I—"

"You can call me Sergeant Jackson," she said angrily.

"Okay, fair enough," Coletti said. "I just want to clear the air so we all understand each other."

"Oh, I think we understand each other perfectly," she snapped. "I heard about what you said to Charlie this morning about shooting at one of his own."

"Yeah, and I said I was wrong! What more do you want?"

"Yo, you need to calm down," Mann warned.

"I will *not* calm down," Coletti said through clenched teeth. "We've got a killer to catch, and that's more important than anything either one of you think about me. So I'll tell you what. Either we can get along, or we can stand here bickering while more people die. It's up to you."

Mann wanted to argue the point, but he knew Coletti was right, and though he hadn't forgiven his new partner, he no longer felt the same anger that Sandy did.

He took a deep breath and turned to her. "If you want me to rough him up later, I'll do it," he deadpanned while glancing at the old detective. "Right now we just need to know where the guy was when you spotted him."

Sandy glared once more at Coletti. Then she walked about fifteen feet from the corner and stood in front of the apartment building. "He was right here."

"What was he doing?" Coletti asked.

"He was standing still. That's what caught my eye, because nobody stands still down here. Most people are on their way to the train or work or home."

"And this guy you saw, he had on a big hat, right?" Coletti asked.

Sandy nodded.

"So how'd you see his eyes?" he asked.

"A breeze turned up the brim of his hat."

"And were you able to see his whole face, or just part of it?" Mann asked.

Sandy thought about it. "I mainly remember his eyes, but I did notice how pale his skin was. Most people aren't that pale in August."

Coletti rubbed his chin and closed his eyes. "Maybe he spends a lot of time indoors."

"Could be," Mann said. "But that still doesn't explain how he walked around the corner and disappeared."

"Can you show us exactly where he went?" Coletti asked.

"He went this way," Sandy said, tracing the man's footsteps around the corner as Mann and Coletti followed.

"This is where I lost him, but there's nowhere he could've gone. We checked that apartment building up the street, but the doorman said nobody came in or out, and I had Harris, the officer who was coming down the street, check every house on the block. Nobody saw anything."

"Maybe the guy had an accomplice with a car," Mann said. "Since the traffic goes the same direction he was running, he could've jumped in and nobody would've seen him."

Coletti looked across the street at a store on the corner. "Hopefully, no one needed to see him," he said, pointing to the surveillance camera above the entrance. "We might have it all on tape."

It was eleven fifteen when they reached the store's owner. She lived only a few blocks away, on the cusp of affluent Rittenhouse Square, and arrived within minutes of receiving the call.

When she pulled up at the corner and got out of her Toyota Prius, they could tell right away that she was well-to-do. Not from the car she drove or the clothes she wore. They could tell because she carried herself with the kind of regality that came with old money.

Brushing a shock of wiry brown hair away from her

inquisitive hazel eyes, she pulled her Burberry trench coat tight around her waist, and ambled toward the police car parked in front of the store.

"Where did they break in?" she asked as Coletti approached with badge in hand.

"Actually, there wasn't a break-in," he said as Mann and Sandy came alongside him.

"Then why did you call me?"

"We were hoping we could ask for your help," Coletti said. "There was a man out here a few hours ago who we'd like to talk to. We think your video camera might've caught him on tape."

"So you called me in the middle of the night for that?" she asked with a half smile. "What's he wanted for? Murder?"

Coletti didn't smile. Neither did Mann or Sandy. When she saw their reactions, the woman's smile faded, too.

Having come from a wealthy family, she'd spent all of her forty years away from the more unsavory aspects of the city. She'd been divorced for the past two years, and the store was a way for her to interact with people outside the society circuit. Thus far she'd enjoyed the chance to spend time with everyday people. But this was more than she'd bargained for.

"Can you give me any details about what he supposedly did?"

"Not really," Mann said, speaking up for the first time. "But I can tell you this. It's an ongoing investigation and time is an issue."

"Will I be in any danger if I cooperate?" she asked.

"We can put a car at your house for the night," Sandy said. "The detectives could put you up somewhere in the morning."

Coletti thought back to the notes and the bodies and the

dreams and the feeling that none of it was within his control. "The truth is, we can't guarantee your safety no matter what we do," he said with a sigh. "But I can guarantee this: The longer we wait, the more people we put in harm's way."

The woman stared at Coletti with a look of concern rather than fear, and just beneath that look, there was an odd sort of exhilaration playing in her eyes. She liked the thought of danger. She liked it a lot.

"Wait here a minute," she said, unlocking the store.

When she opened the door, the alarm went off. As the beeping echoed in the still night air, she pushed a few buttons on the console beside the door, silencing the alarm.

"Come in," she said, turning on the lights.

Coletti and the others followed her inside and looked around quickly at her wares. The lighting fixtures she sold ranged in style from antique to postmodern and everything in between. Nothing cost more than five hundred dollars, and every single piece was unique.

"The security system is set up in the back," she said, unlocking her office door.

When all of them were inside, she sat down in front of a computer with two monitors. Then she pressed the power button and booted up a state-of-the-art video suite. There was editing equipment and graphics software and feeds from four cameras. It was a techie's dream.

"The store keeps me busy," she explained when she felt them looking at her curiously. "The cameras keep me entertained."

She hit a button, and the image from the outside camera filled the screen. "What time did he pass by?" she asked.

"About eight ten," Sandy answered.

The woman isolated the digital images from five minutes after eight to eight fifteen. Then she ran the images at twice the normal speed. It didn't take long for them to find what they were looking for.

"There!" Sandy said excitedly as the man in black appeared on-screen, rounding the corner from Twenty-first to Locust.

The store owner slowed the images to half speed, and the four of them watched as the man dove toward a black pickup being driven down the street. A pigeon flew by the camera, obscuring the view for half a second. When it disappeared, the man did, too. Only the pickup remained.

"That's impossible," Coletti said. "Can you run it back again?"

She hit rewind, this time running the images one frame at a time. When she did, the pictures showed a different story. The man had run toward the slow-moving pickup. He dove toward the bed, the pigeon flew by, and when it disappeared, the man lay flat in the back of the pickup, his black clothes blending in perfectly with the truck's black paint. It had happened so quickly that it was almost impossible to see.

"Can you stop it there and zoom in?" Sandy asked.

The store owner did so. The frame showed the back window of the cab and a driver dressed in a dark shirt or jacket. His face was unclear, and shadows from the roof of the cab made it difficult to discern his hair color. She tried zooming in farther to get a better view, but the picture just got blurry.

"The two of them were definitely together," Coletti said.

"There's no way someone jumps in the back of a pickup like that and you don't feel it in the cab."

"Yeah, but what were they doing together?" Sandy asked as she looked at the image.

"That's the million-dollar question," Mann said, leaning in closer. "Can you rewind it one more time and zoom in on the license plate?"

The store owner did as she was asked.

Mann asked for a print of that frame and a longer shot of the pickup. Coletti called the plate in on his police radio. A few seconds later, the dispatcher responded.

"The plate comes back on a 2002 Ford Ranger," she said. "It's registered to a Frank Kelly. It was reported stolen this morning."

CHAPTER 9

The house was one of several on the block that were marked with "For Sale" signs. In trendy Northern Liberties—an area on the east side of North Philly that had undergone massive gentrification over the previous ten years—such sights were becoming more common.

During the real estate boom, the neighborhood was on the verge of becoming a mecca for young professionals. Property values tripled. Homeowners refinanced. When the bubble burst, many of them were caught holding the bag. Frank Kelly was among them.

Tonight, like most nights, he sat alone in the dark in his beautifully refurbished home on North Sixth Street, unable to sleep, unable to think, unable to awaken from the nightmare his life had become. At thirty-five years old, the former chemist at Rohm and Haas was out of work, out of hope, and nearly out of time. He didn't believe things could get worse. That is, until they knocked at his door.

"Police officers!" Coletti yelled as Mann looked through the window of the darkened house. "Mr. Kelly, we need to talk to you!"

Frank Kelly flipped open his cell phone and looked at the time on the screen. It was eleven forty-five. He'd never been in trouble in his life, and he didn't know much about the police, but he knew they weren't there close to midnight to deliver good news.

Getting up slowly from his seat on the couch, he shuffled to the door and opened it.

"Frank Kelly?" Coletti said, holding up his badge while Mann stood behind him.

Kelly nodded.

"Your pickup was spotted downtown a few hours ago," Coletti said. "We think it was used in a crime."

"I reported it stolen this morning," Kelly said with a shrug. "I don't have anything to do with any crime."

Coletti peered around Kelly at the darkened living room. "Maybe we should talk about it inside."

Kelly hesitated for a second before stepping aside to let them in. "I'm sorry I don't have anything to offer you," he said, turning on a lamp before flopping down on the couch. "Things have been a little tight lately."

"That's okay," Coletti said as he and Mann sat down across from Kelly. "I'll get right to the point. My partner here got a copy of your stolen car report on his iPhone on the way over here. Apparently you told the officer who took your complaint that you saw two guys hotwire your pickup a couple nights ago. Funny thing is, you didn't report it until thirty-six hours after it supposedly happened. We're wondering why."

Kelly sighed. "That's the same thing the insurance company asked me," he said, laughing nervously. "I guess they thought I was one of those people who report their cars stolen and torch them for the insurance money."

"That's not what we thought," Mann said. "We thought you might've known the people who took the pickup and knew what they were going to do with it. We thought they might've given you some money to keep it quiet, but you got a conscience at the last minute and decided you'd report the truck stolen."

Frank Kelly looked genuinely shocked. Then he looked angry. Finally, he just laughed. He laughed because he hadn't done so in such a long time. He laughed because he didn't want to cry in front of strangers. He laughed because the accusation was hilarious.

"I wish I would've thought of doing something like that," he said, his tone angry and sarcastic. "If there was ever a time I needed to hook up with criminals, it would be now. I was laid off, and unemployment just ran out. My house is in foreclosure. My truck was just stolen. My life is in a shambles. I never thought of turning to crime, but who knows? Maybe it's not too late."

"You think this is a joke?" Coletti said, his eyes boring into him. "There are at least three people who've caught tougher breaks than you tonight. They're dead, and we think the guy driving your pickup had something to do with it. So if you don't want to go to jail as an accomplice, start talking. We don't have time to play."

Frank Kelly's laughter disappeared as quickly as it had surfaced. "Look, I didn't mean . . ." He stopped to compose himself. "I didn't know you were talking about a murder case."

Mann handed Kelly one of the printouts from the video camera. "This is your truck in the picture, right?"

He nodded.

"Do you know the guy who's driving?"

He took a closer look at the picture. "I can't see his face, but it might be one of the guys who stole it."

"What did the guys look like?" Coletti asked.

Kelly looked up, clearly afraid. "There were two of them. Both of them were white, kinda pale, wearing black clothes with hats pulled down over their faces. It was late, around this time Sunday, and it was quiet out. I was about to go to bed when I heard this tapping sound and a door creaking open. I looked out the window and I saw these two guys. One of them was in my pickup and the other one was on the sidewalk, standing guard right under the streetlight.

"I rushed outside and the guy on the sidewalk turned around with a sawed-off shotgun in his hand. I guess he was about four feet away from me. I froze.

"A few seconds later the guy in the pickup got it started, and the guy with the shotgun said something to me in this really freaky voice."

"What'd he say?" Coletti asked.

"He said the war had already begun, and he told me not to pick the wrong side, because if I did, I'd be dead in a day." He looked Coletti in the eye. "That's why it took me so long to report it. I was afraid he might be right."

Coletti looked at Mann, who stood up before asking a final question.

"Was there anything about either of them that stood out?

Anything you might've forgotten when you filed the stolen car report?"

"Yeah," he said. "There was one thing I forgot to mention. The guy with the shotgun had a tattoo on the back of his right hand. It looked like some kind of skull. Right underneath the skull it said, 'Daniel 10.' "

It was midnight when Lynch walked into homicide with a Box o' Joe from Dunkin' Donuts. Smiling, he opened the door to the captain's office, where Mary Smithson was at the computer, scrambling to put together a profile on the killer.

"How's it going, Lieutenant?" he asked pleasantly.

She looked up at his smiling face and thought of all the things he'd implied the last time they spoke. She remembered the way he'd glared at her when she returned from Graterford with Coletti. She didn't trust him.

"I'm . . . fine," she said warily.

"That's good," Lynch said, pouring a cup of coffee and taking a large gulp. "Want a cup?"

She wanted to refuse it, but Smithson was as tired as everyone else. She'd been going since early that morning, and her eyes felt like they were ready to shut. "Yes, thank you."

Lynch poured the coffee and handed it to her. Then he sat down. "I didn't get a chance to say it earlier, but we're glad to have you working this case," he said.

Smithson decided to slice through the pleasantries. "Why are you being nice to me?" she asked in an icy tone.

Lynch laughed. "I guess I deserve that for being so rough on you earlier. I'm sorry. It's just that I've never seen an attractive woman pay attention to Coletti. It seemed a little strange."

She took a sip of the coffee. "Oh, I get it," she said with a grin. "You think I'm attractive, so you want me for yourself."

"No, I'm married, and since the kid's finally off at college, I figure I might as well stick it out with the wife."

"That doesn't answer my original question," she said. "Why are you being nice to me?"

"We need you now," Lynch said frankly. "That's the first reason."

"What's the second reason?"

"I saw the way he looked at you. Who am I to stand in the way of that?"

He took a last gulp of coffee and stood up to walk around the desk. "So, what've you got so far?"

"Father Douglas got me curious, so I looked up the passage he was talking about," she said, scrolling her mouse over an online Bible concordance. "What I found was that Daniel, chapter 10, is just part of a bigger picture."

She was about to explain when there was a knock at the door and Mann and Coletti walked in. When Coletti saw Lynch leaning over her shoulder to look at the screen, jealousy flashed across his face. Then Mary smiled at him, and his eyes lit up. Both Mann and Lynch saw the silent exchange and looked at each other knowingly.

"Have some coffee," Lynch said, walking around the desk to greet them. "I'm sure you both can use it."

Coletti poured two cups and handed one to Mann, who

gratefully accepted. Both men seemed more at ease with each other. Lynch was happy to see that.

"So, what've we got on the killer?" the commissioner asked as he sat down.

"From what we've learned, there are at least two people involved, and maybe more," Coletti said.

"Do we have descriptions?"

"That's the thing," Mann said between sips of coffee. "The shooter at the church in Logan matched the description of the guy Sandy saw on Locust Street. He was caught on a store surveillance camera jumping into a stolen pickup driven by another man. We ran the pickup's tag and found the owner."

"And what did the owner say?" Lynch asked.

"He saw the guys who stole his truck," Coletti said. "There were two of them, both dressed in black, and one of them had a sawed-off shotgun."

"Did he see their faces?" Lynch asked.

"No," Mann said. "But one of them had a skull with angel wings tattooed on his hand. It said 'Daniel 10' underneath the skull."

"That means he's one of the other two," Smithson mumbled.

All three men looked at her, waiting for her to explain.

"In Daniel 10 and 11, there's only one angel, and he tells Daniel how the great war plays out. In Daniel 12, two more angels appear, and Daniel gets two time frames: twelve hundred ninety days between the sacrifice and the abomination, and thirteen hundred thirty-five days until the blessing."

She looked up at the three of them. "If this killer's operating according to Daniel's time frames, we'd better figure out what they mean to him, because Father Douglas was right. Daniel is about a war between good and evil. The good guys win in the end, but the world has to die for it to happen."

The pink neon sign towered above the city's premier gentlemen's club, inviting men to come inside and examine its dancers' wares. Located on Delaware Avenue, just a stone's throw from the river and mere steps from the city's voter registration offices, the club hosted businessmen from all over the world and high rollers from up and down the East Coast.

It was the place where well-heeled men escaped the realities of their mundane lives, and where silicone and stilettos shaped a fake world where fake love was exchanged for twenties and fifties. The gleaming poles and colored lights made every girl appear to be a star, and from their comfortable booths and tables, the men watched each performer claim her fifteen minutes of fame.

The round-faced, bespectacled man in the tan leisure suit was a regular. He worked as a CPA at a downtown firm, spending each day with numbers and forms. Every Tuesday, he worked late, and at 7:00 PM sharp, he stacked his papers in two piles on his desk and went to the washroom, where he neatly parted his red hair, smoothed out his unruly eyebrows, and sprayed on two squirts of Old Spice.

After maneuvering his ten-year-old Honda out of the underground lot, he drove the two and a half miles to the strip club, pulled into the outdoor parking lot, and parked in the third space from the end. He sat in the car and counted out exactly four hundred dollars in tens for the other girls, and eight hundred dollars in twenties for Misty.

Tonight he'd adhered to his routine, sitting at the bar for two hours, then moving to the booth in the middle of the room. Because the troubled economy made Tuesdays even slower than usual, the girls were grateful for his presence and gave him just enough extras to make sure they got their share of his bounty. They moved across the stage with a fluidity that was alluring, their hips swaying and their hair flipping as their bottoms clapped and their breasts bounced to the rhythm of techno mixes.

The man in the tan suit was duly impressed by their attempts to turn his head, and he rewarded them with several tens from his tightly guarded roll. But he was never truly excited until Misty came to the stage.

It was she who he'd come to see, after all. With her golden brown complexion and lithe, athletic build, she was supple skin and flowing auburn hair, hazel eyes and sparkling white teeth. She was exotic and sensual, sexy and accessible. She was real, and she was right there in front of him.

She always made a point of looking in his eyes, letting him know that the show was just for him. She lay onstage and arched her back until her nipples pointed at the ceiling. She rode the pole with deftness and skill as he imagined she'd someday ride him. She accompanied him to a private room for the lap dance he desperately desired. And when he was done, he went out to the parking lot, prepared to return to the one-room dump where he slept on a cot.

It was worth it, he thought, as he crossed the parking lot at twelve fifteen in the morning, fumbling in his pocket for his car keys. After all, he loved Misty, and if the twelve hundred dollars a week he spent at the club wasn't enough to show her that, he didn't know what was.

He smiled as he thought about the swing of her hips during the lap dance, and he swallowed hard as he remembered the way she'd looked over her shoulder and licked her lips as he sat mesmerized by the view from the back.

He was whistling by the time he made it to his car. He knew that someday, when she came to her senses, she'd gladly leave the stage for the quiet life he was preparing for them. He'd already saved fifty thousand dollars as a down payment on the house he'd have built in Delaware, away from the grind of the city. She needed only say the word, and he'd take her away from those fools who were corrupting her. He told himself she would say the word soon.

When he reached his car and pressed the button on his security system to shut off the car alarm and open the door, nothing happened. He pressed it again. Silence.

"Oh, come on," he said as he tried to stick the key into the lock. It didn't work.

"Is something stuck in there?" he whispered, bending down to look at it.

When he stood up, he saw a dark reflection in the driver's side window. He looked over his shoulder in much the same way Misty had looked over hers. There was nothing sexy about his gesture, though. In fact, the fear in his eyes made him look oddly pathetic.

He squinted and craned his neck to see if anyone was there. Though he felt like someone was watching him, he saw no one, so he turned back to the car and forced the key into the lock. Quickly, he got in, locked the doors, and drove to the next part of his ritual.

This was the part where the fantasy inevitably fell to pieces, and tonight was no exception. As he rode down Spring Garden Street with his windows tightly shut, the solitude left room for reality to squeeze past fantasy. There would be no house in Delaware for him and Misty. The dancer wouldn't come to her senses. He could never save her with money, because only the willing could be saved.

He passed Broad Street, turned at Fifteenth, and as always, reality gave way to regret. He hated the lust that fueled his strip club visits. He was shamed by the pleasure he derived from Misty's body. He was, after all, a man who believed in a power beyond his desires, and just as he did each week when he fell short, he went to a place where he could seek forgiveness for what he'd done.

Turning on Ridge Avenue, he parked his car near Broad and Fairmont. Then he walked across the street to a magnificent church that stood along the rapidly changing boundary between North Philly and Center City.

He saw a light shining out from the sanctuary and saw two men inside with vacuum cleaners and dust cloths. He knocked on the church's glass doors. They didn't hear him. He knocked again, harder this time, and the whir of the vacuum cleaner stopped. A man in blue work clothes came to the door, looked into his face, and shook his head sadly before reaching for the locks.

"Why don't you just come on Sundays like everybody else?" said the manager of the two-man cleaning crew.

"Because I need forgiveness on Tuesdays," the CPA said, pressing two twenties into the man's hand.

The manager took the money and stepped aside to let him in. Then, with a facial expression that was equal parts reverence and contrition, the CPA walked into the sanctuary and made his way to the altar. He fell to his knees and began to pray for forgiveness. What he got was something else altogether.

The sound of breaking glass made him leap to his feet, and the echo of two shotgun blasts made his eyes grow wide with fear.

He turned and looked down the aisle and saw blood running down the wall. The manager with whom he'd spoken stumbled into the sanctuary and fell atop the other worker, who'd already been shot dead.

The CPA fell back to his knees as a slightly built man in a black suit and hat walked slowly down the aisle. He was holding a sawed-off shotgun, and his intentions were all too clear.

"He that keeps company with harlots spends his substance," the man said in a gravelly voice.

The words made the CPA shrink back against the altar. He'd been raised in the church, and he knew scripture when he heard it. Even so, he never thought that God would send an angel to quote Proverbs while meting out his punishment.

"Please," he said, trying desperately to get a glimpse of the face beneath the wide-brimmed hat, "I won't do it again."

The man in black moved closer, revealing the bottom half of his face. His sunken cheeks framed thin lips arranged in an angry line, and as he raised the shotgun, he raised his eyes. They were blue and merciless.

"Please," the CPA whimpered as his back slid down against the altar. "I'm begging you. I got the message."

"You *are* the message."

The weapon spat fire and hot steel pellets, crushing the victim's chest. As the blood poured down and his life faded to black, his mind replayed echoes of the last sermon he'd ever heard.

Its title was simply this: "Demons Know Scripture, Too."

CHAPTER 10

The call went out over police radio, and every local and national media outlet sent a contingent to the scene of the latest carnage.

With talk of the angel of death being bandied about and people being slaughtered in churches, it was obvious to the media that these were more than random acts of violence. These were the actions of a serial killer.

As such, the killing spree had the makings of a story that could morph into an international scandal. The reporter who could gain exclusive access would earn book deals, movie rights, and fame beyond his wildest dreams. They all understood the stakes, and they acted to stake their claims.

By 12:45 AM, they had gathered at the intersection of Broad Street and Fairmount with satellite trucks and spotlights, helicopters and cameras, notepads and microphones. Philadelphia was in the belly of the beast that is twenty-four-hour news, and nothing was going to prevent that beast from being fed.

Knowing that the city would be under siege from the media, Commissioner Lynch made the necessary calls before leaving headquarters with Coletti and the others. He ordered every district to send a car and wagon to the scene. That put a strain on the city police, so he called for help from every other police department that operated in Philadelphia. By the time he arrived at Broad and Fairmount with Mann, Coletti, and Smithson, the scene was chaotic.

There were barricades and crime scene tape, K-9 units and wagons. A hodgepodge of officers from Temple, Penn, Drexel, La Salle, and the Pennsylvania state police were all under the command of the homicide captain. Thus far, they'd kept the media at bay. When Lynch pulled up and got out of the car, things changed.

Television cameramen swarmed the commissioner while police locked arms and formed a human chain around him. As the police yelled for the reporters to back away, helicopters hovered and their spinning blades added to the commotion. Reporters shouted questions that Lynch was unable to hear. Not that it mattered. He didn't plan to respond to any questions until he had answers to give.

He walked inside with Coletti and the rest of them following, and when he reached the threshold of the church, he saw a scene that defied explanation.

The outside glass door had been smashed by what appeared to be a gunshot. The hallway wall was splattered with blood and pieces of flesh. A thick red trail led from there to the sanctuary, where the lifeless bodies of the two men from the cleaning crew were slumped over a back pew.

The final victim was at the front of the church, his arms spread wide as he lay against the altar with his face locked permanently in a horrified expression.

"The neighbors heard the shots about a half hour ago," said a homicide detective who'd been among the first to arrive. "It looks like the shooter was after the one on the altar. A guy from the neighborhood saw him follow the victim to the church."

"Same description as before on the shooter?" Lynch asked.

"Yes, sir. Thin white male, black wide-brimmed hat, and a black suit. He disappeared before we could get here, but we might've caught a break," the detective said, holding up a clear plastic bag with a business card inside. "The victim dropped this. It's from the gentlemen's club on Delaware Avenue. We sent a guy down there to check it out, and at least one of the girls knew the victim. She's outside now."

Lynch led the three detectives to the front door of the church, where they saw the woman sitting in a squad car with a blanket around her shoulders. She was holding a steaming cup of coffee, and her face was fixed in a shell-shocked expression.

Coletti descended the church steps and walked over to the car. "How are you?" he asked.

"I've been better," she said, smiling weakly. "He was a sweet guy. Always polite, never pushy. Tipped well."

"How long had he been coming to the club to see you?"

"Ten, maybe eleven months."

"Did you ever, uh . . . do anything extra?"

"No. Never. I dance and that's it. I never get personal, and I never learn anybody's name, not even this guy's. I don't have anything to do with what happened to him, either, if that's what you're thinking."

"I'm not," Coletti said. "We were just trying to figure out

why the killer followed him here. Do you know if anyone might've had a vendetta against him?"

"A what?"

Coletti saw the girl's surgically enhanced breasts bulging against her skimpy top and knew she'd invested heavily in the tools of her trade. But she hadn't invested much in her mind.

"Did he have any enemies?" he asked.

"I don't know. I never saw him outside the club."

"Thanks," he said. "I'll get an officer to escort you back to the club. We have your information, right?"

She nodded.

Coletti climbed the steps and walked over to the commissioner and Mann.

"She's not the sharpest pencil in the stack," Coletti said, looking back at the girl in the car. "Not that anybody wants her for her mind."

Smithson was standing off to the side, glaring at him. She shook her head and sighed angrily. "You're just like the rest of them, aren't you, Mike? The only thing women are good for are their bodies."

"What are you talking about?" he asked, clearly confused.

"You know what I'm talking about," she hissed, before angrily stalking away.

Lynch and Mann watched with raised eyebrows and barely concealed smirks.

"You can't be looking at those young girls in front of your woman," Mann said, teasing him. "That's how you get yourself in trouble."

Coletti blushed with embarrassment. Lynch laughed and clapped him on the shoulder. "Welcome to the club, Mike. Now you know how the rest of us feel."

At that, the three men shared a much-needed laugh. But it didn't last for long. Smithson returned with an officer from the crime scene unit. They were both wearing grim expressions.

"Sir, I thought you might want to see this," said the crime scene officer as he held up a bloody piece of paper in a plastic evidence bag. "It was stuck to the victim on the altar."

Mann read the note aloud. "Detective Coletti, I am the abomination. Now the desolation begins."

"What does that mean?" the commissioner asked, looking at Smithson.

Before she could answer, another voice chimed in. "It's from Daniel 12, and it means we're in the last days," said a tall, elegant black man with soulful eyes.

Lynch looked at him curiously. "And you are?"

"Reverend Lewis. I started this church twenty years ago. I never thought I'd see the day people would be murdered in the aisles."

They allowed him a moment to grieve. Then Lynch spoke with a mix of sympathy and urgency. "What do you think the killer was trying to tell us in that note, Reverend?"

"The abomination is something unholy that sets up a period of misery and death," the preacher said. "I think whoever did this is trying to tell you that the worst is yet to come."

A second later, Mann's iPhone rang. He listened as the detective on the other end delivered the news.

"They found that stolen pickup at Sixteenth and Cecil B. Moore," Mann said after he disconnected the call. "It was parked right outside a church."

Lynch and Smithson remained at the murder scene and Coletti and Mann rode the short distance to the corner where the stolen vehicle was found. Lynch hoped the media would remain at Fairmount Avenue, thus giving Coletti and Mann a chance to investigate without further distractions.

Not that it mattered. The real distractions weren't coming from the media. The distractions were coming from within the fold. Mann could see the source of it on Coletti's face. He'd seen it all along.

"You really like Smithson, don't you?" Mann asked as they rode up Ridge Avenue and turned north on Sixteenth.

"She's all right," Coletti said, his tone nonchalant.

"Just all right?"

Coletti glanced at Mann and decided to take a chance. "Yeah, she's just all right. You saw what happened back there. I interviewed a witness and she flipped."

"No, you made a comment about a half-naked girl. If you were smart, you would've just let your imagination run wild and kept your mouth shut."

"Why should I have to do that?" Coletti asked. "I told Mary I'm not interested in a relationship right now."

"Oh, so you talked about that?" Mann said, his ears perking up. "Now we're getting somewhere."

"Forget I said that. In fact, forget I said anything. I don't want my business all over the department."

"It's too late. Everybody saw the two of you at the art gallery. They saw you talking at headquarters. They know you rode up to Graterford. The only one who doesn't know she's your woman is you."

Coletti glanced at Mann again as they approached Cecil B. Moore Avenue. "She's not my woman and I don't want her to be," Coletti said. "I need my freedom."

"I see," Mann said solemnly. "You've got ED, don't you? They've got pills for that, you know."

"Very funny."

Both men laughed as Coletti pulled onto Cecil B. Moore Avenue and parked near the stolen pickup and the police car guarding it.

There was something almost poetic about the case's taking them there, to the avenue that had hosted everything from riots to the Rizzo-era strip search of the Black Panthers.

The avenue, after all, had once been the center of North Philly. It had given birth to nightspots like the Bamboo Supper Club, where black folks danced to R&B while swilling top-shelf liquor in smoke-filled rooms. The avenue served as the meeting place for Marcus Garvey's Universal Negro Improvement Association and as the birthplace for legendary soul food eateries like Ida's.

Fifty years after its heyday, the landmarks that had made the avenue great were in tatters, and the century-old three-story brick row houses were crumbling. The street the neighbors had come to know was peppered with cheap new development constructed by unions that rarely employed the people who lived there.

In this, the avenue's latest incarnation, the thoroughfare

that had played host to the history of North Philly played host to its future.

Even now, at one in the morning during the work week, Coletti and Mann could see that the avenue was alive. Echoes of jazz floated down from a college radio station. A television played highlights from the Phillies-Pirates game. The sound of a woman's laughter could be heard through an open window.

The history of the avenue was alive not only in its people but in every building, including the church where the pickup was parked. Car 2310 was directly behind the stolen vehicle, and a police tow truck was across the street.

When the detectives got out of the car and walked over to the pickup, Mann pulled out a flashlight and shone the light through the vehicle's window. He didn't see anything unusual. In fact, the inside of the pickup looked immaculate.

Coletti walked around to the back of the truck and shone his own flashlight as he looked in the bed. There was a used needle and a thin, grimy rubber hose near the front end of the bed.

"Mann, take a look at this," he said, walking around the side of the vehicle to get a closer look.

Mann stood beside him and shone his own light along with Coletti's.

"So where do you think the dope fiend went?" Coletti asked.

Mann glanced at the church. Coletti nodded. Then he told the patrol officer in car 2310 to stay with the pickup and call for backup. As the officer did so, the detectives unholstered their guns and walked toward the front of the church.

They climbed the steps and Mann tried the handle of the eight-foot-tall, solid oak door. It was locked, and the stone on either side was a foot thick. Coletti nodded toward Sixteenth Street.

As the two men circled around the dark side of the church, they both took out their flashlights and held them out in front of them along with their guns.

The red door on the side of the church was far smaller than the one in the front, and when Coletti tried the handle, it was open.

He and Mann made their way inside with their flashlights and guns at the ready, and as they crossed the basement fellowship hall and climbed the steps to the sanctuary, Coletti felt the same sensation he'd experienced in his dreams.

A cold breeze blew through the church and into his consciousness, settling there like a pain that wouldn't go away. The door at the back of the sanctuary was open, but everything inside was still. Coletti and Mann shared a knowing glance, and when Coletti flipped on the light, they both saw what they knew to be true.

The body was sitting in a chair on the pulpit, his vacant eyes staring at an invisible congregation while a pistol sat on the floor next to his right hand.

With his gun out in front of him, Coletti signaled Mann to check the right side of the sanctuary while Coletti checked the left. When they were sure that the room was clear, Coletti walked to the front of the church and looked into the dead man's ashen face. His mouth was open. His blond hair was tangled by congealed blood and pieces of flesh. His wide-brimmed hat was on the floor, and his suit hung loosely on his spare frame. His hands were a bit too large for his body, and his eyes, though vacant, seemed ruthless—desperate, even. He looked too young to harbor that kind of desperation, so young that Coletti felt a momentary pang of sympathy.

As the backup they'd requested arrived at the church, Mann walked down the aisle and stood beside his partner. "I wish this was the end of it," he said. "But I think the pastor was right. This is only the beginning."

Sandy Jackson had been home for an hour and a half, trying to relax despite the fact that she couldn't stop thinking about what she'd seen.

If not for her lieutenant insisting that she go home and rest for at least a few hours, she'd still be on the street, helping Charlie and the others to track down the man she'd seen. Instead, she was sitting on her king-size bed after a bath, caressing Thierry Mugler Angel cream onto her thighs.

As she did so, she gazed at her cinnamon-brown skin in her full-length mirror. Then she stood up, turned around, and looked over her shoulder, examining her naked body for the defects that came with time.

Her hips were wider than they'd been when she was younger. Her breasts had fallen just a bit. There was a tiny varicose vein at the crease behind her right knee. She was critical of every imperfection. Still, she was as beautiful at thirty as she'd been a decade before.

Slowly and deliberately, she covered every inch of her body with the cream. She spent extra time on every wrinkle, as if she could rub them away. When she was through, she sprayed on Angel perfume, allowing the mist to land against her neck and her breasts, her thighs and her arms. The mingled scents of caramel and honey filled the room, lingering just beneath the Oriental vanilla fragrance. She fell backward onto the bed and felt the satin sheets whisper against her skin.

Her mind filled with thoughts of relaxing things: Charlie's hands and chamomile tea; candlelight and sweet potato pie; white grapes and long walks.

In five minutes, she was asleep, dreaming that she was jogging near the river. Kelly Drive, the winding road flanked by grass and trees on one side and by the Schuylkill River on the other, was her favorite place in the city. Walking distance from her East Falls home, it was the place where she ran, where she thought, where she cleared her mind of everything it took to be a cop.

There, on the concrete path that wound its way along the riverbank, runners, bikers, skaters, and lovers partook of the gentle breeze that swept in off the water. She could almost feel that breeze in her sleep, tickling her face as she watched teams of rowers make their way to the city's fabled Boathouse Row.

She passed by groups of Canadian geese pecking at the grass to her right and heard the humming engines of cars whipping by on her left. The scent of the trees and grass was sweeter than usual. The sensation of the breeze against her skin was softer than it had ever been. Her feet glided along the path almost effortlessly.

As she approached the section of the running path that went beneath a bridge, things around her began to change. The geese became vultures, staring at her as if they were waiting for her to die. The cars were replaced by a single hearse, its engine idling as it sat on the suddenly lifeless drive. The trees and grass turned brown and brittle, while the gentle breeze grew cold and unforgiving.

Sandy looked around for other runners, but all of them had disappeared. The bikers were gone, the skaters were nonexistent, and the lovers were nowhere to be found. She was alone now, and there was nothing but death to keep her company.

As the sky darkened above her and the river turned to ice, she intuitively knew that turning around would do her no good. She had to get beyond the bridge. If she didn't, she would never wake up.

Sandy broke into a full run, passing through the dark tunnel that ran beneath the bridge. There, she heard echoes from her past. Everything that had ever frightened her whispered from the damp stone walls: her mother's cries in childbirth; the rage she'd seen in street fights; her childhood fear of the dark. She ran as the whispers grew louder, but the faster she tried to move, the slower she seemed to go. It was as if she was sinking into her long-forgotten fears, her life slowly ebbing as the symbols of death moved closer.

The vultures flapped their wings. The branches of the dead trees reached out. The door of the hearse creaked open. Sandy tried to scream, but the sound wouldn't leave her throat. As she sank into the abyss of her fear, she reached out for a nearby bush and grasped at its branches. One of them snapped loudly in her grip, and her eyes suddenly flew open.

Sandy blinked twice, reorienting herself to reality. She

didn't have time to blink again, because she heard the sound of snapping branches once more. That sound wasn't a dream. It was real, and it was right outside her house.

She scrambled across the bed and reached for the gun beneath her pillow. Chambering a round, she looked out the window. Her outdoor post lantern illuminated a figure in black moving quickly away from her front window. Sandy went to her closet and pulled on a robe, then bounded down the steps and out the front door. Frantically, she looked up and down her quiet street for signs of the would-be intruder.

A few minutes later, a voice called out from behind her. "Are you all right, Sandy?"

She wheeled around, startled, pointing the gun in his direction. When she realized it was one of her neighbors, she lowered the gun and sighed in relief.

"I guess you saw him, too," her neighbor said.

"You mean the guy in the black suit?"

"Yeah, it looked like he dropped something in the bushes in front of your house. I just happened to be up watching TV and I heard something, so I came outside, but he was gone."

Sandy held the gun down at her side. Then she went to the bushes and looked around. It took her a few minutes, but she finally found a white sheet of paper. She pulled down the sleeve of her robe, so as not to touch it with her bare hands. Then she picked it up and read it as her neighbor approached and looked over her shoulder.

"Tell Mann to check the confessions," the note said. "The priest is the tip of the iceberg."

CHAPTER 11

By 1:45 AM, the media contingent on the avenue had grown to a full-blown flood. It was as if Cecil B. Moore—the civil-rights activist for whom the street was named—had lit the asphalt like one of his trademark cigars and watched it grow bright with life.

Police barricaded the avenue and Sixteenth Street, cutting off access to the church. Though two bus lines were detoured as a result, there was no traffic to speak of at that time of morning, but curious neighbors and aggressive reporters made up for the lack of cars.

Photographers from local papers held cameras and camcorders aloft. TV reporters did stand-ups for CNN via satellite. They all wanted to catch a glimpse of the dead man who'd declared himself the angel of death, and they wanted to know if the rumors were true. Could there possibly be more than one of them?

In the hours since the killing had begun, nearly everyone in Philadelphia had heard at least part of the truth. A man who'd declared that he was from heaven had killed six people before making his way to hell. But no one was sure if he'd acted alone, and if the police had any chance of catching his accomplices off guard, they had to make sure it stayed that way.

Commissioner Lynch knew that. It was the reason he'd avoided the press on Fairmount Avenue, and it was the reason he'd avoid them now.

Pulling up in a vacant lot adjacent to the church, Lynch and Smithson walked quickly to the side entrance and made their way upstairs. In minutes, they were standing at the edge of the crime scene that police had been poring over since the discovery of the body.

"We were able to get in touch with the pastor and several trustees from the church," Mann told the commissioner as he walked in. "They arrived a few minutes ago. They've offered to help in any way they can."

"Good," Lynch said. "They can pray that we find the others before somebody else dies. Where's Coletti?"

Mann pointed to the front of the church. Coletti was wearing latex gloves and examining the body along with two officers from the crime scene unit. Lynch and Smithson walked up to him.

"So this was one of them," Lynch said, looking at the dead man seated in the chair. "He looks like a kid."

"He *was* a kid," Coletti said, reading an old high school ID he'd found in the dead man's wallet. "Says here his name was Phillip Little, from Fargo, North Dakota." He pulled out his driver's license. "Looks like he was living in a second-floor apartment about a block from here."

"Okay, we'll have north detectives see if they can get in

touch with the landlord so we can get in," Lynch said. "How old was Mr. Little?"

"He was twenty-five."

"That's a problem," said Smithson.

Lynch looked confused. "What do you mean?"

"If this guy's only twenty-five, there's no way he could've been involved in the Confessional Murders. Not unless he started killing when he was fifteen, which most serial killers don't."

"You're right," Coletti said, bending down to get a closer look at the young man's puffy hands. "But we already know our killer has helpers. Mr. Little here was obviously one of them."

"But what kind of hold could he have on this kid that would make him want to kill all those people, then kill himself?" Mann asked.

"From the needle in the truck and the look of Mr. Little's hands, I'd say drugs had something to do with it," Coletti said. "He's got lesions that I'd guess came from skin popping, and the puffiness is pretty common in IV drug users."

"That's what's making it so hard to come up with a profile on the ringleader," Smithson said.

"What, the drugs?" Coletti asked.

"No, the fact that he's working with other people. Serial killers normally work alone. They don't recruit people to work with them, and they don't breed the kind of loyalty that would make someone kill for them. The only killer I know of who was able to do that was Charles Manson."

Smithson stopped, and a smile spread across her face.

"What is it?" Lynch asked.

"I've got the profile," she said. "We're looking for a white male who's a charismatic leader. He uses drugs and scripture to convince young people that they're fighting evil in preparation for the apocalypse. The war he talks about is real to them, and the people they kill are merely a means to an end. That's how Manson did it, and that's how this guy's doing it, too."

She turned to Lynch. "I've gotta get back to headquarters and start going through some records. If we can narrow it down to two or three people, we can find him before his followers kill again."

Just then, Mann's radio crackled. He reached down and turned up the volume. "Person breaking in. Thirty-eight forty-two Midvale Avenue. The suspect is a white male wearing a black suit and hat. Use caution, the occupant is a 369."

"That's Sandy's house!" Mann said, snatching off the latex gloves he was wearing and running toward the back of the church.

Coletti was right behind him.

The media were like hungry jackals when the two detectives emerged from the church. But even as the reporters nipped at their heels, trying to bring them down in the midst of the pack, the detectives ignored the shouted questions and pushed the microphones aside. Quickly, they jumped into Coletti's car and hung a U-turn on Cecil B. Moore Avenue.

"This is Dan 61, we're en route to Midvale Avenue," Mann shouted into the car radio. "Have all units use caution. That male is wanted for investigation in connection with multiple murders."

Within minutes, Coletti was flying through Fairmount Park

on the way to Kelly Drive while Mann frantically dialed Sandy on his iPhone.

She answered on the first ring. "I'm all right," she said. "The guy is gone."

"Gone where?" Mann asked as Coletti sped along the twisting drive that ran along the river.

"I'll talk to you when you get here," she said, sounding a bit shaken.

Sandy disconnected, and in the next few minutes, every possible scenario went through Mann's mind. Coletti could see that his imagination was running wild. He wasn't cruel enough to say anything.

In minutes, they were in the East Falls neighborhood where Sandy lived. On one end, the neighborhood housed some of the city's most powerful politicians. On the other, it was a hodgepodge of mixed-income housing, unfinished commercial development, and trendy bars that catered to the young professionals who worked and played nearby.

That was where Sandy lived—in a house that was just two blocks from Kelly Drive. When she moved there, it was the house of her dreams.

"Are you all right?" Mann asked as he jumped out of the car and ran past five thirty-ninth district squad cars to get to her.

"I'm fine," Sandy said as she melted into his arms.

They embraced with their eyes shut tight, thinking of what they meant to each other. Then Mann held her at arm's length, his eyes jumping frantically from her face to her body and back again. When he was sure that she looked all right, he allowed his other senses to take over.

She was still wearing her robe, and the scent of the Angel cream and perfume was emanating from her skin. She smelled like a slice of heaven, but her eyes said she'd been through hell.

"You keep saying you're fine, but you don't look it," Mann said as Coletti came alongside him. "What happened?"

"Somebody tried to break in," she said, looking angrily at Coletti.

Clearly, she wasn't as forgiving as her boyfriend, and as the seconds passed, it was equally apparent that she wasn't about to talk until Coletti left.

"I'll take a walk," he said.

Mann glanced at him, and his expression was almost one of gratitude. He turned back to Sandy and placed an arm around her shoulders. "Let's go inside."

She allowed him to lead her into the doorway, but as soon as they were out of earshot of the other officers who were milling about outside, she turned around with fire in her eyes. "I want you off this case," she said.

"What are you talking about?"

She looked into his eyes with an urgency he'd never seen before. "I'm talking about letting somebody else handle it. If you promise me you'll do that, I'll tell you what happened."

He reached out and stroked her hair. She stiffened, trying to maintain her urgent demeanor. His hand went from her hair to her cheek, and soon she was quaking in his arms. Mann held her for a few minutes more, waiting for the truth he knew she'd eventually tell. She rewarded his patience with a whisper.

"I wasn't scared at first," she said in a small voice. "I saw him outside my window, and I came down with my gun."

"Did you see his face?" Mann asked in a soothing voice.

"No. He was gone by the time I made it outside. We didn't see him run. He was standing there one minute, and the next, he was gone. Only this time he didn't jump into any pickup. He just disappeared."

"You said 'we,'" Mann whispered. "Who else saw him?"

"My neighbor. He's the one who told me the guy dropped something in the bushes. I found it after a few minutes, and . . ."

Her words trailed off and she disengaged from Mann's embrace, turning away from him so he couldn't see the fear in her eyes.

"If he left something behind, it's evidence, Sandy."

"I know that," she said in a trembling voice. Slowly, hesitantly, she walked into the kitchen and took a plastic sandwich bag out of the drawer. The note was inside.

"I never touched it," she said as she handed it to him. "I thought there might be prints."

He looked through the bag and read it aloud. "Tell Mann to check the confessions. The priest is the tip of the iceberg."

He looked up at Sandy as Coletti walked in through the open door.

"Sorry," Coletti said, sounding almost sincere. "I thought the two of you were done."

"We are," Mann said quickly.

"No, we're not," Sandy said, looking at both of them. "The guy dropped another note like the ones he addressed to you, Coletti. This time, the note was to Charlie."

Mann handed the plastic bag to Coletti, who read the note inside and looked up, confused.

"If that were the only thing, I'd be all right," Sandy said. "But when I came back inside and went up to my room . . ."

She tried to finish, but the words were choked by a flood of tears. Mann and Coletti looked at one another. Then they ran upstairs to the bedroom. Mann pushed the door open and stood there, gazing in amazement.

The walls were covered with a series of dates, each of them written in red lipstick. The mirror to her armoire was broken. The drawers of her dresser were flung open. The satin sheets on her bed were shredded. Written on the wall above her headboard were two gigantic words: *I confess*.

The scarred metal desks in homicide looked especially worn at 2:15 AM. It was then that the heavy burdens they bore during the day seemed to take their toll. The arguments between the detectives, the interviews with witnesses, paperwork piled high in corners.

All of it existed beneath pale fluorescent light that never seemed to fill up the room. There was always darkness, and that darkness reflected the morbid business that was conducted there.

The names and faces of suspects and victims mingled in a death dance that never seemed to stop. Even when cases were solved, the most egregious never went away. Death was around them all the time, and the dead spoke out from file cabinets and papers, from sketches and jotted notes. They especially spoke out from boxes.

Box cases were the murders that spoke in muffled voices

from the paper-filled cartons lined up against the walls. In these files were cases for which detectives had spent years gathering evidence, only to arrive at dead ends. In these files were the victims who'd never been avenged, and every file cried out for one thing: justice.

When Smithson walked in and began going through the files, she knew that justice was near. Somewhere in those manila folders and tattered cardboard boxes, there were men who fit the profile she'd assembled.

She started with Coletti's old cases, both the solved and the unsolved, and when she opened up the first of the files, she found an incident form 75-48 and a mug shot of Danny Olivieri, who'd been convicted in the shooting death of a fellow mobster. She reviewed the file on a homeless man named Dennis Leland, who'd been convicted in the beating death of another homeless man in a West Philly alley. She read the file on a schizophrenic named Tommy Moses, who was convicted in the murders of two lovers found dead in a movie theater.

Each of the cases was a solid arrest that resulted in a conviction. Then she opened the file for the Confessional Murders.

The incident form 75-48 was fairly straightforward. Written in Coletti's neat block print, it said that officers arrived to find the first 5292—the code for dead bodies—on the floor of the cathedral's main sanctuary. The second was close by. The suspect, identified in the report as Father O'Reilly, was on his knees next to the bodies, holding a sawed-off shotgun that had recently been fired. The third body was found near the confessional booth. All three victims appeared to have died from wounds consistent with a shotgun blast.

Smithson went through the short report three times and never saw the words "angel of death." Coletti had never included it.

She turned the page, and Father O'Reilly's mug shot jumped out at her. It was more than just an image. It was a portrait of a man who'd suffered far too much. His eyes looked sad. His mouth appeared to be out of words. His cheeks looked sunken. If there was any faith left in his being, it had been sapped by his arrest.

Smithson turned the page and found forty pictures of the carnage. The bodies were twisted at impossible angles. The floors were smeared with blood and flesh. The sanctuary had been forever desecrated.

After the pictures came the interviews. The bishop issued a statement from the archdiocese pledging cooperation with the investigation. O'Reilly's family and friends vouched for the priest's character. Father O'Reilly never confessed and instead proclaimed his innocence while blaming another man for the murders.

The court transcripts painted a clear picture. The fact that the priest was found with the murder weapon and gunpowder residue on his hands, along with the lack of any evidence to support his claims of innocence, had sent him to death row.

Smithson went through a few more cases before she opened the only file that fit.

The incident report described a murder that took place on February 11, 2006. A woman had been shot to death on a kitchen table at a Ukrainian Orthodox church. The man who was arrested for the murder was her ex-boyfriend, a Ukranian immigrant named Aleksey Petrov.

His mug shot was the oddest Smithson had ever seen. He

looked neither defiant nor angry. Rather, he looked confused, as if he was trying to understand why he'd been arrested.

The next twenty pictures in the file depicted the crime scene. The victim, Tonya Ivanova, lay in a pool of blood on a table, her arms folded neatly over her wound. Candles encircled the body. Bloody footprints were on the floor.

Coletti had written exhaustive notes in the file jacket. He'd interviewed Petrov's family members, all of whom insisted that the man was innocent. The detective had interviewed the man's friends, who swore that Petrov was with them at a bar when his ex-girlfriend died. Coletti had interviewed Tonya Ivanova's family and friends and had included everyone's name, contact information, and relationship to the suspect or victim.

A list of dates and times for the twenty disturbances the police had answered at Ivanova's apartment were included in the file. Petrov had been arrested in connection with half of them, but Ivanova never pressed charges. Two days after his arrest in his ex-girlfriend's death, Petrov confessed.

The court transcripts outlined a three-day trial in which the prosecution presented a damning case centered on Petrov's confession. He took the stand to recant, but that allowed the prosecution to cite his ten previous domestic violence arrests.

Smithson turned the page and saw a pile of news clippings in connection with the case. In each of them, Aleksey's cousin, Ivan, was pictured and quoted.

A high-powered lawyer and an official in the church, Ivan had fought hard for Aleksey's acquittal. With blond hair, blue eyes, and a magnetic personality, Ivan never missed a chance to slam the police department and Coletti for their sloppy work in arresting his cousin. In the end, it didn't matter. On the strength of overwhelming evidence and his own damning confession, Aleksey Petrov was sentenced to life in prison without the chance for parole, and Ivan was sentenced to a life of bitterness because of what happened to his cousin.

As Smithson prepared to close the file, she noticed that Coletti had penciled "C.M.?" in the margin of one of the articles on Petrov.

She wondered if the letters stood for Confessional Murders, and why, if Coletti had suspected Petrov, he hadn't pursued it.

Ivan Petrov not only matched the physical description: He had motive. He had means. He was perfect.

By 2:30 AM, officers from the crime scene unit were going over every inch of Sandy Jackson's bedroom. A photographer took pictures, a fingerprint technician dusted surfaces, and officers with latex gloves and plastic bags gathered samples of everything from lipstick to broken glass.

Mann was forced to hand over the note, and Sandy was forced to do something she'd never imagined. She was forced to speak to Mike Coletti.

"It started with a dream," she said, standing outside her bedroom with Mann and Coletti, as the other officers swept the room for evidence. "I was jogging on Kelly Drive, and the river turned to ice. Then the grass and trees died. I heard a branch snap and I woke up. That's when I saw the guy. The crazy thing about it is, I was only out there for a few minutes, and when I came in, I found it like this."

"Look, Sandy, we already know there's more than one of them," Mann said. "You saw them yourself. Even without the one who killed himself at the church tonight, we think there are at least two more, including a ringleader. So the guy out front probably had someone with him."

"Yeah, but how did that someone get up here?" Sandy asked. "They couldn't have walked past me and my neighbor out front, and if they'd come in through the back, the guys from the crime scene unit would've found some sign of it. There was no forced entry. I just mowed the backyard, so if they came in that way, they would've at least tracked some grass through the house. But there's nothing."

"Maybe they were here all the time," Mann said.

"Charlie, you know me. I sense things. If someone was here when I walked into my house, I would've known it. There wasn't. Not when I came home, not when I went to sleep, and not when I walked outside."

"Then who did all this?" Charlie asked.

His question was greeted by silence. It was Coletti who finally spoke.

"What did you feel in the dream?" he asked, his eyes staring straight ahead.

"What do you mean?"

"Was there something else there—something you couldn't put your finger on?"

Mann rolled his eyes. "Come on, Coletti, this is ridiculous. Just because you think—"

"Wait," Sandy said, holding up her hand. "I did feel something, and whatever it was, it was cold."

She stopped to think about it, trying to determine how to best put the feeling into words.

"When everything else in that dream was dead," she whispered with a fearful reverence, "that cold felt like it was alive. It felt like . . . if I stopped running, even for a second, that cold was gonna reach out and grab me."

"I've felt that kind of cold before," Coletti said. "So did the homeless guy who saw him under the bridge."

"That's enough," Mann cautioned.

Coletti ignored him. It wasn't nearly enough. "I'm gonna ask you three questions," he said, looking Sandy square in the eye. "I want you to think about your answers carefully, but whatever those answers are, they'll stay between the three of us. Okay?"

"No, it's not okay!" Mann snapped.

His sharp tone made a few of the officers in the bedroom turn around. Mann saw them looking and pursed his lips in an effort to calm himself.

Sandy reached out and gently pulled Mann back. Then she looked into Coletti's eyes, searching them for something she'd never seen there before. When she found it, she took a deep breath and allowed herself to trust. Slowly, she nodded, and Coletti asked his questions.

"Do you believe the man you saw outside is the same one who did this to your room?"

Sandy nodded.

"Do you believe he was in your dream?"

She nodded again.

"Do you believe he was something other than a man?"

She looked at Coletti. Then she looked at Mann. Then her eyes lost focus and she stared at a spot in her imagination.

"I don't know what he was," she said. "But I almost feel like the spirit of the one who killed himself might still be alive in the next one. It's like they're all one person or something. No. It's like they're all one *thing*. Something that's alive and dead at the same time. Something that can move in a dream and move in reality, killing anytime it wants to."

Coletti thought of his own dreams: the cold breeze blowing through the cathedral, the shotgun blasts in the confessional, the thin layer of reality separating life from death.

"I thought you guys might want to see this," said the sergeant who was leading the crime scene unit.

The three of them looked at the sheet of paper he was holding in his hand.

"What is it?" Coletti asked.

"The dates that were written on the wall," the sergeant said. "Four of them, beginning with July 30, 1999—the day of the Confessional Murders. The other three dates are December 30, 2005, February 12, 2006, and today, August 26, 2009."

CHAPTER 12

It was four in the morning by the time the crime scene unit cleared out of Sandy's house, leaving Mann and Coletti behind to deal with Sandy, who was still shaken but much less fearful.

Though the drama inside was beginning to die down, the streets outside were alive. A media contingent was set up at the end of Sandy's block. They'd heard her address on their police radio scanners, and they knew that a man fitting the killer's description had broken into her house.

The fact that the break-in happened after the body was found in the church on the avenue put the rumors of more than one killer at the forefront. Ignoring the possibility was no longer an option. Not for the media, and not for the cops.

Police cars circled the neighborhood in a manner normally reserved for high-crime areas. A detail was posted in front of Sandy's house. A police helicopter flew overhead with its spotlight sweeping the streets.

Yet in all of this, no one had seen the angel of death or his cohorts. They'd vanished again. As Sandy, Mann, and Coletti stood in Sandy's living room, each of them occupying themselves to avoid each other's eyes, Coletti knew they'd be back.

He'd seen the victims and read the notes, he'd seen the killings in his dreams, and he knew that the angel of death was not the kind who disappeared. After what happened in her house, Sandy knew it, too.

"Turns out we're more alike than we thought," Sandy said, glancing at Coletti.

He looked up from the list of dates the sergeant had given him. "What do you mean?"

"The dreams," she said. "You wouldn't have known about mine if you didn't have them yourself."

Mann stopped scrolling on his iPhone and looked at Coletti. He expected the older man to deflect what Sandy said—to revert to the macho shell that wouldn't allow him to expose his own fears. Mann was wrong.

"I've been having those dreams for years," Coletti said. "They started a few months after the Confessional Murders."

"So did yours ever happen like mine?" she asked.

"Depends on what you mean by 'like mine.'"

"I mean, were they real? Did you wake up and find him near you? Did you think he might be right around the corner when you left your room? Could you *feel* him?"

"No," Coletti said, pausing to consider whether he should go further. He glanced at Mann, who looked curious, and Sandy, who seemed to need to know. He decided to go on, not only to validate Sandy's sanity, but to validate his own.

"I never saw him or felt like he might be close by, but every couple weeks or so, I'd feel this coldness in my sleep, and there he was, walking through that cathedral, killing those people all over again. I ignored the dreams, mostly, hoping they'd go away, but they never did. Instead, they seemed to get more real. I'd wake up sometimes wondering where I was. In fact, that's how I woke up yesterday morning."

Sandy looked at Coletti and felt a surge of empathy for a man she'd spent most of her career hating. She'd always seen him as someone who was just like the rest of them, but now he was just like her, and it was strange.

"Why didn't you tell anybody you were having the dreams?" Mann asked.

"That'd be like standing in the middle of Broad Street yelling that I'm crazy. I don't think that would've gone over too well in the department, let alone in homicide."

Sandy looked at Coletti, whose humanity showed through in his words. Then she looked at Charlie, whose anger from the previous morning had dissipated.

She decided then and there that she would let go of her animosity, as well. She didn't think she'd ever truly like him, but he was partnered with the man she loved, and for that reason alone, she couldn't afford to hate him.

"You asked me something earlier, and you told me it would stay between the three of us," she said, changing the subject. "Did you mean that?"

Coletti nodded.

"So you won't mind if I ask you the same question. Do you believe we're dealing with something other than a man?"

Coletti sat down on Sandy's couch and cradled his chin in

his hand. He didn't look afraid or apprehensive. He simply looked unsure.

"I remember when everything was simple for me," Coletti said pensively. "A man was a man and a woman was a woman. The rich got richer and the poor got poorer. Black was black and white was white. There was no gray area. Then I worked on the Confessional Murders, and everything seemed to turn inside out."

"Does that mean you believe he's an angel?" Mann asked.

"I don't know what to believe," Coletti said with a sigh. "But I do know this: Angels don't pay guys to drop confessions at art exhibits, they don't shoot people in churches, they don't convince kids to kill for them, and they don't try to drive old men crazy just a few days before they retire."

"But they appear and disappear," Mann said, tapping the screen of his iPhone and looking at the words that popped up. "They leave signs, they take vengeance, and from everything I've ever read, they take no prisoners."

"So you're reading up on angels now?" Coletti asked with a sideways glance.

Mann smiled as he tapped the screen of his iPhone again. "Actually, I'm reading up on Daniel. Seems he was more than a man who saw visions. He interpreted dreams."

"I wish he could interpret mine," Sandy said.

"Maybe the killer's already done it," said Mann. "You had a vision by a river just like Daniel, and when you woke up, you found dates written on your wall. Daniel's vision dealt with dates, too. Maybe it's all connected."

"Could be," Sandy said. "But if the killer was only concerned with dates, why did the note say 'check the confessions'?"

Coletti looked down at the list of dates he'd copied from the message on Sandy's wall. "There's only one explanation," he said. "The confessions and the dates are linked."

It was close to 5:00 AM when Coletti and Mann walked into homicide after leaving Sandy's house.

"Anybody here?" Coletti said as he turned on the lights and walked into the office.

No one answered. He walked to the back and opened the captain's door. Mary Smithson was inside. She was asleep with files and boxes spread haphazardly across the floor. Five files were neatly stacked on the desk beside her.

Coletti quietly stepped around the mess, took the files from the desk, and handed them to Mann. Then he closed the door and the two of them walked to Coletti's desk to peruse them.

"I figure we can let her sleep for a few minutes," Coletti said, pulling his hot plate from his bottom drawer. "Meanwhile, we can eat."

Mann looked at him as if he were insane. "What are you gonna make with a hot plate?"

"Spaghetti," Coletti said, plugging the frayed wire into an outlet behind his desk.

Mann shook his head. "If that's your idea of a meal, you've been alone way too long."

"Don't knock it 'til you try it," Coletti said as he placed a can on the plate and reached into his pocket for salt and pepper packets.

As the spaghetti began to simmer, he added his secret ingredient—a packet of liquid garlic from Papa John's pizza.

"Sure you don't want some?" Coletti asked while emptying the concoction into a scarred plastic Tupperware bowl.

Mann's nose wrinkled as the smell of it assaulted his senses. "How can you be Italian and mess up spaghetti?"

Coletti dug into the mushy mess with a plastic fork from Wendy's. "You don't know what you're missing," he said as he jammed the fork into his mouth.

Mann shook his head before going through the folders. The first contained a picture of the Confessional Murders in the blood-spattered cathedral. The second contained a picture of a dead man in a bathroom. The third contained a picture of a body on steps, its face frozen in agony. The fourth looked like a gangland hit, and the fifth contained a picture of a woman on a kitchen table with a hole in her chest and candles surrounding her body.

"These are gruesome," Mann said, going back through the folders again. "Three of them have nothing to do with these murders, but two of them match the dates on Sandy's walls."

Coletti put down the spaghetti and rounded the desk. "Which ones?"

"The Confessional Murders and this one," Mann said, pointing to the incident report from the Petrov case.

Coletti looked like he'd seen a ghost when he saw the three-and-a-half-year-old pictures. There was no more joking, no more playfulness, only a face filled with regret.

Slowly, he shuffled back to his seat and flopped down, as though the weight of the world was on his shoulders.

"I'd almost forgotten about the Petrov case," Coletti said, his voice mournful. "Maybe I just didn't want to remember."

Mann looked down at the file and quickly scanned some of the court transcripts. "It looks like an open-and-shut case," he said. "You had footprints at the scene, a confession, a record of domestic violence—"

"I had fifteen people who said the guy was somewhere else when it happened," Coletti said. "I had his cousin telling everyone I was trying to railroad him."

"Were you?"

Coletti paused. He bit his fingernails. He looked at everything in the room to avoid Mann's eyes. "You know, Charlie, when I started in homicide, you couldn't kill someone and get away with it in Philadelphia," he said wistfully. "We had a ninety-five-percent closure rate. Now, it's a little more than half that. Know why? We've got a thousand rules and the criminals don't have any. It's like fighting with one hand tied behind your back."

"We still have to get it right," Mann said.

"And I did that in the Petrov case. See, I'm real good at fighting with one hand tied behind my back. Some people don't like that, but it works for me."

"So how'd you get him to confess?" Mann asked.

"I had a partner back then. His name was Kowalski. The day after the murders, we went out and questioned witnesses. Then we brought in Petrov and questioned him for twenty-four hours straight. I'd go four hours while Kowalski slept, and Kowalski would go four hours while I slept. Petrov never asked for a lawyer. He just kept saying he didn't do it. There was only one problem. He *did* do it. His footprints were at the scene and his fingerprints were on the murder weapon—a shotgun we found a couple blocks away in the bushes."

"You didn't think about the Confessional Murders when you saw that?"

"I did, but this was different. It wasn't some mysterious person claiming to be an angel. It was the victim's ex. He had a long history of abusing her, to the point where witnesses told us she'd flinch whenever he came around.

"We were sure this guy was guilty, and the evidence was overwhelming. So when we got him in that interrogation room, we didn't let up. We asked him why he beat her. We asked him about his fingerprints and footprints. We asked him why he put candles around her like she was some kind of sacrifice. Eventually, he admitted he wanted her dead. After that, the confession was easy."

"So you coerced him?" Mann asked.

"No, I got him to admit what he did," Coletti said firmly. "There's a big difference."

"Then why did you look so guilty when I brought up the case?"

Coletti lowered his eyes. "Petrov came from a strict Orthodox family," he said sadly. "Killing someone in a church the way he did, literally sacrificing her on his own makeshift altar—it dishonored his whole family, not just him. A few days after his conviction, they found him hanging in his cell. I guess he couldn't live with what he'd done."

"Then you don't have anything to feel guilty about."

"But his cousin has everything to be angry about," Coletti said. "He blames me to this day."

"Well, he shouldn't," Mann said. "You can't blame other people for the things your family does. If that were the case, I'd have plenty of people to blame for my uncles' prison terms and my father's death."

Coletti's sadness and regret began to fade. For a moment, he felt something like sympathy. "How did your father die?" he asked.

Mann sighed deeply as the painful memories came flooding back. "When I was seven, my dad lost his job making truck parts at Budd, and things got tight. First he got a job at McDonald's at Broad and Hunting Park. I still remember the other kids laughing about that. Then he got a job at the car wash on Broad Street, but the manager flew a Confederate flag on his SUV, so that didn't last either.

"When the landlord came around with a final notice on the rent, my father tried selling the only thing that seemed to move in our neighborhood—crack. My mother begged him to stop. She said we could make it on her waitress job if she just worked a few extra shifts. My dad wouldn't listen. He just kept telling her he wasn't going to see his family on the street. For the next fourteen days, he stood on a corner making five hundred dollars a day. On the fifteenth day, they shot him in the back."

Mann paused as his voice caught in his throat. "At the funeral, my mom told me I was all she had left. She made me promise to go to school. I did, and I found out I was pretty good at it. Got a scholarship to Temple, went to Wharton for my master's, and threw away all that good education to be a cop. I guess after what happened to my dad, I knew that's what I wanted to be. I thought maybe, in some small way, I could make a difference for the next little boy whose father was murdered."

"Did they ever lock up the guy who shot your father?"

Mann shook his head no. "It's hard to get witnesses at Broad and Butler. They've seen dead kids carried out of firebombed houses and witnesses beaten with bats. There were people who wanted to speak up about what happened to my dad, but they were afraid. There's not a lot of witness protection in the 'hood."

Coletti was quiet as he contemplated Mann's words. Then the captain's door creaked. Coletti and Mann looked up to find Smithson staring at them from the doorway.

"How long have you been standing there?" Coletti asked.

"Long enough," she said, crossing the room until she was standing in front of Coletti. "I wondered why you didn't connect Ivan Petrov to this from the beginning. Now I know." She turned to Mann. "And I guess what happened with your father explains a lot about you, too."

There was an awkward silence. Coletti tried to lighten the mood. "So what are you going to do now that you know our secrets?"

"This." Smithson took Coletti's face in her palms and kissed his cheek.

Coletti's eyes began to dance. Mann glanced down at the files and pretended not to watch. Then something in one of the folders caught his eye. Mann pulled out his iPhone and began to scroll through the calendar, counting days while referring back to two of the folders.

"Did you find something?" Coletti asked as he tore his eyes away from Smithson's.

Mann spent another few seconds double-checking what he saw.

"Actually, yes," Mann said. "The Petrov murder happened on one of the dates they wrote on Sandy's wall. February 12, 2006—twelve hundred ninety days ago."

"Twelve hundred ninety," Smithson slowly repeated. "That matches one of the time frames from Daniel 12."

"I know," Mann said gravely. "So does December 30, 2005. That was thirteen hundred thirty-five days ago."

"So the dates from Sandy's wall not only match the time frames in Daniel 12," Coletti said. "They match the dates of murders."

"There's only one way to know that for sure," Smithson said. "We have to find out what happened in December 2005."

"She's right," Mann said. "And the sooner the better, because the last date they wrote on Sandy's wall was August 26, 2009. That's today."

By five thirty, the crowd outside the church on Cecil B. Moore Avenue filled almost half the block. Police barricades had been hastily erected to keep the gawkers at bay, but the media contingent was increasingly impatient, and the rest of the onlookers grew ever more frightened and restless. Even so, no one dared cause a disturbance.

Everyone from thugs with their low-slung pants to students with half-empty backpacks knew that this was no ordinary crime scene. People of every stripe were there, waiting for a single glimpse, and all of them were frightened enough to show reverence for what they were about to see.

The crowd spoke in hushed tones, staring up at the church

as if it were a shrine. They'd all heard that the dead man had proclaimed himself the angel of death, and each of them was trying to attach his or her own meaning to that moniker.

The church folks stood next to each other and swayed, eyes closed and palms raised as they waited for divine revelation. The students on their way to the Broad Street subway craned their necks and kept their distance, afraid that God, or whoever had sent this angel, would strike those who questioned his veracity. The commuters walked slowly, hoping to catch a glimpse of this so-called angel.

Neighbors filled out the quiet crowd, standing next to the media members who only came to the avenue for occasions marked by death. The calm was eerie, and it served as an odd contrast to the smell of baked goods and brewing coffee emanating from the nearby Dunkin' Donuts. It was as if the smell of life had been attached to the stillness of death, and neither knew how to react to the other.

All that changed very quickly. The rumbling sound of a diesel engine rose above the hushed voices. The cops moved one of the barricades to allow for the truck to back up to the side door of the church.

As something upstairs began to move, the crowd pressed forward as one. With the sound of each step on the rickety wooden staircase inside the church, the flashbulbs came to life. When finally the two cops carrying the body emerged from the front door, pushing ensued. Shouting broke out. Police officers brandished batons.

The crowd, led by camera operators desperate for the definitive shot, looked to be ready to charge. Then, in a moment when almost everyone was close enough to see, the unthinkable happened. The policemen dropped the body. It rolled onto the ground and the body bag ripped, exposing an arm and part of the forehead that had been smashed by a bullet.

Suddenly everything stopped. The crowd was once again quiet and still, staring at what they'd come to see. The stillness extended for a second more, and then there was chaos. Photographers pushed for the money shot, while the crowd turned on itself with a mix of revulsion and glee. The police who'd dropped the body picked it up and hoisted it into the van, while those around them locked arms and held the crowd at bay. After ten long seconds, the door to the van was closed, and the diesel engine kicked into gear.

Police held back the crowd. Reporters waded into chaos. Cameras caught it all.

When the body was gone and the avenue was restored to order, the sound of footsteps once again echoed from the church's rickety stairway.

Lynch emerged from the door flanked by his deputies, and personalities from national news outlets vied with hardened reporters from local newspaper and radio. The national folks were quickly marginalized, forced to ask their questions from the edges of the pack.

"Commissioner, has the man who was just brought out been identified?" asked a woman from 6ABC.

"We have a preliminary ID and we're trying to locate his next of kin before releasing his name to the public."

"Can you confirm an age?" a radio reporter shouted.

"He was in his early- to midtwenties."

"And what about his claim that he was the angel of death?" said a reporter from the *Philadelphia Daily News.*

"We can neither confirm nor deny that," Lynch said.

"Our sources tell us that several of the notes the killer left were addressed to Detective Mike Coletti," said an *Inquirer* reporter. "Do you have any idea why?"

"I can neither confirm nor deny that any notes were addressed to anyone," Lynch said. "This is an ongoing investigation, and unfortunately, we can't conduct it in the media."

"Has there been any discussion of the fact that there seems to be more than one of these killers?" the *Daily News* reporter asked.

"No comment," Lynch said.

"What's the time frame on the completion of the investigation?" said a reporter from CNN, who'd managed to squeeze past the local media.

"We're working around the clock," Lynch said.

"Is Detective Coletti still involved in the investigation?" asked the reporter from the *Inquirer.*

"Several detectives are working on the case," Lynch said with a warning glance.

"Does that number include Detective Coletti?" the reporter pressed. "I mean, if the killer was writing notes to him, it seems improper to have him working on the case."

Lynch took a deep breath and pursed his lips in an effort to hold in the stream of profanity that had made its way to the tip of his tongue. Then he looked at the reporter and spoke in a calm, steady voice.

"I'll make a deal with you," he said. "I'll decide what's

proper in this department, and you can decide what's proper in your paper."

The reporter shrunk back in the face of Lynch's withering stare, but another rose up to ask the most salient question.

"Does this young man's death mean that the killing spree is over?"

"No comment," Lynch said.

Then he got in his car and drove to headquarters. He had a few questions of his own.

CHAPTER 13

Coletti, Mann, and Smithson tore through the handful of files pertaining to the homicides that took place in Philadelphia on December 30, 2005.

When none of them fit the pattern, Smithson went into the captain's office to search online police records, while Coletti sat at his desk and searched his soul.

Mann could see the pain in his partner's eyes, and though he wanted to tell the older man not to blame himself for all that had happened, the young detective first had to deal with himself.

Mann needed time to reflect on the life he'd taken at the train station. He needed time to check on Sandy after chasing angels and demons. He needed time to hold her and whisper things a man says to a woman. But when Mary Smithson came out of the captain's office with a printout, he knew, just as they all did, that time was a luxury they couldn't afford.

"I think I found our other murder," Smithson said, tossing the sheet of paper onto the desk in front of Coletti.

Mann joined them at the desk.

"It wasn't in the records here because it didn't happen in Philadelphia," she explained. "It happened in Darby, right outside the city, in a storefront church."

"So where did you find it?" Coletti asked.

"State police records."

"Any press on it?"

"A one-paragraph mention on page 20 of the *Daily News*. Frankly, I'm surprised there was that much coverage, considering it happened between Christmas and New Year's and the victim was a drug addict."

"So what were the details of the case?" Mann asked.

Coletti leaned forward and read from the report in front of him. "A white male, armed with a shotgun, entered the Mt. Pisgah Baptist Church on Darby Road, at 2:00 PM on December 30, 2005. He shot the victim, twenty-two-year-old Harley Thompson, in the chest. At 3:00 PM, David Atwell was apprehended three blocks from the scene. The murder weapon was found on a nearby rooftop. Atwell subsequently confessed to involuntary manslaughter."

The blood drained from Coletti's face.

"Did you know these people?" Smithson asked.

He nodded. "I arrested David Atwell about a year before that. I caught him with a gun that was used in a murder in Northeast Philly. He got off on a technicality. Prosecutorial misconduct. If I remember correctly, Harley Thompson's family blamed us for getting him killed. They said we let a murderer walk."

"Did you help with the investigation in Darby?" Smithson asked. "I didn't see your name anywhere in the records."

"That's because there wasn't much of an investigation. Everybody in Darby knew Atwell was a meth dealer, and Thompson was the preacher's strung-out nephew. The theory was that a drug deal went bad and Atwell caught Thompson in his uncle's storefront church and shot him. The only thing Darby wanted me to do was testify about Atwell's prior arrest. I told them I would."

"So did you?" Mann asked.

"They didn't need me. Atwell gave up his meth suppliers and the Darby DA let him plead to involuntary manslaughter. Funny thing about it was, Atwell always insisted he didn't kill Thompson. Even after he copped his plea, he swore he'd been set up."

"So where's Atwell now?" Mann asked. "We're gonna need to talk to him."

"I don't think that's gonna be possible," Coletti said. "Atwell was beaten to death in Graterford about a month into his sentence. His suppliers didn't appreciate the information he shared about them."

They fell silent as they reflected on the apparent dead end. After a few moments, Smithson spoke up.

"You mentioned Harley Thompson's family being angry with you over his death," she said. "Do you remember anyone specifically who might have taken that anger a step further?"

"No. I just remember that he had a few uncles who were involved with the church. I never met them or talked to them, but they sent a bunch of letters to homicide complaining about our handling of that first gun arrest. Nothing ever came of it."

"I'll follow up and see if any of them fit the profile," Smithson said quickly.

Coletti didn't respond. He just sat there, staring into space as if he could see into the past. Smithson stopped and watched him. Mann did too. Coletti didn't look up. Rather, he looked inside himself.

"Suppose it's all true?" he asked in a faraway voice. "The angels, the prophecy, everything. I mean, it all fits, doesn't it? Thirteen hundred thirty-five days between Harley Thompson's murder and today. Twelve hundred ninety days between Tonya Ivanova's sacrifice and the abomination in those churches last night. Now all we need is the desolation—the death, the misery, and the pain. Then the whole thing would be complete."

Neither Mann nor Smithson knew what to say.

"Maybe this whole thing is God's way of punishing me for my mistakes," Coletti said.

"What mistakes did you make that God would punish?" Mann asked.

"Father O'Reilly's on death row. David Atwell was murdered in prison. Aleksey Petrov killed himself. A killer's on the loose who's responsible for seven murders in the last twenty-four hours alone. And it's all because of cases I botched."

"You went with the evidence you had and worked within the system," Mann said. "There isn't a detective in the world that would've done anything different."

"Yeah, but that doesn't bring anybody back, does it?" Coletti asked bitterly.

"Neither does blaming yourself," Smithson said. "But if we figure out who this killer is and bring him in, maybe we can stop him and his followers before they kill again."

Mann thought back over everything that had happened

over the past day—from the notes to Coletti to the bodies in churches to the dates on Sandy's walls.

"I don't think we'll have a problem bringing him in," Mann said, staring at Coletti. "I think he wants to be caught, and he wants to be caught by you."

"What do you mean?" Coletti asked.

"Why would he spend years killing people, then give us the dates of the murders? Why would he put notes on dead bodies and address them to you? Why would he tell me to look at the confessions, knowing they would all point back to you? I'll tell you why. He's fighting a war, and you're the enemy. And the prophecy he chose, the message he mapped out with all those dead bodies, isn't about the end of the world. It's about the end of you."

"But why?" Coletti asked.

"Because his war is a fight between good and evil," Smithson said, warming to Mann's theory. "Maybe in this killer's mind, he's good, and you're evil. You might even represent something that hurt him as a child. If that's the case, this is classic transference. He's projecting all the evil in his world onto you, and he's determined to stamp that evil out."

"So why would he recruit other people to help him to do that? Why not just do it himself?"

"In his mind, this is a crusade," Smithson said. "So convincing other people to join him not only fulfills the prophecy, it makes him feel like he's right. But the bottom line is this: Whoever's fighting this war against you has got to have a hell of a reason for doing it.

"Now, I think Ivan Petrov is as good a suspect as we're going to get. He's smart, charismatic, he fits the psychological profile and physical description, and with what happened to his cousin, he's got an axe to grind. Maybe Harley Thompson's uncles are good suspects, too. But this goes all the way back to the Confessional Murders, so unless Petrov or one of the others started killing ten years ago, we may have to look at someone else altogether. And you've got to ask yourself if there's anyone else who's hated you long enough to spend a decade planning this."

Coletti was quiet, thinking back over the enemies he'd made over a lifetime. "I honestly don't know."

"Well, we have to find out," Mann said. "Otherwise we're just flying blind, and you're walking around with a target on your back."

"All right," Coletti said after a long silence. "Here's the plan. Mann, since we've got an address on Phillip Little and you know North Philly better than I do, you can start there. If we find out who he was connected to, we can find the guy who's behind this. Mary, when you find Harley Thompson's uncles, don't stop there. Go back as far as you can. Check my cases from ten years ago and beyond. See if any of them fit."

"And what are you going to do?" Smithson asked.

"I'm gonna make sure we get the warrant on Petrov. Then I'm gonna hit the street."

"Be careful," she said, staring into his eyes.

He looked back at her longingly. "I will. I've got a lot to live for."

It was six o'clock when Mann left police headquarters wearing a hoodie, jeans, and Timberlands.

As the sun rose against the morning sky and the city woke up to the reality of an overnight killing spree, Mann drove west on Ridge Avenue and passed the church on Broad and Fairmount where three of the murders had taken place. The barricades were gone. Commuters were out. The only thing to indicate what had happened was a two-cop detail and a satellite truck. The sight of them reminded him of the detail at Sandy's house. He called to check on her.

"What do you want?" she asked in a playful tone when she answered the phone.

"I want you," he answered in a throaty whisper.

"No, you don't. If you wanted me, you wouldn't have left here to be with Coletti. I think you're cheating on me."

"You know I wouldn't do that."

"Smart man. You never cheat on a woman with a gun."

He laughed flirtatiously. "I've got a gun, too. Maybe I'll show it to you next time I see you."

"And when will that be?" she said with a girlish giggle.

"Whenever we find the angel of death."

As soon as he spoke those words the laughter stopped. The flirting ceased. A tense, uncomfortable silence hung between them. When Sandy spoke, she sounded angry.

"You better hope you find him before I do," she said ominously. "Because if I see him and his little helpers first, we're gonna find out if they're angels or men."

"Sandy, don't do anything crazy."

"It was sweet of you to call and check on me," she said, ignoring his plea. "I'm going in for the early shift today. I have to get ready for work. You should, too."

Before he could say anything else the line went dead. Mann held the phone for a moment, knowing that Sandy wouldn't rest until the men who had violated her home were caught.

Mann didn't plan to rest, either. He quickly dialed a second number and spoke to an old friend. When he'd finished making arrangements to see him, he took Sandy's advice and went to work.

He parked his car along Cecil B. Moore Avenue, within sight of the church on Sixteenth Street where another police detail and satellite truck stood by.

He walked north on Fifteenth, between the multilevel parking lot and Temple University's Student Recreation Center. He walked west on Montgomery, past the police department's north central division headquarters, then north on Seventeenth to Berks.

Along the way, he passed refurbished houses that were rented out to students and saw firsthand the uneasy coexistence of the neighborhood and the university.

Going west on Berks Street, where a wide swath of undeveloped land still lent itself to North Philly's underground economy, Mann looked around for the drug dealers who sometimes did business in the area. They knew the rhythm of the neighborhood better than anyone, but he wouldn't be talking to them today. They'd retreated from the corners. The TV cameras made the streets too hot.

As Mann turned on Eighteenth and headed back toward Montgomery, he took a dirt path through a weed-filled lot, his broad shoulders dipping as his Timberlands dug into the packed earth.

The path, which wove through a tract of land where houses had once stood, was one of many shortcuts that crisscrossed North Philly's most desolate corners. Such paths helped people avoid the right angles of the sidewalks, but they rarely helped them avoid the wrong angles of the streets.

Running through vast spaces adjacent to row homes that had survived the demolitions of the nineties, the paths and the lots around them were home to loose bricks and condoms, panties, and bottles discarded by passersby.

The good people—and there were many—often walked those paths with the others, but the good people always ended up at different destinations.

Charlie Mann knew North Philly's paths. He'd seen the harm that came to those who walked them with bad intentions, and he'd reaped the rewards that came to those who overcame the obstacles. It was precisely this perspective that allowed him to see the neighborhood for what it was.

When he reached the end of the dirt path and approached one of the many pockets of new development spurred by former Mayor John Street's Neighborhood Transformation Initiative, he thought of the complaints he'd heard from those who couldn't understand the need to revitalize poor neighborhoods and allow the poor to stay.

Mann understood, though. He understood that the worst consequence of poverty was never seeing one's name on a title, that using Laundromats cost three times the amount of owning a washer and dryer, that the threat of eviction could drive a man to the corner that would orphan his son. Charlie Mann understood because he had lived it.

He reached Ninteenth and Montgomery Avenue and walked up to an old house with a crooked screen door and peeling paint. Before he could knock, a man came to the door wearing a tattered robe and a grin. Half of his hair was cornrowed. The other half was standing on end, waiting for his niece's nimble fingers to finish the job.

"Charlie Mack!" his old friend said, calling him by the nickname that he'd given him as a boy.

"Wussup, Lighty?" Mann said, his face creasing in a genuine smile as he reached for a handshake with one hand and hugged the man with the other.

After the greeting, Lighty stood aside and opened the door so Mann could come in. He directed him to a chair and limped to a couch on the other side of his sparsely furnished living room. It was starting to get cloudy, and the humidity was bothering the nub that remained after he lost his lower left leg to Gulf War shrapnel.

"I heard about what happened at the church on Sixteenth Street," Lighty said, sitting down with a heavy sigh. "That better be the reason you called me at six in the mornin'."

"My fault," Mann said, slipping easily into the language that he'd grown up speaking. "I ain't mean to call you this early."

"You damn right it's your fault. If I ain't know your mom I woulda slammed that door right in your face."

"Your door don't slam, Lighty," Mann said, pulling down his hood with a sideways grin. "It's barely on the hinges."

"Don't get smart wit' me! I'll still do ya."

Mann laughed. He felt at home. Ever since 1996, when Jerome Lightfoot worked as a short-order cook at a Fifth Street greasy spoon where Mann's mom waitressed, the man they called

Lighty had always fascinated him. With his prosthetic leg and easy smile, he was both off-putting and alluring. He was smart in his way, and in between collecting disability and working odd jobs, he kept up with everything and everyone in the three-mile stretch of North Philly from Girard Avenue to Hunting Park. He was an observer, and that was invaluable to Mann.

"All right, Charlie, what you need?" Lighty said, turning on the television and sitting back against the couch.

"Damn, you can't even offer a brother a glass o' water before you start askin' questions?" Mann said as he placed a picture of the suicide victim on the coffee table. "You rude, Lighty. Real rude."

"Yeah, whatever," Lighty said, getting up and snatching the picture from the table.

He looked at it for a few moments, studying the bullet hole in the man's temple.

"What you know about him?" Mann asked.

Lighty put down the picture. His smile had disappeared. "I know he wasn't wrapped too tight," he said, glancing at the television as *Good Morning America* flashed yet another picture of the Cecil B. Moore Avenue crime scene.

"You talk to him before?"

"I didn't, but the boy up the street who work in that Temple guard shack on Fifteenth Street had words with him."

"When?"

"Like two, three days ago. The guy was walkin' down Montgomery Avenue wearin' them black clothes and kinda stumblin'. The boy thought he was drunk, so he got out the guard shack to help him. When he asked him if he was okay, dude started talkin' all this crazy stuff 'bout princes and angels and wars. Then he started noddin', right in the middle o' what he was sayin'. He just leaned up against the wall and dipped. The boy tried to wake him up and the guy started yellin' again. It didn't last long, though. After while he just started scratchin' his face and talkin' real slow. Next thing you know, he was slumped on the wall again. The boy ran to the guard shack to call the cops, but by the time he came back to check on him, he was gone."

"So he was on heroin," Mann said.

"Sure as I'm sittin' here talkin' to you," Lighty said. "My cousin Eugene Brown used to see him a lot before he got strung out. He told me he used to come down to Thoughts From The Heart and Soul and the two of them would talk poetry for hours. Then he just stopped comin'. After while, I heard he was goin' cross town coppin' yellow bags from the Ricans up there on Second and Indiana."

"You know this for sure?"

"I know everything, Charlie," Lighty said with a grin. "The question is, what you know?"

This was the moment that always came right before the biggest revelation. Above all things, Lighty was nosey, and before he dropped a significant bit of information on Mann, he wanted his curiosity satisfied. Mann knew he'd have to give Lighty an appetizer if he wanted to get the entrée. If he didn't feed Lighty's thirst for gossip, the flow of information would stop.

"I can't give you a lot 'cause it's still under investigation," Mann said. "But I can tell you he wasn't from here."

Lighty sat back, folded his arms and waited. He wanted to know more. He deserved that much after losing his leg for his country. God knows he'd gotten little else. He lived in a place that had come to life around him, while his home and his body died debilitating deaths. He slept with a woman who'd settled for him because his check came like clockwork on the first of the month. He served as the heartbeat for a community that too often saw young men's hearts stopped cold. He lived vicariously through the people around him, and that was what got him through the day, so if he asked for a bit of information here and there, the least Mann could do was oblige him.

"If I tell you this," Mann said impatiently, "you can't tell other people."

"I won't," Lighty said, leaning forward on the couch.

"The guy was from North Dakota and he was twenty-five," Mann said. "We don't think he worked alone and we don't think it's over, so if you got somethin' else, I need it now. I can't wait."

"You think they'll kill some more people?" Lighty asked.

"I don't know, but I know the longer I sit here the harder it'll be to catch 'em if they do."

Lighty wasn't one to play games with death. He'd seen it up close too many times and knew it better than he knew himself. He was keenly aware of the fact that death never hurt those who experienced it. Death only devastated those who were left behind.

"He was messin' with a girl named Desiree, Desi for short," Lighty said. "She live on Twenty-fifth Street, on the corner 'cross the street from the church on the avenue."

"Don't waste my time, Lighty," Mann warned. "If I can get what she know somewhere else, I don't need to talk to her."

Lighty chuckled. "Unless you 'bout to go out to Fargo and find the boy's mother, you won't find nobody that know more about him than Desi."

"How do you know?" Mann asked.

Lighty looked Mann in the eye. "She carryin' his baby."

Charlie Mann tried calling Coletti right before he reached the house at Twenty-fifth and Cecil B. Moore, but the old man's cell phone just rang.

Mann shook his head. If Coletti was going to be his partner for the next couple of days, he at least had to have a working cell phone.

A few moments after he disconnected the call, Mann climbed the steps of the house and knocked. A young woman wearing a flowing skirt and a fitted brown top that accentuated the slight bulge in her belly cracked the door. Almost everything about her was youthful—from her waist-length braids to her taut brown skin. Her eyes were the exception. They were red and filled with pain.

"Are you Charlie?" she asked warily.

"Yeah," he said, reaching into his hoodie and showing her the badge he wore on a chain around his neck.

"I'm Desiree," she said as she pulled open the door. "Lighty called and said you were on your way. Come on in."

"So you know Lighty, too, huh?"

"He knew my grandmother before she died. She left me two things: this house, and people like Lighty to stay in my business."

Mann laughed as he walked in and glanced at the pictures

on the mantelpiece. The young woman's high school graduation picture was there, along with a copy of an associate's degree in psychology. Next to it was a picture of her grandmother, and in the middle, there was a framed snapshot of the young woman with the man who'd died that morning. His eyes were blue and playful. His dirty blond hair fell down into his face. They were both laughing.

"Please sit down," she said as she followed him into the living room. "I'll be right back."

Mann took a seat on the couch as she walked into the kitchen. A moment later she returned with two glasses of lemonade. She handed him one before sitting down in an easy chair and taking a sip from her own.

"I assume you're here about Phillip," she said, her enunciation clear, but her tone muddied by grief.

"Yeah, I am," he said, looking up at the pictures on the mantelpiece. "I'm sorry you had to lose him this way."

A single tear rolled down her cheek. She wiped it away quickly. "I lost him way before today," she said with a sniffle.

"What do you mean?"

Another tear fell. It was quickly followed by several more, and suddenly her head was on the arm of her chair and her body was shaking with ever-expanding waves of grief.

"I'm sorry," she said, wiping her eyes with a tissue as she got up and walked to the mantelpiece. "It's just hard right now."

She took down the picture of her and Phillip and stroked it lovingly with her free hand. "We met about a year ago," she said. "We were both going to Community College, trying to get our lives back on track. That's where we took this picture. It was right after a math class we had together. We were out on campus around lunchtime and this guy dared Phillip to try to do the Wu Tang," she said with a muffled laugh. "He was, like, this white boy from North Dakota, and he was jumping around in the grass outside the student life building, trying to do this crazy ghetto dance. It was the funniest thing I've ever seen in my life."

"Is that when you knew you liked him?" Mann asked.

She sighed sadly, looked at the picture once more, and gently placed it back on the mantelpiece. "I never really knew I liked him, because I never saw myself being with someone like him. I always imagined myself with someone who looked like me. Someone who understood what it meant to be black, and not only black, but dark black. I thought that was the most important thing in the world, because when you grow up in the 'hood looking and talking like me, you're teased for everything from talking white to looking black, and if you're not careful, you can end up hating who you are."

She went back to her armchair and took another sip of her lemonade. "I never hated me," she said. "My grandmother saw to that. She taught me to speak well and walk proud and carry myself like a lady. She died when I was in eleventh grade, and my grades and test scores went way down. That's how I ended up at Community instead of Penn."

"What about Phillip? Did he ever tell you how he ended up there?"

"His parents wanted him to go to school at North Dakota State, but he didn't want to stay there. He wanted to meet new people and see new things, and he'd been in trouble in Fargo.

Nothing major, just stupid stuff kids do. Drinking, rebelling, trying to figure things out on his own. After a while, he just left. A friend of his was already going to school at Drexel, but Phillip's grades weren't good enough to get in, so his friend agreed to help him find an apartment while Phillip got his grades up at Community College."

"Did you ever meet this friend?"

"Not until recently," she said. "By then it was too late."

Her eyes lost focus as she stared through Mann and into the past that had died just a few hours before.

"Phillip was kind of aimless at first," she said with a far-away smile. "All he knew was that he wanted to get away from his parents. He told me all the time that he loved them, but he just couldn't be in a place where everybody looked alike and thought alike. That's why he loved it here so much. He liked to sneak into poetry slams and listen to the rhythm of the words. He liked to sit in the back of that church across the street and listen to the choir sing. He liked Philly—the pace of it, the feel of it, he even liked that funky smell that hits you when you walk into the subway. He liked it because it was real. I guess that's why he liked me, too."

Mann watched her hand roll into a fist as she squeezed the tissue she was holding in an effort to avoid the tears.

"He used to tell me I was the best thing about this place. I never believed him, but I liked the way he sounded when he said it. He just seemed so honest about himself and about life. He knew he wasn't cool. He knew he wasn't tough. He just knew he wanted to be happy, and he treated me like I was the one thing he needed to be happy. Well, me and his music."

"Music?"

"Phillip messed around with guitar. Nothing serious, but he liked it."

"How long were the two of you seeing each other?"

"It would've been a year next Friday," she said, her voice wavering as she spoke. "We started out as friends, having lunch every now and then and taking walks downtown after school. After the first three months, it grew, and it seemed like it was going to be something special."

"Nobody gave you a hard time about dating a white boy?"

"Nobody cared," she said. "The guys around here never paid much attention to me. The girls called me stuck up because I never dressed like them or talked like them or slept with every guy in the neighborhood. By the time Phillip came around, I was isolated. My grandmother wasn't around anymore, and Phillip didn't have his parents, so we hung on to each other. It happened so naturally that it didn't feel like we were dating. It just felt . . . right. His friend changed all that, though."

"The same friend who helped him come here?" Mann asked.

"Yes," she said. "His name was Steven. He was a mechanical engineering major at Drexel. Had a co-op job at Boeing and a 3.0 GPA. At first, he seemed to be a good influence. Then, about four months ago, he started calling Phillip at all hours of the night, and the two of them would go out to these parties. I didn't really care, because I figured they wanted to do the college-boy thing, so I let Phillip do Phillip, as long as he came back to me."

She chuckled at her own naïveté. "That didn't last too long. I was never the type who could put up with other people's mess, so I left him alone. I didn't argue. I didn't get in his face. I just backed away. That was before I found out I was pregnant."

Desiree's voice caught in her throat, and she covered her eyes in an attempt to stem the flow of tears.

"I tried for a month to forget about him," she said in a pain-choked whisper. "I figured I would raise the baby on my own, but after I thought about it, I knew I was just being silly. I was thirteen weeks when I decided I had to tell him. When I finally made the call a month ago, I thought we should meet in a place we both liked, so I asked him to meet me at Community College, in that same little space where we took that picture. Everything was fine until I saw him."

She paused as the memory stifled her words and stabbed at her heart, but she swallowed hard and went on.

"His face was all white and sweaty," she said sadly. "His eyes were droopy and his lips were dry. He was wearing this crazy black outfit."

"What did he say when you told him about the baby?" Mann asked.

She lowered her head in shame. "I, um, I didn't tell him. I couldn't, because I knew he was on drugs the minute I looked at him."

"So what *did* you say?"

"I asked him where he'd been and why he looked that way. He was quiet for a few minutes. Then he started rambling about wars and legions of angels. I asked him what he meant by legions, and he just smiled and said he was never coming back, because the archangel had an assignment for him that he couldn't tell me about. I never saw him again after that."

Desiree wiped her eyes and curled her feet beneath her in the chair. Touching the life inside her belly, she swayed side to side with pain etched on her face.

"I just have one more question," Mann said quietly. "Was his friend Steven supposed to be the archangel?"

"No. Phillip said Steven was part of the legion, too. In fact, Steven was there the day we talked. He was sitting across the street watching us. No, watching is the wrong word. It was almost like he was guarding us."

"Do you remember what he looked like?"

"I couldn't forget it if I wanted to," she said in a distant voice. "He looked exactly like Phillip."

CHAPTER 14

The autopsy technician looked dispassionately at the waxy white face that was marred by a single bullet to the temple. He'd seen countless bodies like this one in his twenty years at the medical examiner's office. Bodies that had been sealed in a plastic body bag, transported in a police van, and delivered to a nondescript ramp at the back of a concrete building that smelled of formaldehyde and congealed blood.

The technician was a fixture there. He'd gone from wearing an afro to sporting a shaved head. He'd gone from picking up bodies to wielding a scalpel and saw, and, having seen everything that had passed through over two decades, he was unimpressed with the dead man who'd proclaimed himself the angel of death.

There was nothing ethereal in the body's appearance. There was nothing supernatural about its aura. It was simply a body, and when the police officers who'd dropped it off left the inconspicuous building located just a stone's throw from Penn's Ivy League campus, the technician processed it as he normally would.

He and another autopsy technician loaded the body onto a gurney. They stripped it of the black suit and hat, removed the black T-shirt and underwear, and took off the Doc Martens and socks. They took a single key from his pocket, along with his wallet, which was empty except for a North Dakota driver's license and a Community College of Philadelphia ID. They filled out a property form listing all his personal effects, and the senior technician and an investigator from the medical examiner's office signed it. Next, they rolled the gurney onto the scale. The body was 170 pounds and five feet, eleven inches tall.

They took pictures of the face, the torso, and the lower extremities. Then they wheeled the body into the doctor for inspection.

"So this is the angel of death," the doctor said, looking at the body.

"I guess it is," the technician said. "At least, it was."

The doctor turned on the light above the gurney, pulled on a pair of latex gloves, and started the tape recorder as he began his examination of the body.

"White male, early- to midtwenties, with short, dirty-blond hair and a penetrating wound in his temple consistent with a bullet wound," the doctor said. He reached down with his gloved hand and opened both eyes. "Blue eyes. Nose has no visible contusions. Lips are dry and extremely chapped." He took a single finger and opened the mouth. "Teeth are in good condition."

Systematically, the doctor moved down the body, noting

that the outer appearance looked fairly normal. When he got to the arms, however, he stopped. "There are small round lesions on both the right and left forearms consistent with skin popping, and several puncture wounds near the veins."

He paid close attention to both wrists and found what he was looking for on the right one. "There are black marks on the right wrist consistent with gunpowder residue," he said. "There's also some bruising on the webbing between the thumb and index finger."

After examining the lower extremities and the back of the body, he noted that the remainder of the body looked normal.

"Let's get him on the table," the doctor said. "We need to expedite this one."

The technician rolled the gurney into the autopsy room, where another technician was waiting. They washed their hands thoroughly and donned latex gloves and masks before pouring water onto the stainless steel autopsy table and sliding the body into place.

One of the men placed a four-by-four under the shoulders while the other placed two scalpels, four pairs of scissors, a Stryker saw, a large knife, and a long needle on an instrument tray.

The senior technician picked up the scalpel and began his first incision at the left clavicle, cutting across to the right clavicle, then down around the chest and back up to the top. Next, he made a long incision from the sternum to the pubic area and peeled back the skin, exposing the lower organs.

He used the Stryker saw to cut down both sides of the rib

cage, and the smell of blood and burning bone filled the room as the saw did its work. With the scalpel, he cut away the muscle holding the ribs in place, then removed the ribs, exposing the upper organs.

As they extracted the organs and placed them in a pan, blood ran along the stainless-steel table and disappeared down a drain at the end. With a swipe of the scalpel, the technician cut out the dead man's tongue and placed it in the pan as well.

"You gentlemen just about ready for me?" the doctor asked as he entered the room.

"Just about," the lead technician said as he made an incision across the top of the head from ear to ear.

When the cut was complete, he pulled half the skin forward over the face, and the other half backward to the base of the neck. With the skull exposed, he used the Stryker saw to cut a circle around the head. Then he removed the top of the skull and reached down into the space at the back of the brain to cut the spinal cord.

He put the brain into the pan while the second technician weighed the remaining organs. Next, a needle was inserted into the bladder to remove a urine sample and the testicles were removed from the scrotum.

"Do me a favor and get that urine sample up to toxicology," the doctor said as he placed the brain onto a separate table and began slicing it in an attempt to find the bullet. "We need the results back today."

"Okay, doctor," the second technician said, screwing a cap onto the sample and taking it upstairs.

"There's a lot of swelling in here," the doctor said as he cut through the tissue using a technique known as bread-loafing. "I'm guessing the bullet's a .22. What do you think?"

Over the years, every doctor who'd passed through the ME's office had posed similar questions to the old technician, and each doctor was keenly interested in his answers. This stately black man from working-class roots often noticed things the well-heeled doctors didn't. Not just because he'd been performing autopsies longer than most of them. He simply knew more about the world outside the morgue.

"I think you're probably right," the technician said. "But if it is a .22, you might have a hard time finding it."

The doctor chuckled as he made another incision. "I wouldn't be surprised if it disappeared altogether, considering."

The technician stepped back and looked at the doctor. "Considering what—this angel nonsense? Come on, Doc, you don't believe in that, do you?"

"No," the doctor said as he sliced through a third section of the brain. "I'm just wondering why this guy would kill all those people and then kill himself. Usually people who do murder-suicides do it all in one place. They don't get away scot-free and then go across town and put a bullet in their brains."

The technician shrugged. "If I were a gambling man, I'd say the drugs made him kill himself. But I don't gamble, and if I did, I wouldn't take that bet."

"Why not?"

"It's a sucker's bet," the technician said. "Every drug addict I've ever seen come through here either died of an overdose or they were murdered. They almost never kill themselves."

The doctor sliced into another section of the brain. The

scalpel hit something hard. He reached in with a pair of tweezers, pulled out an intact slug, and dropped it into a pan.

"If they never kill themselves, how do you explain this bullet and the gun residue on his wrist?" the doctor asked.

The technician glanced down at the body as he considered the doctor's question. He was about to shrug it off when he noticed something the doctor had missed.

"Look at his left hand, Doc," the technician said, leaning in closer. "You see that little callous on the side of his middle finger?"

The doctor looked closer. "Well, I'll be damned," he said. "He's got some tiny yellow paint fragments there, too. They almost look like they came from a pencil."

The technician handed the doctor a petri dish. The doctor found a fresh scalpel and gently scraped the paint fragments off the dead man's finger.

"You know what I think, Doc?" the technician said as he looked at the body.

"What?"

"I think this guy was left-handed, but whoever shot him didn't know that. So when they tried to make it look like a suicide, they put the gun in his right hand and fired it. And when they did that, he was already dead."

When Sandy Jackson's squad car turned onto Chestnut at Seventeenth, she quickly scanned the block, hoping to see someone who matched the description that had been etched in her mind the night before.

She didn't see anyone, and it left her feeling helpless.

She hated being in that position. It always caused her mind to wander.

Sandy's thoughts were everywhere as she sat in traffic so heavy that not even her police car could pass. She thought of the wasted MAC lipstick that was smeared on her walls. She'd paid good money for that. She thought of the lieutenant's exam and wondered how she'd do. She thought of finding the man who'd turned her life upside down.

She inched the car forward and looked up at Liberty Place, the sixty-one-story structure of glass and steel that towered overhead. Then she turned her attention to the people around her. The man in the Mazda was picking his nose, no doubt believing that the car afforded him a level of invisibility. The woman in front of her was frantically applying makeup. Pedestrians on the sidewalk moved quickly, hustling to offices and stores.

Slowly, the traffic began to move again, and as she pulled up at the corner of Sixteenth Street, the light turned red once more. Sandy glanced quickly to her right as she prepared to make a left turn, but something on the corner caught her eye.

A pierced and bearded man with pasty skin and steel-blue eyes sat cross-legged on the sidewalk, his filthy blond Mohawk refusing to stand on end. He was rail thin but heavily tattooed, and he was wearing an olive green wifebeater and cargo pants. The steel toes of his boots had worn through the leather, and he was holding a handwritten sign that read, "Traveling and hungry. Anything will help."

A small dog reclined at his knee, its eyebrows arching sadly as he looked up at passersby. Sandy watched a woman glance at the dog before placing a dollar in the young man's cup. When he reached over to retrieve the money, Sandy saw a tattoo on his hand. It was a picture of a demon's skull with angel's wings. "Daniel 10" was written underneath.

A chill went up Sandy's spine. She hastily pulled over and jumped out of the car with her gun drawn. The young man looked up, startled. Then he leaped up from the sidewalk, knocking down his cup and sign, and ran down Chestnut Street with the dog barking loudly behind him.

As Sandy gave chase, frightened pedestrians moved aside and drivers stopped their cars to watch. The young man turned to see where she was and tripped and fell hard on the concrete sidewalk.

Sandy jumped on his back and flipped him over. The dog grabbed at her pants leg. Enraged, she swung her gun and clipped the dog's jaw. The animal yelped in agony and limped away with its tail between its legs.

"What the hell are you doin'?" the young man asked, looking up at Sandy with streaks of dried sweat on his dirty face.

"Shut up!" she said, pointing her gun at his head.

He raised his arms in surrender as he lay flat on his back, looking up at Sandy with fear in his eyes.

"This is 9A," she said, breathing hard into the radio that was perched on her shoulder. "I need a wagon on the sixteen hundred block of Chestnut. I've got a prisoner."

"What did I do?" the man asked earnestly. "What are you locking me up for? Panhandling? I'll stop, I'll go someplace else, just . . . please, don't lock me up."

"I told you to shut up," Sandy hissed as a crowd began to gather.

She made him lie on his stomach. Then she knelt on one knee and handcuffed him before grabbing a fistful of his hair and jerking his head back.

"What's Daniel 10 mean to you?" she asked in a low voice.

His eyes began to shift nervously. His breathing pattern changed. He looked like he was considering running again, but Sandy placed the gun against the back of his head, and out of the corner of his eye, he could see that she was more than willing to shoot.

"Answer me," she said, her tone low and angry.

"It's just a tattoo," he said with an anxious smile.

"And you're just a liar," she said, grabbing the handcuffs and pulling them up toward his shoulders.

He screamed in pain and someone in the crowd said something about abuse. Sandy ignored it. The only thing that mattered now was getting the truth.

"He wasn't alone, was he?" she asked as the man lay on his stomach, turning his head sideways in an attempt to look back at her.

"I don't know what you're talking about," he said, his tone more fearful than it had been just moments before.

She holstered her gun, took out her nightstick, and used it to put him in a choke hold. Sitting on his back and pulling his neck toward her, she whispered menacingly in his ear.

"You know exactly what I'm talking about. The man who came to my house last night wasn't alone, was he? He had help. That's how he was downstairs and upstairs at the same time."

He tried croaking an answer, but Sandy wasn't listening anymore.

"Were you in my house?" she shouted. "Was it you?"

He was gasping for air and unable to speak. The only thing that stopped him from passing out was the arrival of a detective who'd detoured from headquarters after hearing Sandy's unit number on the radio. When he pulled up on the sidewalk in his black Mercury Marquis, the crowd began to disperse. He jumped out of the car and knelt beside Sandy Jackson, knowing that her anger had already gotten the best of her.

"Let him go, Sandy," Coletti said in a soothing voice. "If you kill him, we'll never find out the truth."

Her eyes were wild and sweat dripped down her face. She looked like she was someplace else, and Coletti spoke calmly to try to bring her back.

"I know what happened last night was wrong," he said. "But you're going to be a lieutenant soon. You can't throw your career away over this."

She loosened her grip on the nightstick and gently laid the suspect on the ground. Two ninth district patrol officers picked him up and placed him in the back of another squad car.

As Sandy made her way back to her own car, the rage still simmering inside, Coletti walked beside her. "Are you all right?" he asked.

"Of course I'm all right," she said. "We got one. I just wonder how many more of them are out there."

"At least one," he said. "Maybe more."

"So what were you planning on doing about it?" she asked.

Coletti stuffed his hands in his pockets and looked off into the distance. "Charlie's connecting the dots between the guy we found this morning and whoever he's working with. Mary's putting together a list of men who fit the profile of the ringleader."

"And what are you doing?" Sandy asked.

Coletti thought for a few moments before he spoke. "I'm praying a lot."

"And what's that gotten you?"

"I don't know," Coletti said. "I guess we'll see soon enough."

CHAPTER 15

Commissioner Lynch strode into the radio room, and the civilian dispatchers looked up in disbelief. Many of them had been there for twenty years or more, and they had never seen a commissioner on the second floor, let alone walking through the radio room.

The lieutenant in charge spotted him and became anxious. There had been problems in the radio room before. The signal had been knocked out, leaving patrol officers with no communication. On-air shenanigans had exposed bitter love triangles between dispatchers and officers. Heads had rolled, and the lieutenant was determined to make sure his wasn't next.

"Good morning, Commissioner," the lieutenant said nervously. "Everything okay?"

"I need you to raise Dan 60, Dan 61, and 9A on M band," Lynch said, the urgency evident in his voice. "Tell them to report to homicide, and tell them to expedite."

"Yes, Sir."

As Lynch left the radio room and boarded the elevator, he

thought about the phone call he'd just received and knew that if they were going to beat the clock, they'd have to move even faster than he'd anticipated.

He got off the elevator at the first floor, walked through homicide and into the office where Smithson was working.

"We're having a meeting," Lynch said to her as he looked at his watch. "Everyone should be here in a few minutes."

The door opened and Mann walked in. Coletti and Sandy were a few steps behind him.

"Close the door," Lynch said as they all crammed into the small office.

When they did, he looked around at all of them and delivered the news. "I called you all here because the game has changed. I just got a call from the medical examiner's office. They're about to announce that the Phillip Little shooting was a homicide, not a suicide. Toxicology reports showed he died from a heroin overdose and that the gunshot was fired by somebody else after he died. They also found something in his stomach: a handwritten note sealed in a small plastic baggie about the size of a dime bag of marijuana."

"What did the note say?" Coletti asked.

"It said, 'We are legion.'"

"I don't understand," Coletti said.

"It means we are many," Charlie said, "and it's the same thing Phillip told his girlfriend a couple months ago when she saw him for the last time. She said she knew he was on drugs as soon as she looked at him, and that he was rambling about war and legions of angels. Apparently he thought he was part of one of those legions, and he had a friend named Steven who believed he was part of one, too."

"Where's this Steven now?" Lynch asked.

"Phillip's girlfriend told me he was a mechanical engineering major at Drexel and had a co-op job at Boeing," said Mann. "I had a friend at Drexel check into it. His name is Steven Carrier. He was a few credits from graduating when he dropped out a couple months ago. Nobody's seen him since."

"Until today," Sandy said, almost to herself.

They all looked at her expectantly.

"At first I thought he was just another one of those kids who come here and get strung out on heroin. But something about him made me take a second look. It was a tattoo on his hand—of a burning skull with angel's wings and 'Daniel 10' written underneath."

"Wait a minute," Coletti said. "Was the tattoo on his right hand?"

"Yeah."

"That ties him to the stolen pickup," Mann said. "The owner saw that same tattoo on one of the guys who took his truck."

"Maybe that's why I felt so angry when I saw it," Sandy said. "That tattoo made me think of this morning—the man at my house, the note in the bushes, the words on the wall, my dream where everything died. I saw that tattoo and something inside just snapped.

"I jumped out of the car, and when he saw me coming at him, he ran. I caught him and cuffed him, and as soon as I touched him, I knew."

"Knew what?" Lynch said.

"He's involved in this somehow," Sandy said firmly. "He didn't have any ID, so I can't say for sure that he's Steven or that he's even involved until we get his fingerprints or until the owner of that pickup comes in and identifies him. But I know he's part of this. I saw it in his eyes."

"Where is he now?" Lynch said.

"He's in the lockup downstairs."

"As soon as we finish here, I need you and Coletti down there questioning him," Lynch said. "I need the owner of the pickup in here, too. We haven't got much time. When the medical examiner announces that Phillip Little's death was a homicide, the media's going to go into a feeding frenzy, and that's going to make our job harder. We can't afford that, because if we don't catch this guy soon, more people are going to die."

Everyone in the room fell silent as the truth of the matter sunk in.

"Okay," Lynch said, looking each of them in the eye before focusing on Smithson. "Coletti told me about the dates and the profile, and he said Ivan Petrov looks like a match. But I understand you were looking at some others."

"Yes, Commissioner. Based on the dates on Sergeant Jackson's wall, I found a case from December 2005. A man Detective Coletti previously arrested confessed to a murder in a Darby church. The victim's family was livid. I'm still trying to pull some records, but it looks like at least two of the victim's uncles fit the profile. I'm looking at some older cases, too."

"Okay, I want those names on my desk in fifteen minutes. Hopefully, one of them is our so-called angel of death. In the meantime, Mann, I need you working with the narcotics unit. If he had these guys on dope, we might be able to find them in the drug houses. Jackson, you're off the street for now. I want you with Coletti when he interviews the guy you arrested, and I want you looking at everybody Mann brings in, because you've seen these guys a couple of times."

Lynch's cell phone vibrated in his pocket. While the commissioner took the call, Mann tapped Coletti on the arm and handed him an iPhone.

"I picked this up for you," he said with a grin. "I might need to reach you."

Coletti nodded and put the phone in his pocket just as Lynch disconnected his call.

"The medical examiner's office is sending over the autopsy results," the commissioner said with a grim expression. "We're going to need to prepare a statement, because if I know the medical examiner's office, the press is going to have that report before we do."

The young man sat on a cold metal bunk in the eight-foot cell, his eyes shifting from the bars to the rust-stained toilet. His neck was sore from the nightstick, and his nerves were frayed from the ordeal. His stomach churned from the jailhouse cheese sandwich, and he knew that his whole body would soon quake with heroin withdrawal.

"Yo," the cop in charge of the prisoners said as he unlocked the door to his cell. "You got people here to see you."

The young man was confused. He had no family in Philadelphia, and his only real friend was his dog. He hesitantly got up from the metal bunk and ventured slowly out of the cell.

"Hurry up!" the cop said, grabbing his arm and pushing him into the hall. "We ain't got all day."

He looked up and saw Detective Coletti standing a few feet away, waiting for him. The other prisoners watched curiously as he walked down the hall with the detective, knowing that he'd be asked for information and most likely would provide it.

As they reached the end of the hallway and walked through a heavy steel door, the cop pushed him into a room where Sandy Jackson was waiting. They cuffed him and took him down a hall and into a plain white cinderblock room with a clock and a fluorescent light.

"Sit down," Coletti said, pushing him toward a table and chairs in the middle of the room.

The man sat down while warily watching Sandy as if he were waiting for her to choke him again.

"I'm not here to hurt you," she said as she reached down to unlock his handcuffs. "At least, not yet."

Sandy sat on the edge of a metal table at the other end of the small room as Coletti sat down in a chair across from the suspect. He crossed his legs and pulled a pack of Marlboros from his pocket. "Smoke?" he asked, holding out the cigarettes like a lifeline.

The man looked around like a nervous rodent, unsure of what to do. Finally, he took the cigarette with shaking hands and held it up to his lips. Coletti leaned over and lit it for the man, who greedily sucked down the smoke.

"I understand your real name is James White," Coletti said.

"Your fingerprints came back with a couple hits from Tulsa, including a stolen car, just like the pickup you stole from Sixth Street Sunday night."

"I didn't steal any pickup."

Coletti nodded toward Sandy, who walked out of the room and stood with the pickup owner, Frank Kelly, who was watching through two-sided glass.

"Is that him?" she asked, as Coletti grabbed James's hand and made him hold up the tattoo.

Kelly looked confused and unsure. "I never saw his face because of the hat," he said. "But yeah, the tattoo on his hand was just like that."

"Thank you," Sandy said. "The patrolman will take you home. We'll call you soon about your truck."

"Thanks," he said as a cop led him away.

Sandy came back into the room and nodded knowingly at Coletti.

"So the owner of the truck just identified you as the man who pulled a sawed-off shotgun and stole his truck," Coletti said. "We know you didn't come here from Tulsa to kill anybody, right?"

The man shook his head vigorously while nervously puffing the cigarette.

"So why'd you come here? Was it the dope?"

"I don't use dope," he answered while blowing a plume of smoke into the air.

"Okay," Coletti said with a skeptical smile as Jackson stared menacingly.

"Does she have to look at me like that?" White asked.

Coletti ignored the question. "Did you know Phillip Little—the guy who died this morning on Cecil B. Moore Avenue?"

"I didn't kill him, if that's what you're asking."

"I didn't say you killed him," Coletti said. "But since you've got that demon-angel and verse tattooed on your hand, and both of you like to shoot dope, I thought you might travel in the same circles."

White puffed the cigarette again, his drooping eyes cutting from Coletti to Jackson and back again. "I didn't know him," he said, leaning back in the chair with a nonchalant attitude that set Coletti off.

The detective dove across the table and snatched the cigarette from James White's mouth. "I don't have time to play games with you," he said, grabbing the prisoner's arm and twisting it until the needle marks showed. "Here's your choice. You can answer my questions and get outta here, or I can put you in a cell until the withdrawal has you twisted up like a pretzel in the corner."

The silence in the room was palpable as Sandy and Coletti watched White's facial expression go from defiant to fearful.

"I can't tell you anything," White said with a slight stutter. "They'll kill me as soon as I hit the street."

"Who's *they*?" Sandy asked.

White looked up with a clarity he hadn't shown since they'd pulled him from the cell. "They're the people who came to your house last night."

"What people?" Sandy pressed.

The young man looked down at the table and back up at

them. "Who's going to protect me if I tell you what you wanna know?" he asked.

"You tell us what we want to know, and we'll send you back to Tulsa," Coletti said.

"I don't wanna go back to Tulsa."

Coletti smiled. "You don't want to go back to the street, either. You think those prisoners didn't see you walk that hall with me? I guarantee you at least one of them knows these people you're running from, so it doesn't matter whether you talk to us or not. People think you did, and that's enough to get you popped."

White thought about Coletti's words, and as he did so, his skin turned gray and clammy and his hands began to shake. "I need to get outta here," he said as the withdrawal began to creep up on him. "I think I'm gonna be sick."

Sandy nudged a trash can over to him with her foot. "Don't get any on the floor," she said coldly.

White looked at both of them and knew that they were serious. The combination of the sickness and their withering stares made him willing to do almost anything to get out of that room. He was even willing to talk.

"Who was at her house last night?" Coletti asked.

White grabbed his stomach and winced in pain. "Two guys I know from near Kensington and Allegheny."

"How can you be so sure?"

He hesitated before answering. "Because they went in my place."

Coletti and Sandy Jackson looked at each other knowingly.

"You're a part of the legion, aren't you?" Coletti said.

He nodded. A few seconds later, he opened his mouth as if he wanted to say more, then thought better of it and sat looking around uncomfortably.

"Did they use the dope to lure you in?" Coletti asked as he lit another cigarette and handed it to him.

James White leaned back in his chair and took a short drag. He looked terrified.

"Look, these people have killed at least seven times in the last twenty-four hours," Coletti said firmly. "The minute you walk outta here, they'll kill you, too. Now, if you don't want to go down for those seven murders, or be the next one to die, I suggest you start talking."

With shaking hands, White took another drag of the cigarette and nervously exhaled the smoke. As it cleared, his mind did, too. For the first time he saw the past four months for what they were, and before he knew it, he was reliving them out loud.

"We met at this rave up in Kensington," he said as he stared into the past. "Me and Gabe were friends, and Phillip and Steven were friends, and when the four of us got under those red and purple lights in that funky little warehouse, the first thing we noticed was that we all kinda looked alike. Same hair, same eyes, same height, more or less. We all liked music, too. After a while, we started messing around with a little garage band. We stunk, but if we smoked enough weed, we thought we sounded pretty good. It was just something to do, ya know? Something to pass the time.

"In real life, Steven and Phillip had their college classes. Me and Gabe had jobs at a little market in Old City. We were just holding on, making enough to pay our rent, because we all figured we'd make it doing something else one day.

"After a while, the band thing got a little more serious. We learned to play a song or two, and every now and then, we'd play a rave. There were always drugs or girls or something else to keep us playing. It damn sure wasn't the money, because we almost never got paid, and we were always stoned out of our minds. That's how we met the guy."

Coletti was about to ask a question, but he didn't need to, because James White was caught up in memories he needed to purge.

"We'd just finished a set at this party," he said. "The DJ was playing techno and the lights were flashing, and up walks this guy dressed in all black. He tells us he's been watching us forever, and says we have a bigger purpose than we know. It was kind of scary, now that I think about it, but it was what we wanted to hear, so we listened."

"What did the guy look like?" Coletti asked.

"He was thin, about five nine. Blond with blue eyes, average face. Crazy as it sounds, I don't ever remember getting a really good look at him. He always had on that hat."

"About how old do you think he was?" Coletti said.

"I'd say he was in his forties, maybe younger. It was hard to tell."

"What else do you remember about him?"

"I remember what happened at the end of that party," he said, puffing the cigarette and wincing as the withdrawal took its toll. "He led us into a back room and handed us these little plastic bags. He told us if we wanted to see our lives the way they were supposed to be, we could open up the bags and snort what was inside, but if we didn't want to see our destiny, we could always walk away."

He shook his head sadly. "None of us walked away," he said. "We snorted it and we were glad we did. It was better than anything we'd ever done before. It didn't make us paranoid like coke, or silly like weed, or out of control like ecstasy. It made everything hazy and beautiful, and when he talked to us through that haze and told us we were in heaven, it wasn't that hard to believe. He told us in this gravelly sounding voice that we were a legion of angels who'd been called to fight a war."

White closed his eyes and swallowed hard against the nausea rising in his throat.

"When did you see him again?" Coletti asked.

"We all met at Phillip's apartment the next two nights in a row, and each time, he gave us a little more dope. By the fourth night, we were hooked, so when he told us to meet him in this old warehouse in North Philly, we did it. That's when it started getting scary. We snorted the dope and he told us he was the angel of death. He said he'd been sent to help us carry out God's will, and that eventually, we'd have to let everything go.

"By the time the first month passed, everybody had given up their place, and the guy put us up in an apartment in Kensington. Halfway into that first month, we were shooting dope instead of snorting it. At two months, we couldn't function without it. At three months, we turned our backs on everyone we knew. We were dressing like him and talking like him and believing everything he told us. I was so deep into it that I got this tattoo, and when he told us there were thousands of angels in the legion who would find us and kill us if we ever turned against him, we all took it as the gospel."

There was silence as Sandy and Coletti digested the story. A few seconds later, it was clear that Coletti wasn't sold.

"If you were so afraid you'd die for going against him," he asked cynically, "why didn't you go to Sergeant Jackson's house when he told you to?"

White was quiet for the next few moments, his body continuing to quiver from the withdrawal.

"When he started talking about killing people, I knew I couldn't do it," he said solemnly. "So last week, I took some money I'd stashed, and copped like twenty bags of dope. Then I left. I walked a couple miles until I ran across this abandoned house in North Philly and I hid there, waiting for the angels he told us about to find me. When they didn't, I knew that everything I believed was a lie.

"Yesterday morning, I went back to tell the others. I begged them to just leave, but they wouldn't. They said the war was about to start, and we all had our assignments. Mine was to go to your house," he said, looking at Sandy. "They said if I didn't they would kill me, so I put on the black suit and agreed to do it, but when they went into the kitchen to cook up some dope, I slipped out the back door, took off the clothes, took the dog, and never came back."

"Do you know what happened to Steven and Gabe?" Coletti asked.

James White shivered. "No, but I know what happened to

Phillip," he said gravely. "And I wouldn't be surprised if the same thing happened to them."

Charlie Mann was in the passenger seat of a black van with tinted windows, which was parked near a house in Kensington. He was wearing a helmet and bulletproof vest, and his right hand was resting on the butt of his Glock nine-millimeter.

A narcotics sergeant was in the driver's seat, and ten other officers were sitting in the back of the van, their M16 rifles at the ready and their helmets and vests firmly in place.

A half block away, there were three twenty-fifth district wagons and two unmarked cars from homicide. At the rear of the house was a second narcotics van. They were all waiting for Mann to utter the word *go*.

The house on tiny Tulip Street had long been the most notorious shooting gallery in Kensington. It was the place where addicts went to shoot heroin so pure it boasted brand names like Playboy and X-Factor. In that house, dealers provided creature comforts like fresh needles and prostitutes, rented rooms and fishscale cocaine. Veteran addicts rubbed shoulders with young beginners who learned firsthand that Philadelphia had the most potent heroin in the country.

"This is Dan 61," Mann said into his radio. "I need 2501 and 2502 to take up positions on the north end of the block. Dan 25 and Dan 27, you're on the south end with 2503."

"Okay," each officer said, as they moved their vehicles into position.

Mann looked at the narcotics officer on the seat across from him. He nodded, and Mann set the raid in motion.

"Squad one, go," he said into his radio.

The van's back door swung open and the cops jumped out in pairs.

"Squad two, go," Mann said, and the officers in back of the house jumped out in pairs as well.

Mann and the sergeant exited the van just as battering rams hit the front and back doors in unison. They could hear the sounds of people scrambling inside the house. In five seconds, however, the door was forced open and the sound of scrambling footsteps was overshadowed by the sounds of shouting voices.

"Police! Don't move! Get down!"

Women screamed and men shouted. There was the sickening thud of billy clubs against skulls and the unmistakable click and slide of bullets being chambered in guns. Ten cops ran upstairs with their rifles poised to fire. Ten cops ran downstairs with their weapons at the ready.

Three people who tried to escape were quickly subdued and cuffed. Within five minutes, the messages began coming through on the radio.

"Second floor secured. We're bringing down twenty."

"First floor secured. We've got ten."

"Basement secured. We've got eleven."

"Any injuries to police?" Mann said into the radio.

"No injuries," said the three team leaders.

It was over in minutes, and as the wagons met in the middle of the block, prisoners were marched out single file. Among them were the usual suspects: wild-eyed men and used-up women, toothless addicts, and callous dealers. Mixed in among them were the people no one expected to see. There were men and women in business suits, suburban mothers, and rosy-cheeked teens.

Mann looked through the crowd and saw only four white men. Two of them appeared to be in their twenties, and two of them looked as if they might fit the profile laid out by Mary Smithson.

"See those four?" Mann said to one of the homicide detectives. "Let's take them straight to headquarters."

The detective pulled the men out of the line and placed them in the back of the two unmarked cars as shocked neighbors who'd spent years calling for such a raid lined up to watch.

While workers from the city's department of licenses and inspections moved in to board up the house and the remaining prisoners were loaded into wagons, Mann got into the narcotics van and checked on the status of two other raids that had taken place simultaneously. Forty additional prisoners were in custody. On the surface, the raids were successful, but Mann knew there was only one real measure of success, and they had only a few hours to attain it.

His phone vibrated in his pocket. He looked at the screen and smiled when he saw the number. "So you figured out how to use that iPhone, huh?" Mann asked.

"It's not like I'm blind," Coletti said. "I can see numbers and a send button."

"Okay, old head, what's up? I'm kinda busy," Mann said.

"Turns out your girl Sandy's got great instincts," Coletti said. "The guy she arrested this morning was knee-deep in this thing. He claims he had nothing to do with the murders, but he knows what the ringleader looks like."

"Okay," Mann said, taking out a pen and paper. "I'm ready."

"He's about five nine and in his forties, maybe younger," Coletti said. "He's got blond hair and blue eyes, and he talks with a gravelly voice."

"Did he tell you his name or where we could find him?" Mann asked.

"No, but he confirmed what Phillip's girlfriend told you. One of his followers is named Steven. The other one's named Gabe. They're in an apartment at 3179 Kensington."

CHAPTER 16

The cameras and microphones were lined up in the parking lot of police headquarters, trained on the portable podium bearing the police department's crest. Ten microphones with logos from local and national media outlets were mounted there, and dozens of reporters waited anxiously for the press conference to begin.

Lynch stood inside the front entrance, watching as the media frenzy took shape. Flanked by the homicide captain, a deputy commissioner, and Lieutenant Mary Smithson, Lynch made it clear that he was more interested in the progress of the investigation than the progress of the public relations campaign.

With special units deployed and ready to move, he was in no hurry to satisfy the needs of the press, especially if it meant compromising the safety of his people.

"Is the task force on location up in Kensington yet?" Lynch asked.

"Yes, sir," the captain said. "They're in position and ready to move."

"And Coletti's with them, right?"

"Yes, sir."

"Where's Sergeant Jackson?"

"She's downstairs eyeballing the guys they brought in from the raids this morning. So far she's had us pull two of them aside."

"Good," Lynch said, turning to Mary Smithson. "Based on the information Coletti got out of his interview, I think congratulations are in order. Your profile was right."

"I appreciate that, Commissioner, but I don't think anybody should be congratulated until we catch this guy."

"Fair enough," Lynch said as he pulled a piece of paper from his pocket and looked at the two additional names she'd submitted to him an hour before. "Have we been able to get warrants on these guys yet?"

"They should be coming down from the bail commissioner's office any minute," the deputy commissioner said. "They'll call me when they're ready."

"Okay," Lynch said, looking at his watch. "I'm going to go out here and make a statement, and the minute you get that phone call, I want you to tap me on my shoulder. Right after that, I want you to give the order for everyone to move."

"Yes, sir."

Lynch walked out into the summer air, the stars on his shoulders gleaming in the noonday sun. Flashbulbs popped and tape recorders hissed as he spoke into the microphones.

"Good afternoon," he said. "I'm Commissioner Kevin Lynch. To my left are Deputy Commissioner Halsey and Captain Riley. To my right is Lieutenant Mary Smithson of the Pennsylvania state police. As you know, over the past twenty-four-plus hours, there have been multiple homicides in the city of Philadelphia that have been connected to a killer who has dubbed himself the Angel of Death."

A loud humming sound suddenly burst through the speakers, causing everyone in the immediate area to cover their ears. A technician came out and made an adjustment to the main microphone, and Lynch stood back, thankful for the interruption. He cast a sideways glance at the deputy commissioner, who shook his head slightly to indicate that he hadn't yet received the call. Slowly, Lynch made his way back to the podium.

"Testing, one, two, three," he said, prompting laughter from the assorted media who were gathered in front of him.

"As I was saying, we have been working diligently to come to some resolution on this case, and we have conducted multiple operations in an attempt to find the person or persons responsible for these heinous acts. As you all know, a male fitting the description of the perpetrator was found dead of a gunshot wound early this morning."

A breeze whistled through the parking lot and blew his paper off the podium. When he bent down to pick it up, the deputy commissioner was on his cell phone. He tapped Lynch on his shoulder as Lynch retrieved the paper and went back to the podium.

The commissioner paused long enough to allow his deputy to call the radio room and give the order. When he saw him disconnect the call, he spoke slowly and purposefully into the microphones.

"The male we found dead of a gunshot wound this morning

in a church on Cecil B. Moore Avenue has been identified as Phillip Little, twenty-five, of Fargo, North Dakota," he said, pausing once again. "We have also been informed by the medical examiner's office that the cause and manner of death have been determined. One Phillip Little died twelve to fifteen hours ago, according to forensics reports. The cause of death was a heroin overdose. The manner of death was homicide."

The press corps exploded. Questions were shouted from every direction. Cameras were thrust into the commissioner's face. Voices overlapped in a cacophony of sound that made it impossible for any one person to be heard above another.

Lynch was in no hurry to respond to any of them. His answers would come from the raids.

Everything about the house was dark. The bricks, worn and weather-beaten over the course of a century, were dark from the carbon exhaust of cars and buses. The steps were dark with years of grime.

Its windows covered with yellowing newspapers and its door falling slowly apart, the house appeared to be abandoned. Were it not for the fact that a single lightbulb was on in the vestibule, no one would believe it was inhabited.

"Team one in position," Mann said, as he and the narcotics officers from the prior raid pulled up near the front of the house.

"Team two in position," Coletti said, as he and four homicide detectives pulled up in the back.

The department had never been able to pull so many resources together this quickly. Then again, the city had never faced killers so deadly. As homicide and narcotics took up their positions, sharpshooters from the SWAT team lay prone on rooftops across the street.

Twenty-fourth district wagons were stationed at both ends of the block, cutting off traffic just one minute before Mann uttered the key word.

"Go," Mann said, and the narcotics officers scrambled out of the van, easily battering down the dry-rotted front door. The homicide detectives did the same in the back.

The two teams moved methodically up the stairs to the second floor, each man covering the officer in front of him. When they made it to the second-floor apartment, they found the door ajar and smelled a strange odor coming from inside.

"Police!" Coletti shouted as he stood on one side of the door.

Mann, who was on the other side, gave a hand signal, and the two of them went in, their guns pointed at either side of the room. Six officers from homicide and narcotics came in behind them, and the eight men conducted a quick search of the two-bedroom apartment.

There were needles and thin rubber hoses scattered across the worn carpet. Spoons with black stains on the bottom and dried residue on the top were on every table. Small plastic bags—hundreds of them—were in corners and on chairs, on the TV stand and on the stove.

It was there, in the kitchen, that Coletti found the source of the odor.

Holstering his gun, he called his partner inside. "Mann," he said, the frustration evident in his voice. "Take a look at this."

Mann came in and saw a small nonstick pan on the stove with the fire burning underneath.

"They must've just left," Coletti said, turning off the fire. "Otherwise, the place would be full of smoke."

One of the narcotics officers called from the bedroom in the back. Coletti and Mann both ran to the room and looked out the open window at a pile of trash that was high enough to cushion a fall.

"Here's how they got out," the narcotics officer said to Coletti.

"Somebody warned them," Coletti said, "but they couldn't have gotten far."

Mann grabbed his radio. "This is Dan 61," he said quickly. "Flash information on two white males wanted for investigation in multiple homicides. The males are both around five foot ten and in their early twenties. They may be on foot in the area of Kensington and Allegheny and dressed in black. These males answer to the names Steven and Gabe, and both should be considered armed and dangerous."

Five seconds of static filled the room before someone spoke up over the radio.

"This is 2411," a patrolman said. "I think I have a visual on one of those males walking north on H Street from Westmoreland."

"Twenty-four command," the shift lieutenant said. "I'm en route to that location."

Coletti and Mann ran out of the apartment and down the stairs. By the time they made it to the first floor, they could hear the sound of sirens filling the air as officers rushed to assist the patrolman who'd spotted one of the suspects.

They jumped into Coletti's car just as the officer attempted to stop the suspect.

"Twenty-four eleven!" the officer yelled over the air. "I've got a foot pursuit! North on H Street from Cornwall!"

The radio erupted in chaos, and so did the streets. Coletti gunned the engine and rounded the corner, skidding onto H Street. Two patrol cars sped down the street in front of him. Three detectives rushed to the scene on foot. The van from narcotics fishtailed and nearly flipped.

As quickly as they all responded to the chase, none of them could prevent what happened next.

The sound of a shotgun blast split the air. A woman screamed. The chase stopped. A body hit the ground with a sickening thud.

It took only seconds for a crowd to gather at the scene. Coletti and Mann skidded to a stop, and Coletti jumped out first. Frantically, he pushed through the crowd, fearing that the officer had fallen victim to the blast. When he got to the center and saw what had happened, he almost felt like this was worse.

Falling to his knees, he looked to the heavens to ask God why. Then he looked down at a face too young for this fate.

"What's your name?" Coletti asked, gazing at the young man who'd shot himself in the stomach.

"Gabe," he said in a near whisper.

"Gabe," Coletti repeated. "Where's Steven?"

Gabe tried to speak again, but the blood was bubbling up in his throat. He managed to swallow most of it before uttering a few important words. "Steven left after he shot Phillip," he said.

"Do you know where he went?" Coletti asked.

Gabe shook his head slowly.

"What about the man who got you to join the legion?" Coletti asked. "Can you tell me his name?"

"He's not a man," Gabriel said as a tear slid down his face. "He's . . . an angel."

Mann was standing behind them now, watching Coletti whisper to a boy who'd decided that freedom in death was better than bondage in life. He could almost see the grief in Coletti's posture. But the grief didn't stop Coletti from doing his job.

"Gabe," Coletti said softly. "I need you to listen to me. Where can we find the angel who talked to you?"

Gabe winced as the blood pooled in his self-inflicted wounds. He started to shiver from the loss of blood, and Coletti took off his own jacket and placed it on top of the young man. Coletti knew it wouldn't be long now, but he still needed to know one final thing.

"He told you to fight against evil, didn't he?"

"Yes," Gabe answered, his face twisting in pain.

"Then I need you to tell me where to find him," Coletti said. "If we're going to win the fight against evil, we have to find him."

Gabe suddenly turned his face toward the heavens. He saw the purple haze he'd tried so hard to chase with needles. It was there, all around him, warming his cold body and touching his tortured soul.

"He's up there," Gabe said, smiling. "Can you see him?"

Coletti's face crumpled in sadness. He glanced over his shoulder and pretended to see the angel that the boy's dying mind had conjured up.

"I see him, kid," Coletti whispered with something approaching sympathy. "He's coming to take you away from all this. The war's all over for you."

Gabe closed his eyes just as fire rescue arrived. When they made their way through the crowd and knelt down beside him, Coletti got up, loosened his tie, and staggered back to his car.

"I'll go to headquarters and check on the identifications," a worn-out Coletti told Mann. "You escort the body to the medical examiner's office."

Neither of them spoke of the warrants being executed downtown. They didn't want to risk having hope.

Three officers from the warrant unit and two homicide detectives stepped off the elevator on the sixtieth floor of a downtown high-rise. Their weapons at the ready, they banged on the locked glass doors of one of Philadelphia's most prominent law firms, startling the receptionist.

"Police!" one of them shouted. "We have a warrant for Ivan Petrov!"

The receptionist was about to disengage the electronic lock, but then thought better of it. Instead, she picked up the phone and tried to call a senior partner. The cops raised their weapons and broke through the door.

The sound of the shattering glass was followed by heavy footfalls as police conducted a room-by-room search of the luxurious suite of offices. Secretaries screamed when they saw the heavily armed men. Lawyers who asked questions were slammed facedown on conference tables.

When finally a partner stepped into their path and refused

to move aside, the detective in charge raised his nine-millimeter in one hand and a picture of the suspect in the other.

"Where's Ivan Petrov?" he asked.

The senior partner started to speak, but he was silenced by the sound of a voice that spoke from behind him.

"I'm Ivan Petrov," said an elegantly dressed man who looked much younger than his forty-five years. "What's this about?"

"Murder," said a homicide detective as he handcuffed the high-profile criminal defense attorney.

"I don't know what you're talking about," Petrov said with a puzzled look on his face.

"You will," the detective answered.

A few moments later, just as two more raids were taking place in other parts of the city, the cops walked Petrov past his shocked coworkers and out the shattered door. Secretaries wept and colleagues were aghast as the detectives deposited him on the elevator. Petrov, however, was composed—almost eerily so.

At five feet ten inches, with blond hair and blue eyes, he was the man who best fit the physical descriptions they'd received from those who'd seen the angel of death. He also was the one who'd most loudly expressed a motive for wanting to hurt Coletti. He'd been outspoken in his criticism of the detective's tactics while representing his cousin Aleksey in the 2003 murder case. Ivan Petrov had been determined in his attempts to get the conviction overturned on appeal.

More than his physical appearance or potential motive, however, his personal story fit the profile. Raised by a single mother who worked for near-slave wages in his native Ukraine, he spent much of his childhood by himself. When his mother died, they were penniless, and he was shipped to an orphanage, where he was abused at the hands of those who were supposed to care for him. It was only by happenstance that his cousin Aleksey's father came back to visit the village from which their family hailed. When he learned of young Ivan's fate, he spent a year dealing with the legalities of the international adoption, and the boy was eventually allowed to leave Ukraine for a new life with his cousins in America.

Ivan Petrov used his reprieve as a springboard to success. He graduated with honors from Masterman High School, one of the top one hundred schools in America. He won full academic scholarships to Yale and then Harvard Law. He graduated at the top of his class and made partner at his firm in just two years.

As a means of giving back, he'd spent the last five years sharing his story of success in the face of childhood neglect. He'd been featured on television talk shows all over the world.

Now, his story of empowerment and hope was being used to paint him as a serial killer with the motive, the background, and enough star power to convince disaffected young people to kill for him. The insinuation alone was enough to damage the reputation that had taken him a lifetime to build. They'd disgraced him in front of his colleagues, and as the detectives led him off the elevator and through the Italian marble lobby, the media took his humiliation worldwide.

"Mr. Petrov, are you the angel of death?" a newswoman from NBC asked as she thrust a microphone in his face.

"Are you going to represent yourself?" a *Philadelphia Daily News* reporter shouted.

"Do you have any comment about the man who was killed this morning?" asked a radio reporter.

Flashbulbs exploded in a hail of light as voices rained down on him from every angle. Faces moved in and out of his sightlines as he tried to maintain his already shattered dignity. Shouted questions and angry expressions assaulted his senses. Heavy hands clung to his arms as if he were a common criminal. It was as though he'd been thrown into a pool of sharks, and his blood was in the water.

The normally talkative lawyer was silent as they walked him through the throng of reporters and out the door to a waiting van. Petrov, a veteran of many high-profile criminal trials, smiled at the irony.

He'd often been involved in perp walks that had been set up as media events. While his client remained silent, he would walk alongside in tailored suits, loudly proclaiming the innocence of the accused. In most cases, his protestations were quoted at length in the media. His handsome face was repeatedly shown throughout the course of the trial. His humorous quips and acid-tongued rebuttals were grist for the media mill.

Today, he was the man who was handcuffed and being led through the media gauntlet. In all his years as a lawyer, he never imagined that his career would come to this.

CHAPTER 17

Steven had spent the night and half the day in the trash-strewn passageway behind the houses on eighteen hundred Oxford Street, watching as the rats frolicked in the trash, listening as the sirens split the morning air, and hoping that he could finish what he'd begun.

Now it was noon, and even though the rest of the city was bathed in bright sunlight, the alley was still dark. That was fine with Steven. Darkness was what he needed. It was the one thing that could shield him from the horror of looking at himself, and knowing that he'd killed his friend.

Having grown up just a stone's throw from his friend in North Dakota, Steven didn't know just how perfect the dirty passageway was. Once used by sanitation workers to collect trash, Philadelphia's alleys were now places where trash languished. Thieves and rapists used them to hide their evil deeds, robbers ran through them to try to elude police, and every now and then, a body would appear, rotting until the stench exposed its presence.

The alley was the ideal place to fight a war against evil, because the alley was the best place to find it. Steven didn't know that, however. He only knew that he had done the bidding of his master, and in doing so, he wondered if he'd become the evil he was supposed to fight.

He pushed that thought from his mind as he looked around and tried to get his bearings. Despite the fact that trash and overgrown weeds gave the alley a junglelike appearance, it was still in the open, and remaining there meant risking capture.

Steven stood up, and his knees cracked. He'd never sat in one place for so long, and his body was feeling the effects. He thought back to what the angel had told him. When the war was over, Steven would get a new body with powers beyond his comprehension. He wouldn't need the sawed-off anymore. He would have wings and eyes of fire, a face that would turn to lightning, and a presence that would make even the most hardened men bow down. Steven would have all those powers and more. He had only to make it through the war.

As he walked toward the end of the alley, he stopped every few feet to listen for unusual sounds. After eight hours in the same place, he knew what he was supposed to hear: the prattle of television sets, the crying baby in the middle of the block, the intermittent yelling from the wife whose husband was out of work. Now, as he walked through the alley, kicking trash aside and trying desperately not to be heard, there was another sound. It was the sound of kids in the nearby school who were out at lunch, laughing and playing the way he used to do, when times were simple and friendships were real. He envied those kids. He hated them, too, because they would never have to bear the burden of saving mankind from itself. That duty fell to angels like him.

When he reached the end of the alley, he looked directly across the street and saw the decades-old school building. He looked to his left and saw new houses being built on the opposite corner. It was a literal intersection of old and new, on a corner where life wasn't easy. Steven had only to look at the construction site, which was devoid of workers due to the fallout from the financial crisis, to know that nothing here was guaranteed.

He ducked into the alley and listened to the children play. When the bell rang, he looked once more at the houses across the street and picked one that was close to completion.

With the children back inside the school and the streets empty because most people were at work, he waited a few seconds to look for passing cars. When there weren't any, he took a deep breath and crossed the street. Then he pressed his shoulder against the door of the house and forced it open. Seconds later, he was inside.

He closed the door behind him and looked around at the exposed wooden beams along the walls. Then he walked into the kitchen area and sat cross-legged against the newly installed cabinets. He would rest there for a few minutes. He would wait for word from the angel. He would shoot dope.

He took off his jacket and fished a syringe, a lighter, a spoon, and a small packet of heroin from one pocket. He removed a thin, six-inch rubber hose from the other pocket and tossed the jacket across the floor. His eyes wide with anticipation, he dumped the powder into the spoon and cooked it with the lighter. When the powder turned to liquid, he placed it on the floor beside him.

Then he tied the hose around his upper arm with one hand and pulled it taut with his teeth.

It had been more than eight hours since his last fix, and desperation was beginning to set in. He bit his bottom lip as he smacked the crook of his arm with his free hand, praying that a vein would rise to the surface. He was about to lose hope when he spotted a thin blue line on his arm. Quickly, he reached for the needle and filled it with the heroin from the spoon. Plunging it into his arm, he emptied the syringe of its contents, and emptied himself of his soul.

His eyes rolled back, and he felt incredible warmth envelop his body. His spirit seemed to float above him, and his mind wandered freely through the fantasies it liked best. Then something went wrong. The slice of heaven he normally attained felt like a burning hell. He reached for his throat as his windpipe began to constrict. He reached for his eyes, which suddenly filled with tears, and he envisioned the friend he'd grown up with in North Dakota.

In his mind, they were children again, running through a field with their hair blowing in the wind. They were laughing like the kids he'd heard on the playground, their voices united in a moment of unbridled joy.

He closed his eyes tightly and tried to leave the memory behind. His mind obliged him and leaped forward to the day he'd come to Philadelphia to study at Drexel. It leaped again to the moment he'd invited his childhood friend to join him. The final leap took him to the scene in the apartment that morning. Not even his tightly closed eyes could hold back the tears.

Filled with the shame and self-loathing that he'd ignored

since obeying the angel's most recent order, he cried through the haze of the heroin and wished the tears could wash away the pain he felt inside.

He sobbed quietly, his mind floating in the grief that not even the drugs could mask. He wanted the images from that morning to go away. They didn't. In fact, they got stronger.

"Why are you crying, Steven?" said a familiar voice.

The words came out slow and thick, spoken as if they'd rolled off a swollen tongue.

Steven looked up and saw his dead friend standing in front of him. His face was pasty and white, his skin was a bit too tight, but the bullet hole in his temple was just as Steven remembered it.

"What are you doing here?" Steven whispered as he shrunk back toward the corner. "You're supposed to be . . ."

"Dead?" his friend said, moving closer to him.

Steven retreated until his back was against the cabinets. The tears fell even faster now. He was shivering, and his eyes were wide with fear.

That made his friend happy. He smiled and knelt down, leaning in until their faces were almost touching.

"Why couldn't you understand when I told you I didn't want to be in the legion anymore?" he asked, his thick tongue marring his words.

Steven was afraid. Not because a dead man was inches away from him, but because he could see what had happened to his friend's body after his death. There was an indentation circling his head, where his skull had been cut open and reattached. There was a line across his chest where his skin had been sliced.

There was stitching in his mouth where his tongue had been sewn back into his mouth.

"It doesn't matter why I couldn't understand," Steven said. "You're dead now."

"Yes, it does matter," the dead man said. "You made me overdose, and you shot me. Then you tried to make it look like I killed myself. Tell me why you did it, or I'm going to kill you."

Steven looked into those lifeless eyes and knew that his friend's soul was gone. Knowing that made Steven more afraid.

Through tears and grief, he tried to explain. "I didn't want to do it," he sobbed. "But he told me he would kill me if I didn't. He said you'd ruin everything if we let you walk away. I couldn't let you."

"You couldn't let me do what?" his dead friend said. "Be happy? Live?"

"I couldn't let you ruin it," Steven said earnestly. "Not now. Not when we're so close to finishing what we started. Don't you see? People die in war. The people in the church in Logan, the people in the church in North Philly—"

"And me," his friend said, standing up and looking down at him.

"So what are you going to do?" Steven whispered in a small frightened voice.

The dead man smiled. "You killed me," he said as he pulled a sawed-off from his jacket. "I'm going to return the favor."

Steven closed his eyes as the blast rang through his consciousness. It shook him to his core, pulled him from his reverie, and landed him in a place where darkness gripped him like a vise.

He was shaking uncontrollably when he opened his eyes, thinking he would see hellfire all around him. Instead, he felt a thin film of cold sweat clinging to his skin. He ran his hands along his face and swiped hard at the tears on his cheeks. Then he breathed deep and exhaled quickly before running his quivering fingers through his hair.

"I'm sorry," he said to the empty room. "There are no friends in war."

As soon as he spoke those words, something buzzed in his pocket. He was momentarily confused, wondering if his dead friend was returning for another visit. When it buzzed again, his mind was transported back to the moment. The buzzing was his cell phone, and there were only two people left to call him.

Steven connected the call without speaking. Then the voice he'd come to know so well moved through his entire being.

"Gabe's dead," the angel said in a cold, rough voice. "It's up to us now. Do you understand?"

Steven nodded.

"Good. They'll find the final message soon, and we'll fight for the last time. I'll let you know where when the time is right. In the meantime, rest, and whatever you do, don't fall for the tricks of the enemy."

Coletti was lost in thought when he walked into police headquarters. Gabe's suicide had struck him particularly hard, in part because he blamed himself.

For years he'd known, deep down in the place where such truisms exist, that the priest was innocent of the Confessional

Murders. That feeling was confirmed in vivid dreams and idle thoughts that gripped him in quiet moments. As he walked into homicide and into the captain's office, the pressures of the case showed on his face. Mary Smithson noticed.

"Are you okay?" she asked, looking up from the paperwork that lined the captain's desk.

"I'm fine," he said.

"Good, because they just arrested the three men who best fit the profile. They should be bringing them down in a few minutes."

"I know," Coletti said. "I just came to check on you and see if you needed anything else."

"No, I don't need anything. I'm still looking through your old cases to see if there's something we missed."

Coletti grunted in response.

"Are you sure you're okay?" she asked, sounding more than a little concerned.

He was hesitant to tell her his true feelings. Not that it mattered. He couldn't hide them if he wanted to.

"I'm just tired," he said. "It's been a long couple of days."

"I know. But it'll be over soon."

"That's what I'm hoping," Coletti said in a weary tone.

"That's what we're *all* hoping," Smithson said earnestly. "Not just for your sake, but for everyone's."

Coletti walked around to her side of the desk and sat down in front of her. Then he reached out and stroked her hair with a gentleness that neither of them knew he possessed. "I never got a chance to thank you for all your help with the case," he said.

"There's no need to thank me," she said, reaching up to guide his hand down to her face.

As he touched her, she looked up at him, and he was once again lost in her eyes, the same way he was the first time they met. Smithson smiled, knowing that Coletti was smitten. Then she stood up slowly until their faces were inches apart. While Coletti's eyes searched hers and his breath came ever faster, she pressed her body against his and gave him a long, lingering kiss. The gesture was sweet. It was gentle. It was unexpected.

When she was finished, she pulled away slowly and looked into his eyes. "I didn't know if I would have a chance to do that when this is all over," she said with a wicked grin. "I figured I'd take my shot now."

Coletti smiled. "I like a woman who knows what she wants."

"That's good," she said, stroking his face with her hand. "Because I always finish what I start."

"Well, you can't finish in this office unless you wanna get me fired," he said with a chuckle. "But I'll take a rain check."

Smithson sat down and looked up at him curiously. "Can I ask you something?"

"Sure."

"Do you have any regrets about the Confessional Murders?"

Coletti leaned back and thought about it. "I wish I would've searched harder for the truth. Maybe then all these people wouldn't have died."

Smithson stood up and walked over to him. "Confessing

your mistakes makes you stronger," she said. "I guess that's why they say confession is good for the soul."

It was one o'clock, and the lineups from the drug raids weren't yielding results, partly because James White's withdrawal symptoms were worsening.

As sweat trickled down his face and his hands began to shake, he looked at the officer who'd beaten and arrested him on a street corner just hours before. He hated being so close to her, but in truth, he was willing to do almost anything to escape the world of heroin and murder that had all but destroyed him. Willingness alone wasn't enough to fight the withdrawal, however, and as he and Sandy Jackson were viewing their third lineup, White doubled over in pain. He began shaking so violently that he fell and banged his head on the concrete floor before vomiting at Jackson's feet.

Minutes later, White was taken to a nearby interrogation room, where a doctor was called in to evaluate him. The doctor checked his blood pressure and vital signs before turning to Jackson.

"He's suffering from acute withdrawal," he said as the handcuffed man sat shivering in a seventy-degree room. "I could administer a small dose of methadone. That would stop the symptoms for at least twenty-four hours."

"Do it," Sandy said.

"If you have a little more time—"

"We don't. Give him the methadone. We've got to get the next lineup in here."

When the doctor was done, Sandy and a detective led White

from the interrogation room back to the cramped space behind the two-way mirror where the lineups took place.

Sandy was tired from the rigors of the morning and frustrated by the fact that none of the men from the three previous lineups looked vaguely familiar to either of them. Not that it truly mattered what Sandy thought. White was the one who knew the angel of death. He was the one who'd followed the man. His was the identification that would matter in the end.

White knew that, and as he stood next to Sandy and waited for the next lineup to be presented, he reached up and ran his hands over his wilting, sweat-soaked Mohawk and contemplated what had become of his friends. He knew that Steven shot Phillip at the angel's behest, and he had learned from the police that Gabe died by his own hand. White knew he could identify the angel if he saw him, but he wondered if the price would be his life.

"They're bringing in the three guys from the profiler's list," said the detective who was running the lineup. "Are you ready?"

Sandy looked at White, and for the first she saw the remnants of what he'd been. Beneath the tattoos and piercings, under the wilting Mohawk, and behind the drug-induced stupor, there was a frightened little boy trying to escape a scary world. Instead of escaping, however, he'd stepped into a realm more frightening than anything he'd ever known. Now he was stuck there, and he wanted nothing more than to get out.

"You okay?" she said.

He nodded.

"I think we're ready," Sandy said to the detective. "Bring them in."

A door opened, and the men walked onto a small stage.

Each of them held a card bearing a number, and each of them resembled the others.

Number 1 had pasty white skin and dirty-blond hair. Number 2 had brown razor stubble and eyebrows to match, with hair bleached almost white. Number 3 was a natural blond, and his blue eyes were fearful in a way that the others weren't. It was obvious he'd never been arrested before.

The detective pushed a button that connected to an intercom. "Number 1, step forward and turn to the right."

James looked at the man and indicated that he wasn't the one.

"Number 2," the detective said, "take one step forward and turn to the right."

The man did as he was told, and James said no again.

"Number 3, take one step forward."

The man stepped forward at the same time that the door beside Sandy opened and Coletti walked in with Smithson. "Hey Sandy, I wanted to—" He stopped in midsentence when he saw that they were still in the middle of lineups. "I'm sorry," Coletti said, turning to leave, "I thought you were done."

"We are," Sandy said as she glanced at James White. "None of these guys is a match, right?"

White's face was ashen. His body was shaking. His eyes were wide with fear. Raising his cuffed hands, he looked straight ahead, as though he'd seen a ghost. Then he clutched at his chest.

"Get the doctor in here!" Sandy said as White fell to the floor and started to convulse. "I think he's having a heart attack!"

The detective running the lineup ran out to get help. Coletti grabbed White's shoulders. Sandy grabbed his feet. Smithson knelt over him and applied CPR. The harder she worked, the whiter his face became. The more she tried to save him, the more afraid he looked.

James White had seen the angel of death, and his heart skipped a beat, then two, before slowing to a snail's pace. As he moved his lips in an attempt to speak, his windpipe began to close. He shut his eyes against the pain and hoped his body would listen.

As the light in his eyes grew dim, the detective rushed back with the doctor and two patrolmen. After a few frightening moments, the doctor managed to stabilize the stricken man, who was immediately transported to nearby Jefferson Hospital.

When he was gone, Smithson turned to Sandy and Coletti, who both looked through the glass at the last man to step forward.

It was Ivan Petrov.

Charlie Mann pulled up in the loading bay at the medical examiner's office and parked next to the police wagon that had transported Gabe's body from the scene.

Mann watched as the autopsy technicians opened the steel double doors so the officers could carry the body inside. Then he walked in behind them.

One of the technicians looked Mann up and down, glancing disapprovingly at his hoodie, jeans, and boots.

"Detective Charles Mann, homicide," he said, pulling a chain that held his badge from inside his hoodie. "I'm here to examine the personal effects."

"Oh, sorry," the technician said as he pulled out a book and donned heavy latex gloves. "I didn't mean to stare."

"It's all right. I get that all the time. Even from people in the department."

The technician opened the book in which they documented personal effects and wrote a number in the second column. A few seconds later, the investigator from the medical examiner's office came down on the elevator.

"Sorry it took me a few minutes," he said to the technician before turning to Mann. "How are you?"

"Overworked," Mann said, only half joking.

"I know what you mean," the investigator said. "This place has been crazy for the past two days."

"We've all been crazy for the past two days," Mann said. "I've never seen anything like it."

The investigator shook his head. "Are you guys any closer to catching whoever's behind all this?"

"Depends on what comes out of Gabe's pockets," Mann said.

The technician went to work, pulling a set of needles from the dead man's pockets. Since there was no wallet or identification, he went back to the personal effects book and started to write the name "John Doe." Mann stopped him.

"It's Gabriel," he said. "We'll get his last name later when the prints come back."

The technician shrugged and followed Mann's instructions. Then he continued going through the pockets. "This guy looks a lot like the one from this morning," the technician said as he pulled two packets of heroin from his inside pocket. "You think this one's a homicide, too?"

"No," Mann said. "This one shot himself."

"That's a shame," the technician said as he went to the book and completed the list of personal effects, including the dead man's jacket, pants, boots, shirt, and hat.

"We're going to need to keep the clothes on this one," the investigator reminded him. "The doctor's going to want to examine the powder burns on the jacket and shirt."

The technician nodded as he finished filling out the paperwork.

"Was that everything?" Mann asked. "There wasn't anything else in his pockets?"

The question annoyed the technician, who looked at Mann and sighed heavily before going through Gabe's pockets once more. He was about to turn to the young detective and say no, but he felt something deep in the dead man's pants pocket.

"It's a phone," the technician said, pulling it out and making note of it in the effects book.

"I need to take that," Mann said.

"Sign for it and it's yours," the investigator said.

"You got any gloves?" Mann asked as he scrawled his name across a property receipt.

The technician handed him a pair.

Mann donned the latex gloves, took the phone, and flipped it open to navigate through the recent calls. They were all from a single number, and each call was placed around the time of one of the murders. The phone didn't contain voice mails or outgoing calls, but there was a single text message. It was received right before the police arrived at the house on Kensington Avenue. It simply said, "Run."

Mann jotted down Gabe's phone number and slipped the phone back into the plastic bag. "Thanks," he said to the technician and the investigator as he rushed out of the medical examiner's office and into his car.

As he sped back toward headquarters, he dialed the iPhone he'd given to Coletti. The old detective picked up on the second ring. "Hello?"

"They just bagged Gabe's personal effects, and I think we got something."

"What?"

"His phone. He got three calls from one number over the last two days, and they all came about fifteen minutes before each murder."

"What number did the calls come from?" Coletti asked.

"It looks like they could've come from one of those throwaway phones."

"Gimme a second," Coletti said. "I've got Petrov's property receipt right here. If you give me the number I'll check it against his phone."

"Okay," Mann said, pulling out the sheet of paper where he'd written the number. When he read it to Coletti there was a pause.

"That's not Petrov's number," Coletti said.

"Doesn't mean anything," Mann said. "Maybe he used the phone and got rid of it after he made his calls."

"Or maybe this is all a bit too neat," Coletti said as a phone began ringing in the background. "Hold on a minute."

Mann listened as Coletti answered the office phone and grunted a few garbled responses.

When Coletti came back on the line, he was speaking in a tone that was clearly strained. "They found a body at Thirtieth Street Station with a note attached," he said.

"What did it say?"

"It said, 'I won't stop until I get to Mike Coletti.'"

CHAPTER 18

Steven awakened at the unfinished house on Oxford Street, praying he wasn't about to experience a repeat of his nightmare. He
looked around nervously to see if his dead friend was back, but
he soon realized he'd been awakened by his buzzing phone.

It vibrated insistently and repeatedly, like the memories
from the night before. By the time it vibrated for the tenth time,
his mind went to a place between consciousness and dreams,
and his imagination began to take over. It took him on a journey
through a heaven he saw only in his mind. There, in his own
private heaven, he was a king rather than an addict.

His heaven never lasted, however. In fact, it often turned
into hell. As the buzzing phone gathered strength, the vibration
was like screaming that cut at his very soul. It rang like a hellish
alarm that told him the war was about to begin.

Steven's eyes snapped open, and he fumbled in his pocket
for the phone. When finally he connected the call, he heard the
sound of heavy breathing and voices in the background saying
words he couldn't quite understand.

"They've found the body," the angel said in a voice that grated in Steven's ears. "Prepare yourself. Take up your weapon. The war is about to begin. Do you understand?"

Steven nodded.

"Good. There's an old factory at the corner of Stillman and Oxford," the angel said. "Be there in exactly one hour."

Steven didn't nod. He didn't respond at all. He simply waited, knowing that the angel understood his responses even before he spoke them. If he just waited, Steven would receive the reassurance that he needed. The angel would never disappoint.

"What is it, Steven?" the angel asked.

Steven breathed deeply and tried to gather his thoughts. In a war he was unafraid to fight, in a place he was anxious to go, for a cause that was worth his life, he wanted nothing more than to join the final battle. But even in his drug-addled mind, Steven knew that if he stepped outside and tried to go the seven and a half blocks to Stillman and Oxford, he'd be apprehended before he could reach his destination.

"I'll need power to get there," Steven said in a sheepish voice. "If you give me the power you promised, I can get there."

"The power isn't given, it's earned," the angel said. "Find a way to get there, win the final battle, and prove you're worthy. Then you'll have all the power you want."

The line went dead. Steven sat still, the numbness from the drugs replaced by grim determination.

He walked across the room and picked up his jacket and the sawed-off shotgun. He reached into his pocket, retrieved his shells, and began loading them into his weapon.

Somehow, he would make it those seven and a half blocks. Then he would finally make it to heaven.

By one thirty, 30th Street Station was a madhouse. Trains were backed up. Amtrak police with dogs and rifles were patrolling the station and platforms. Sandwich and coffee shops were closed. Commuters were afraid, and it was all because of an angel.

With outstretched wings and stony expression, the bronze *Angel of Resurrection* was a tribute to war dead and a symbol of protection for travelers passing through Philadelphia's ornately appointed train station. Today, that depiction of the archangel Michael lifting a fallen soldier, flanked by Greco-Roman columns stretching nearly a hundred feet from floor to ceiling, was surrounded by crime scene tape, and the dead man at the statue's base was not about to be swept up to heaven.

When Mann pulled up at the train station and ran inside, Coletti and Lynch were entering from the other end. Between them were ninth district patrol officers, Amtrak police, and cops from SEPTA, the local transportation authority.

All of them were focused on the sight that both repulsed and fascinated everyone who saw it: a duffle bag propped up against the angel statue with a dead body crammed inside.

"How long has it been here?" Lynch asked a captain from the Amtrak police.

"About thirty minutes," he said. "We've got our folks in the back right now reviewing videotape, but it's the damnedest thing. We isolated the video a minute before and a minute after the bag showed up, and on it you never see anyone bring it here, and you never see anyone walk away. It's like it just appeared out of nowhere."

Lynch glanced at Coletti, who looked around the station trying to gauge the possibility of someone entering unnoticed. There was far too much open space for that.

"Who spotted the note on the body?" Coletti asked.

"I did," said a sergeant from Amtrak's K-9 unit. "We didn't move anything. It's still there."

Mann joined Coletti and Lynch as they looked inside the duffle bag at the body. All three of them gasped when they saw the thinning black hair, the priest's collar, and the slight frame. Father Douglas had been stuffed inside in the fetal position, and he was still wearing the same fearful expression he'd worn when he told them he'd seen the angel of death kill three people in his church. From the nature of the priest's wounds, the MO appeared to be the same as the other church murders—a shotgun blast.

"I guess angels don't like to leave witnesses," Mann said.

Lynch grunted in agreement. But Coletti was silent, staring at the dead priest as anger and guilt wrestled for control of his mind. Coletti still blamed himself for every body they found, and a quiet rage was building inside with each moment that the killers remained free.

"We've got to stop this now," Coletti in a near whisper.

"We've already got Petrov," Mann said. "We're halfway there."

"Maybe," Coletti said. "But we've been wrong before."

"So how do we make sure we're not wrong this time?" Mann asked.

"We give them what they want to draw them out of the woodwork," said Lynch. "We offer them a meeting with Coletti."

They both turned to the old detective, who returned their stares with unflinching resolve. "I'm in," he said. "But how do we set it up?"

"I have a feeling they'll be reaching out to us," Lynch said.

Coletti looked at the duffle bag once more and clenched his jaw. "I'm going to the bathroom," he said, walking across the station floor in an attempt to cool off.

Lynch and Mann barely acknowledged him. They were too busy trying to figure out how they were going to track down the killer. It was just as well. Coletti needed a few minutes alone. It was the only way he'd be able to sort things out.

He was halfway across the station, passing the automatic ticket kiosks, when his iPhone began to ring. He looked back at Mann and was about to yell that he shouldn't abuse the phone. Mann wasn't on the phone, however. The young detective was kneeling near the body and saying something to Lynch.

Coletti felt a cold breeze whisper through the station. It was the same breeze he'd felt in his dreams. As time began to slow and his hands began to tremble, he turned to his left. The horses in the bas-relief sculpture on the far wall seemed to move. The light around him seemed to dim. His face sweating and his eyes darting to and fro, he extracted the phone from his pocket and looked at the screen. "Private number," it said.

He connected the call and listened. A few seconds of silence passed before he heard a sound he never thought he'd hear in waking moments.

"Only you can end this," said the raspy voice from his dreams.

"How?" Coletti asked, the word coming out as a hoarse whisper.

"Meet me in the old factory at Stillman and Oxford," the angel of death said. "You have ten minutes to get there. Be alone. If you're not, more people will die."

The line went dead and Coletti looked around him, knowing that he had no choice. If they were going to get the truth that would finally set things right, Coletti would have to be the one to find it.

As Lynch and Mann and all the other officers swarmed around the priest's body that lay beneath the angel's wings, Coletti moved toward the door. He was going to fix this, or he was going to die trying.

It was two o' clock when Steven began his trek down Oxford Street, braving the fearful stares of those he encountered as he made his way toward the factory.

"Ain't that him?" a woman whispered to her friend, nervously regarding his blond hair, black suit, heavy black boots, and steely blue eyes.

Steven looked up at her defiantly, his brow knit together in anger. He had no choice but to continue to walk. If he was going to see the glory of the final battle, he would have to walk by faith, believing far beyond what he could see.

Both women crossed the street. Steven didn't care. He'd made it as far as Nineteenth Street. There were six and a half blocks to go.

With his arm hard against his side, he held the sawed-off shotgun in place beneath his jacket, his eyes fixed on the ground as an increasing number of people stepped silently aside to let him pass.

When he crossed Twentieth Street he felt more powerful, as if the very act of moving closer to the battlefield made him stronger.

"Oh my God!" a woman screamed as she watched him walk past. "That's him!"

Soon, other voices joined in the growing chorus of recognition. Steven ignored them, held his gun even tighter, and walked ever faster toward the factory.

As people watched him pass with a mixture of fear and awe, he looked up from the ground and drew strength from the only thing he had left.

"Then I lifted up mine eyes, and looked, and beheld a certain man clothed in linen, whose loins were girded with fine gold of Uphaz," he said, quoting from the book of Daniel.

The voices of fearful neighbors grew louder, and Steven grew bolder, loudly reciting the words he'd come to know intimately over the past four months.

"His body also was like the beryl, and his face as the appearance of lightning, and his eyes as lamps of fire, and his arms and his feet like in color to polished brass, and the voice of his words like the voice of a multitude. And I Daniel alone saw the vision: for the men that were with me saw not the vision; but a great quaking fell upon them, so that they fled to hide themselves."

As he shouted those words the neighbors took flight. Some

ran blocks away, scrambling toward the high-rises of the Blumberg housing projects. Some ran to cars, driving as far from him as they could get. All of them ran to safety, because no one could convince them that the man in black was anything less than a demon from the depths of hell.

The streets were deserted now, but the power Steven had gained with his initial push toward the factory was beginning to wane. The sleepless nights and heroin, the murders and the hiding, all of it was coming down on him at once. Still, he continued to shout the words he had committed to memory, clinging to them as he moved toward his final destiny.

"Therefore I was left alone, and saw this great vision, and there remained no strength in me: for my comeliness was turned in me into corruption, and I retained no strength."

The sound of sirens rose in the distance, and as the hum of powerful engines hurtled toward him from every direction, Steven pulled the sawed-off from his jacket and held it at his side. There was nothing left for him to do but stand.

When the police rolled to a stop all around him, jumping from their cars and pulling guns, the man who had done the bidding of the angel of death looked around slowly.

"Drop the gun!" one of the officers said.

Steven wouldn't. He couldn't. Not if he wanted his power. He threw his head back and shouted the words he remembered to the heavens, knowing that those words would be his last.

"Then said he, Knowest thou wherefore I come unto thee? And now will I return to fight with the prince of Persia: and when I am gone forth, lo, the prince of Greece shall come. But I will show thee that which is noted in the scripture of truth: and there is none that holdeth with me in these things, but Michael your prince."

He raised the sawed-off and fired twice. A hail of bullets flew through the air. He fell to the ground in a bloody heap, still waiting for the power he'd been promised.

Mike Coletti looked at the four missed calls from his partner and turned off the iPhone as he walked through the factory's open door. There would be no backup on this one.

As he looked around for some sign of life, he heard the sound of gunshots from four blocks away. Coletti wondered if the killer had been caught. Those thoughts were put to rest when he heard the voice echo through the darkness.

"The gunshots were for Steven," the gravelly voice said ominously. "I sent him to his death so we could be alone. Now, close the door."

Coletti did so, and the long-shuttered factory was immediately thrust into darkness as the dank air inside swirled through the empty space.

"The prophecy is about to be fulfilled," the voice said. "The sacrifice has been made, the abomination carried out, and the desolation has begun."

As the voice echoed though the factory, a shaft of sunlight peered through a hole in the roof. Coletti's eyes began to adjust. He could see the dim outlines of trash that trespassers had thrown inside over the years, and the hulking shapes of old machinery and rusting deep freezers the previous owners had left behind.

He crouched low and ducked behind one of the old freezers. Then he removed his gun from its holster as sweat trickled down the side of his face. He hoped to hear the voice again, but he didn't hear a sound.

"What do you want from me?" he shouted through the eerie silence.

The voice exploded in full-throated laughter before it spoke again. "I want you to die."

Coletti stuck his head out and spotted another freezer about ten feet in front of him and to his left. Staying low, he scrambled along the floor and hid behind it.

"There's no use hiding," the gravelly voice said. "I can see you. I always have."

Coletti released the safety on his gun. "Then let me see you, too," he said. "Come out and show yourself."

Again, he heard the laughter, but this time it sounded closer.

"I've shown myself many times, and you ignored me. I killed in the cathedral. I killed in the churches. I killed in each case where you got a false confession, and still you never found me. Why should I show myself now?"

Coletti was starting to get a bead on the voice. It seemed to be coming from just beyond a wall fifteen feet in front of him and slightly to the right.

Coletti crawled out from behind the freezer and ran to the wall. He was breathing hard now, but he knew he couldn't rest, so he leaned against the wall with his gun in front of him, and asked a question to keep him talking. "Why did you call me here if you weren't going to let me see you?"

Silence.

"Where are you?"

No response.

Coletti took a deep breath and slid along the wall until he reached the edge. He raised his gun and held it in front of him with both hands. Slowly, carefully, he peered around the corner. Then all hell broke loose.

A two-by-four smacked against his forehead, and he saw a flash of white light as a stream of thick red blood ran down his face. He managed to fire one shot before another swing of the two-by-four knocked the gun from his hand.

Coletti dove for the gun, but a kick landed in his midsection, flipping him onto his back. Through rapidly clouding vision, he saw a booted foot rear back for a second kick, and he managed to grab it and pull his assailant to the ground.

The figure moved quickly, rolling away from Coletti and reaching for his weapon. Coletti pulled the dark figure back and managed to retrieve the gun. Rolling onto his back, the detective held the weapon out in front of him, but he couldn't see.

His adversary got up in a flash and disappeared into the recesses of the factory.

Coletti groaned and got to his feet. He walked slowly past the wall and into the factory's next room, wiping his bloody forehead on his sleeve.

"Show yourself!" Coletti shouted, his breath coming heavy and fast as he ducked behind another old freezer.

Something ran behind him and he turned to find a scurrying rat. He turned again as something much larger ran in front of him. A drop of water fell from the ceiling and he jumped as something hard struck the freezer. The burst of movement left Coletti disoriented. His reaction left the angel amused.

Laughter floated through the room like a whisper on the

wind. Then the words came in that gravelly voice he'd heard so often before. "Do you remember the first time you came to the cathedral?" the voice said.

Coletti's mind flashed images from his time as a patrolman: a little girl covered in blood; a green-eyed, bearded homeless man; a bathroom off the entrance to the sanctuary.

"Thirty-one years ago," the voice said. "A little girl was attacked in the bathroom, and you were the patrolman who answered the call. The man who hurt that child was never brought to justice."

Coletti sat back against the freezer, his mind racing with thirty-one-year-old memories. "I caught that guy," Coletti said, sounding confused. "I remember because he tried to resist arrest and I had to subdue him. Right after I cuffed him he admitted that he'd raped that little girl. He went to jail for that. I know he appealed, but I thought . . ."

"You thought wrong," the voice said. "They let him go quietly on appeal. What you called subduing a suspect, they called coercing a confession. And because of you, that little girl was scarred for life."

"That's not my fault," Coletti said, his eyes darting about as he tried to dig the truth from his memories.

"It *is* your fault!" the voice shouted. "And now you're going to pay."

A figure dashed in front of him, and Coletti took a shot. The figure ran to his left and Coletti took another. The sound of the growling voice began to fill his ears. Coletti tried to look through the darkness to find the source of the sound. Suddenly the figure sprung from the shadows and cracked the two-by-four against his shoulder.

Coletti raised his gun and shot until the magazine was empty. Only then did the angel of death stand up in front of him and level a sawed-off shotgun at his face.

Coletti blinked several times to clear his blurry vision. Between the head injuries and the blood, it was difficult to focus. When finally his vision cleared and he looked up at the truth, Coletti refused to believe what he saw.

"I almost changed my mind about killing you," Mary Smithson said, abandoning the grating voice that she'd used as the angel of death. "But in the end, I really had no choice."

Coletti tried to speak, but the words wouldn't come. Seeing this woman standing over him, dressed in black, blue eyes filled with simmering hate, his heart broke as his mind recalled what he already knew deep down. He remembered how she'd articulated the killer's motives and childhood pain. He envisioned the ease with which she'd broken down the prophecy and explained the killer's war against him.

She watched his face as he digested it all and remembered the lust she'd seen in his eyes. She almost laughed when she saw it replaced by hurt.

"I was that little girl in the cathedral, Mike," she said, while pointing the gun at him. "I was the one you let down when you let that rapist walk."

"That couldn't have been you," he said, sounding confused. "The family was named O'Hanlon."

"My name was O'Hanlon, too, before I got married and

divorced," she said. "But that marriage was just like my family. It fell apart because of what happened to me in that cathedral. I still remember the months right after the rape. I stopped talking and created my own little place inside my mind where I was a perfect angel. My parents' marriage was disintegrating, my faith in God had failed, but as long as I stayed in that place where I was an angel, nothing could ever hurt me."

"Mary, you don't have to do this," Coletti said. "Let me help you."

"Shut up!" she screamed with an anger she'd thus far managed to mask. "If you would've helped me in the beginning, my mind wouldn't have twisted the way it did. I would've never gone back to that cathedral to kill those people. I would've never believed that murder could make things right."

A tear rolled down her cheek and sparkled in the factory's dim light.

"If killing didn't make things right the first time, why did you keep doing it?"

"I did it to punish you," she said. "Each time I made it look like somebody else committed a murder, and watched you arrest the wrong people, I pulled you down a little further."

"But it wasn't just me you punished. You killed innocent people."

"I exposed you for the failure you are!" she screamed.

"How? By getting four boys strung out on dope and telling them they were fulfilling a prophecy?"

"Those boys were a means to an end," she said, her face crumpling as her eyes filled with tears.

"What about Father Douglas and Father O'Reilly?" Coletti

said, as he placed his hands flat on the floor. "Why did you punish them?"

"They preached for a God who failed me."

"And all those other people you got those boys to kill? Did they deserve to die?"

"I died in that bathroom thirty-one years ago!" she shouted. "Did anyone care about me then? Did *you* care about me then?"

Suddenly, Coletti rolled to his right and Smithson pulled the trigger. He scrambled to his feet and lunged at her, but she dodged him, and he landed on the floor.

"The prophecy was right," she said as she leveled the gun at him. "Good does triumph over evil in the end."

Just then, bright light poured in through the door, and everything slowed down for Coletti. He could hear the sound of his heart beating against his chest, and feel the air rushing into his lungs. He could see the dust particles dancing in the light, and feel the hate that filled Mary's eyes.

Her finger tightened on the trigger. The light seemed to grow brighter. The room felt oddly silent. And then there was a gunshot.

With a look of shock etched on her face, Mary fell as Charlie Mann stood in the doorway, the smoke rising from his gun.

"Coletti!" Mann called out frantically. "Coletti!"

"I'm over here," Coletti said, as he retrieved his gun from the floor and stood over the body.

Mann came in and stood next to Coletti as he grieved for the little girl he barely knew, and for the woman he almost loved.

"How did you know where I was?" Coletti said as he stared at Smithson's dead blue eyes.

"I put a GPS tracking key on your car yesterday, in case you stopped answering the phone."

"You're a wise man," Coletti said with a wan smile. "Must be from hanging around old guys like me."

Mann looked down at Smithson's body and shook his head. "I'm sorry it was her," he said with genuine sadness in his voice. "I know how you felt about her."

"Yeah," Coletti said, trying his best to mask the true depths of his feelings. "I'm sorry, too."

"The commissioner should be on his way," Mann said. "I guess I'll meet him out front." He patted Coletti on the shoulder and took a last look at the body before going outside. "Take all the time you need."

As the sound of approaching sirens filled the air, Coletti stared at Smithson and knew he couldn't retire. There were too many lives to be touched and too many wrongs to right.

As he turned to leave, a cold breeze blew through the factory, causing a cloud of dust to form in the air. Coletti covered his eyes, and when he opened them, there was a figure kneeling near Smithson's body.

He was dressed in white linen and his legs shone like gold. His face glowed like lightning and his eyes burned bright as fire.

The angel took her spirit up in arms of polished brass. He rose into the air and paused at the ceiling. Then he dove through the floor and disappeared.

Coletti wasn't sure if he was dreaming or awake, but as he clutched at the golden crucifix around his neck, he knew that the war was over and that Mary Smithson was about to find out that vengeance is indeed the Lord's.